THE ISLAND BOOKSHOP MURDER

JAMES LONDON

Acorn Books

The Island Bookshop Murder
Published in 2025 by
Acorn Books
West Wing Studios
Unit 166, The Mall
Luton, LU1 2TL
acornbooks.uk

Cover design inspired by a
photo from Darren Hudson

For Mark Watkins,
whose skill in deciphering my handwritten manuscripts
transports Bruno Peach onto the printed page.

Contents

Everyone is a potential murderer. In everyone there arises from time to time the wish to kill, though not the will to kill.

—Agatha Christie

Prologue

That Tuesday evening Sheila Catchpole let herself in through the front entrance to clean the bookshop. The weather had been gloomy and overcast all day. By 6:45 p.m., the time she always arrived, the sun had been set for an hour, and it was properly dark. At her fifty-nine years, she felt the cold and damp, and this evening her shoulder was aching with what she thought might be the onset of rheumatism. Although she didn't particularly enjoy dusting the bookshelves and hoovering the floors every night after hours, it was reliable employment at a time when jobs were not easy to come by.

At night, the shop front was well lit by streetlights. The books in the window display were illuminated from above to attract customers with the latest titles. Local Authority cameras were sited at street level as security for local businesses. The downlights in the window spilled a glow into the front room of the shop, but it was still shadowy.

Inside, Sheila locked the door behind her, leaving her keys in the mortice lock. The premises at the back were entirely dark, so she put on the pendant lights, starting from the front door and moving through the shop. As always, she started to clean from the back, where she tackled the kitchen and lavatory first. She didn't usually switch the lights on in the private office, situated between the shop at the front and the storerooms, kitchen and lavatory at the back, until she got to that stage of her cleaning ritual. The shop had closed as it always did at 5:30 p.m., with the staff usually leaving by 6 p.m., so it was empty and quiet as she expected, and she had it to herself to clean.

This evening, one thing was different: the alarm warning signal did not go off when she opened the front door. Usually, the beeps would sound, and she would present a small fob attached to her keys in order to turn the alarm system off. The fact that it was not set did not unduly trouble her – occasionally the last person to leave forgot to set the alarm or it could mean that someone was still in the shop or the offices working late. This evening she called out to see if anyone was in but there was only silence, so she concluded that there had been an oversight in setting the alarm.

When Sheila had finished the back rooms, she cleaned the shop at the front and then proceeded to tackle the office. The office was the quickest part of the ground floor to clean and she usually just emptied the bin, flicked a duster around the few areas of uncovered surfaces, and hoovered the floor area. As she opened the door, the light from where she stood flooded the office. She was shocked to see her boss, and the owner of the shop, Simeon Calafifi, asleep at his desk in the dark.

"Oh, Mr Simeon, I'm so sorry to disturb you!" she exclaimed.

The office had been in pitch darkness. The thought occurred to Sheila that he must be very tired to be sleeping at his desk, so she didn't disturb him by switching on the overhead lights. Tiptoeing up behind him, she got closer. His head was down, and she couldn't see his face.

"Mr Simeon?" she whispered gently. "You gave me such a fright! Do you want me to clean in here?"

No answer came. No sound could be heard in the silent darkness. Not even a breath.

"Are you alright, Mr Simeon? Don't you think it's time for you to be getting home? I've cleaned the shop already. Your wife will be wondering where you are, won't she? Are you alright?" Sheila's words came out in a babble reflecting her surprise at discovering him in the office.

When he didn't answer or make any movement, she approached gingerly. Putting her hand on the shoulder of his tweed jacket, she tried to nudge him, and then to shake him. The light from behind her was enough to illuminate the dark liquid that had seeped out of his mouth. Blood. Sheila realised that he wasn't asleep.

Simeon Calafifi was dead.

Sheila felt a shock run through her. In an instant, the shock turned to fear and then to panic. Standing there in the semi-dark, locked into the shop from the inside, with the dead body of her boss, she suddenly realised she might not be alone in the bookshop, or even here in this office part. Terrified, she fled to the front door. A lock never opens quickly when you're in a hurry, but she managed to unlock the mortice and turn the Yale; pulling the door open with all her might, she ran from the shop, leaving her keys in the back of the door and the door wide open behind her.

Standing on the pavement shaking with fear, she looked around her. There were no passers-by or cars at that moment. She rummaged for her mobile phone which she always carried when she was working in a zipped side pocket of her work trousers. She tried dialling 999 but her hands were shaking, and her phone signal was weak. On her third attempt, she got through. She told the emergency services operator her name, Mrs Sheila Catchpole, and her location, Simeon's Bookshop, and the shop address in Shanklin.

"Please, come quickly! Someone's inside the shop… the bookshop I clean every night. I found my boss inside. I think he's dead! I'm not sure but he's not moving… He needs help."

The operator asked a number of questions, but Sheila wasn't listening. She couldn't keep the panic from her voice: "Please send someone quickly! I got out as fast as I could but he's still there in the dark!"

It was unclear whether she meant the victim or the murderer.

*

Susan Buckley was walking on the other side of the street when she saw Sheila Catchpole ahead of her, standing under a streetlight and screaming into her phone. As Sheila hung up her 999 call, she saw Susan, who was a stranger to her, approaching. It did not occur to her that this stranger might be dangerous or connected to the murder; Sheila was simply so pleased to see another human at that moment – a walking, talking live one.

Having explained what had happened to Susan, who lived around the corner and was walking to post a thank you note through a friend's door before settling down for an evening of television, the two women waited together for the police to arrive. They watched the door to the shop fearfully, as if someone could emerge at any moment. No one emerged from the shop. Mrs Catchpole wished she had kept her coat on, because it was a cold February night, and she now felt a chill in her bones and was shivering.

Fifteen minutes after making the 999 call, a police car arrived. Sheila told them what she had seen inside the shop. Seeing that she was in a distressed state, going into shock, and because it was cold, the junior officers sat her in their police car. They had been the nearest car to Shanklin and, listening to her story, felt rather daunted at the thought of what lay inside the shop. They were relieved when they heard on their radio that an ambulance and another police car with a detective would be arriving almost immediately, having both driven with blue lights from Newport. The uniformed officers took down Susan Buckley's name and address before she left the scene in case they needed to contact her again, but she had nothing relevant to report other than the facts of what had happened over the past half hour. As the discoverer of the body, Mrs Catchpole was the person of interest to the police, and she remained inside the police car.

*

Detective Sergeant Andrew Bowen managed to get to the bookshop soon after 8 p.m., abandoning his microwaved dinner and jumping in his car as soon as the call came in. The Scene of Crime Officers, known as SOCOs, also arrived quickly and went straight in to secure the scene, photographing the body and the interior of the shop. Andy made a cursory examination of the premises, ensuring that nothing was touched or moved.

The victim, Simeon Calafifi, the owner of the bookshop, had been sitting at his desk, presumably reading something in front of him, and was now slumped forward, face down. The single visible puncture wound on his clothing suggested that he had been stabbed once from behind, most likely with a very long narrow-bladed knife, administered by a person who possibly understood anatomy, being able to penetrate the heart from behind through the victim's fully clothed body. No weapon could be seen on or around the desk.

Lights were on throughout the ground floor. Sheila Catchpole told them she had discovered the body in the office in the dark, but it was not clear whether those office lights were on or off at the time of the assault. After a brief interview with her, Andy asked a junior officer to get her bag and coat, which she had left inside the shop in her panic to leave. Apart from the passer-by, Susan Buckley, she was able to confirm that she had not observed anyone in or near the shop since her arrival. Mrs Catchpole could offer no explanation of why anyone would murder the bookseller, who was both her employer and a friend. Mrs Catchpole was now completely overcome with shock, fear and grief, and she started to cry. She had discovered a brutal, ruthless murder and it had shaken her to the core.

Andy Bowen asked a junior officer to drive Mrs Catchpole home. This gave them the opportunity to verify her identity and see where she lived; they also did not want her walking alone in a traumatised state with a killer potentially still in the vicinity.

By now it was after 9 p.m. Andy left the SOCOs and the other police officers to do their jobs and proceeded to undertake the worst part of any murder investigation: informing the next of kin that their loved one had been killed at the hands of another person. He drove to Ryde to see the victim's wife, slowly and apprehensively dreading the task before him. At this stage he knew almost nothing about the victim, and this first task of informing Mrs Calafifi of her husband's shocking death would be where the detective work would begin.

Chapter 1

Detective Chief Inspector Bruno Peach had been off sick with flu for ten days. His GP told him every year to take a two-week break in February in Barbados, because some winter sun would set him up for the rest of the winter and remedy his deficiency of vitamin D. Bruno had never yet taken his doctor's advice, but this year he thought he should have done.

It had been a busy autumn and winter. He had been advanced to Detective Chief Inspector, a promotion he had not necessarily sought, but which had been awarded on his merits, having managed responses to many major incidents on the Isle of Wight, including three murder cases solved successfully. The most recent had been the death of a carnival queen in what appeared to be an accident but turned out to be a carefully staged murder. It had caused quite a sensation in the national newspapers, given the youth and beauty of the victim, and had raised Bruno's profile within the police force.

On that cold Wednesday, the first day of March, Bruno received an early morning visit from his friend and Murder Squad partner Detective Sergeant Andrew Bowen. Sensing that his boss could be ready to return to work, but more importantly because of the nature of the crime which had arisen, Andy needed to open a new police investigation with Bruno's support and investigative skills. There had been a death, again in Shanklin, but this time there could be no doubt that it was murder.

Bruno Peach had mentored twenty-nine-year-old Andy Bowen for three years since he joined the Island Murder Squad from Southampton, encouraging him to sit his Sergeant exams and to get promoted the previous year. Between them, they headed up the Island Murder Unit. Bruno had shown Andy how efficiency, hard work, and enthusiasm, at the beginning of a new case, coupled with serious attention to detail, paid substantial dividends.

The particularly gruesome killing had taken place early on the previous evening of Tuesday 28th February, in a bookshop in Shanklin. This disturbing murder had been committed sometime after 5:45 p.m. when the business was closed for the day. The victim was Simeon Calafifi, the owner of the bookshop.

Chief Superintendent Barlow, the long-standing head of the Island Police Force, had encouraged Andy to call Bruno to bring him back from sick leave. The nature of the killing meant the police needed to be on high alert in case the killer struck again.

The motive for this killing was not immediately apparent. It did not appear to be the result of a domestic or local disagreement. The Island's police investigation would become the subject of intense scrutiny and, eventually, national news coverage; so, if possible, flu or no flu, he needed his best detective, Bruno Peach, to lead the police investigation.

"See if Peach is well enough to give some input," he said, before Bowen set off.

When Andy relayed Barlow's suggestion to Bruno it was a welcome instruction to get back to work from the Chief, who always acted with kindness towards his detectives, and understood their engagement.

*

Bruno felt better and was further rejuvenated by the sense of being needed. So it was that by 11 a.m. on the Wednesday morning, Bruno was accompanying Andy to the scene of the murder that had taken place in the early evening of the previous day.

The shop was closed for business, for obvious reasons, and at Bruno's instruction it was to remain closed. The fingerprint experts were hard at work taking prints from every surface and ledge.

The brief search of the shop on the night of the murder had indicated no obvious murder weapon and an initial conclusion that the killer had removed it. Indeed, Andy Bowen had discovered nothing obvious during his brief visit to the shop that he could connect with the crime and, so as not to contaminate the scene, he had left the bookshop and the SOCOs to complete their documentation of the scene. The SOCOs had sealed the crime scene and left two junior officers sitting outside the shop overnight in a marked car, on guard as it were, until now, on Wednesday morning, when Detective Chief Inspector Bruno Peach arrived.

The body had been removed to the mortuary in Newport to await a post-mortem, and subsequently an inquest. The shop and office premises had been preserved as a murder scene. Bruno was always impressed at the work of the experienced, professional SOCOs and their strict adherence to protocols.

Having assessed the layout of the shop and the front and rear entrances, Bruno entered the office. On the desk lay a leather-edged ink blotter roughly one metre by half a metre in size. Calafifi had presumably been attending to the documents on the desk when the fatal wound was administered. These appeared to be statements and invoices for books bought from distributors for relatively small amounts of money, certainly nothing that seemed significant, though the pages would be examined by forensics.

"I wonder why there wasn't more blood on the blotter?" said Bruno.

"According to the initial forensic pathologist's comments that came in this morning," said Andy, reading from an email on his smartphone, while he spoke: "It says here that '*if the victim was stabbed from the back and through the heart then blood would only be found on blotting paper in front of him if the stab wound involves the anterior chest wall – in which case the amount of blood would be significant. The other possibility is that the stab wound might have injured the oesophagus or the bronchi so that a small amount of blood would seep through the mouth and nose.*' That's what Mrs Catchpole noticed, a small pool of blood."

Bruno nodded and remarked, "So it looks then like the murder weapon went in through his back, damaging his heart and other internal organs, but didn't come out the other side." Both men knew that the investigation and examination of the scene would involve a forensic scientist specialised in any blood splattering patterns, and the location and quantity of blood after a murder of this kind.

"No blood spattering is apparent," replied Andy, "but forensics will be here later today to check for anything we might not be able to see and predict the mechanism of injuries and any movement of the victim after injury."

Bruno paused for thought; he then observed: "Having murdered Simeon, escaping the premises in darkness through the rear exit would be essential, I think. Even a stranger could be sufficiently familiar with the premises, from previous anonymous visits to the shop combined with a nonchalant wander around the back, to move about, do or take whatever they came for, and vanish out the rear door."

"But what was it that they came for?" asked Andy.

The office safe had appeared the previous night to be locked, but the fingerprint team revealed that it had only been closed, and it was empty. The books in the locked glass-fronted bookcase marked 'First Editions', which stood behind Simeon's desk, seemed in order, although of course they could not be sure about that at this stage and, apart from the items on the desk itself, the room was dust-free and tidy.

"This shop seems full of incredibly special and expensive looking books. Rare ones, I would imagine," Andy observed. "If a book or something else from the safe had been stolen by the murderer, or murderers, that could give us a motive and could help our investigation."

"Maybe," said Bruno, knowing that no murder solution was ever straightforward. "We need to find out what was in that safe but, first, we need to find out all we can about the victim. Who was it who discovered the body?" Bruno asked.

"The cleaner, who normally arrives at about 6:45 p.m. Mrs Catchpole. Sheila Catchpole. She is in a state of shock, but we can interview her later, as well as Calafifi's work colleague, Annabel Wilson, who we understand left at 5:45 p.m. She – Annabel – was the last person, as far as we know, who saw the victim alive."

"Can we interview Annabel Wilson now?"

"She was prevented from entering the building earlier, sir, when she showed up, and was sent back home again, but she is available to come in as soon as we call her. She didn't know about Simeon's death, so she came to work as usual, it seems. I'll call her now and ask her to come right away."

Andy called Annabel Wilson at home, and she left immediately at their request to come to the bookshop. Meanwhile he had received a lengthier email from the office with an initial summary of the Scene of Crime Officers' and forensic findings.

The victim had died instantly from a single stab wound that had pierced the heart through his back. The killer had evidently been able to move behind Simeon and to thrust the weapon deeply into his body. There had been no sign of any struggle. This suggested the killer knew Simeon well enough to wander around while he was attending to something at his desk or that the killer had been able to silently sneak up on the victim. Standing in the office, Bruno tried to imagine the scenario where the murderer could have manoeuvred himself into a position where he could forcibly stab the victim in the back. Bruno agreed that it could have been when the killer stood behind Simeon while he was showing or explaining something to the killer that probably lay on the desk, or it could have been when the killer was looking at the books in the cabinet; finally, the killer could have emerged from the concealed darkness at the rear of the shop unseen and unheard by Simeon. At this stage, nothing was clear or certain.

The fact that the murderer came out of normal business hours, on a cold February night, could be significant, suggesting that he, she or they were known to the victim, and did not want to be identified by staff, therefore showing up when the shop was empty but the owner still there. This further suggested someone who knew the dynamics of the shop working day.

There was nothing remarkable to report about the office layout. Nothing appeared to have been disturbed. Without a struggle, Calafifi had slumped forward onto his desk, whereupon the killer presumably made a quick escape through the rear door, through which the bookshop owner might previously have admitted them.

"A very quick death," said Andy, searching for a positive comment to make in the face of such a brutal and calculated killing.

"What do we know about the victim?" asked Bruno, taking a seat in one of the armchairs in the front room of the bookstore.

Andy handed Bruno the brief dossier prepared by the office team, which gave him the following information.

Simeon Calafifi was a well-known antiquarian bookseller with a national and international reputation.

Calafifi was aged fifty and lived with his wife, Miriam, an architect, in Ryde. Their two young sons, Benjamin, aged seven, and David, aged eight, went to Ryde School. The family had moved to the Isle of Wight from Muswell Hill, a north London suburb. At the same time, Simeon had relocated his antiquarian book business from an expensive shop premises in Mayfair in Central London to a decent sized shop in the Isle of Wight town of Shanklin.

Simeon Calafifi ran his business with the assistance of Annabel Wilson, who was described as the manager on Simeon's website, which detailed a short précis of her career. An Oxford University Classics graduate with a first-class honours degree, Annabel had spent several years in New York working in the Public Library cataloguing rare editions of American literature. She then moved to Jerusalem as an assistant in the Hebrew Library of Ancient Manuscripts. Many of these ancient works dated from the time of the Jewish exile from Babylon, when their Prince Zerubbabel was given permission by Cyrus, King of Persia, to lead his people back to the Promised Land. The arduous journey was recorded by the chief Scribe Ezra on parchment, much of which had been found hidden in the vaults of the second temple in Jerusalem beneath the altar erected to King Solomon. Also discovered were the designs of the temple by Hiram Abif, the chief architect to the King.

This unique knowledge acquired by Annabel Wilson, having worked as part of a team authenticating and translating both old and newly discovered parchments, had proved valuable to Calafifi, so that his business became regarded as one of the leading book dealers of antique religious books and manuscripts throughout the UK and

Europe. Her experience in Simeon's field was second to none and immensely helpful in developing the business on the Island, and beyond.

*

When Annabel Wilson had arrived for work first thing that Wednesday morning, she had apparently anticipated business as usual. She had been noticeably surprised to see a uniformed officer at the entrance to the shop, and was sent away having been told her workplace was now a crime scene. Her details had been taken by uniformed officers and passed to Andy Bowen when he and Bruno arrived. After Andy's phone call asking her to attend, she expected the detectives to be waiting inside to see her.

After introducing himself to her, Bruno observed that Annabel looked about forty, about five foot six, blonde, with a fair complexion and sparkling eyes. She was exceptionally clean and tidily dressed, wearing a trouser suit and leather boots appropriate for the weather. She gave no indication whether she was married or had a family.

It was Bruno's sad duty to tell her about the death of her employer the night before in suspicious circumstances. Overnight, they had sought to keep the news private, for a number of public and private reasons. Her reaction was a stunned silence, as she clearly had no idea what had taken place. Bruno related what Mrs Catchpole had discovered and confirmed that, as yet, the detectives had reached no conclusions about the cause of death.

"Before we go any further, Miss Wilson, please can you tell us a little about yourself, your background and your connection to the deceased?" Bruno said.

Annabel explained that she had retired from her University of Jerusalem post to move to the Isle of Wight three years earlier to concentrate on writing. She was clearly an authoritative scholar on Ancient Roman history. She had written on the politics of Rome and Greece at the period around the beginning of the first millennium, although she had so far failed to capture the attention of the film and television industry, where she faced competition from other learned female scholars.

Books, she claimed, were her first love. Working for Simeon, an antiquarian bookseller, had given her the opportunity to indulge her passion and use her specialist knowledge, at the same time learning the intricacies and politics of the business, alongside the secrets of buying and selling valuable books. She was fortunate that Simeon's Bookshop was located in Shanklin, where she lived, so she could structure her life accordingly. As every writer knows, she explained, you can only engage in creative or academic writing for a limited part of each day, whatever your subject, and combining writing with the discipline and experience she enjoyed in Simeon's Bookshop created an ideal lifestyle for her.

Annabel's demeanour clearly displayed her distress at the killing of Simeon Calafifi. Not only was he her employer but Bruno detected that he was also a friend who shared much in common with her. Kindred spirits, it seemed.

"Miss Wilson, nothing has been disturbed since you left at the close of business yesterday. Can you have a look around – touching nothing, of course – and tell us if anything looks unusual? Furthermore, what happened during the day, yesterday, before you closed the shop and what time was that?"

"Please, call me Annabel," she said before continuing. "Nothing really out of the ordinary happened during the day, yesterday, but it did seem odd that Simeon was expecting a visitor after closing time."

Bruno and Andy were clearly interested and said, almost in unison: "Who was this visitor Simeon said he was expecting?"

"He didn't tell me who it was. He simply said that someone was calling to collect a book soon after 5:45 p.m. I left as the shop closed, as I usually do."

"And you didn't ask who it was?" asked Andy.

She shook her head.

"Would you be able to work out and tell us from your records who it might have been?"

"No, my records show titles ordered by me for customers, whom I call when the book arrives. As he didn't say who it was and what it was, I have no record," she said.

"Is there any way you could find out who would call at your bookshop to collect a book after hours?"

"I will try, Chief Inspector, but don't expect me to find anything."

Bruno was surprised that she was so sure she would find nothing, and curious that Simeon would have kept details of a sale from her, as surely it would have to show in the sales figures. However, he did not pursue that line of questioning at this stage.

Andy asked Annabel about her own movements on the night of the murder.

Annabel said: "I left at 5:45 p.m. as usual, said good night to Simeon and exited by the rear door. I got into my car, and I saw nothing untoward as I drove home, to prepare supper for a friend."

"Could you show us around the full extent of the premises? How the doors open and shut – that kind of thing," said Bruno.

"Of course," she said. They followed her as she walked and talked. "From the street it is a double-fronted shop premises which you enter by the centre front door, as you can see. In this front area on both sides are the tables on which we stack new publications – novels, thrillers, historical books. There is a section displaying biographies and crime novels in alphabetical order. As you'd expect in a small bookshop, all the walls are lined with shelves. They have to be. Classics take up one wall section, as do hobbies, travel and general fiction, on the other side."

Annabel led them to the centre of the shop. "This is the payment desk. You then come into the antiquarian, rare and first edition books, which occupy about the same floor area as the front section. Beyond that is Simeon's office, where the latest acquisitions are received, considered and catalogued. On the rear wall of his office is a bookcase of first editions and valuable rare books to view by supervised appointment. There is also his computer and business records and so on."

"And that is where the safe is?" asked Bruno.

"Yes, the safe is behind his desk. I'll show you," she replied, and walked them through towards the office she had described, and which they had examined earlier, describing sections which contained special items, maps and manuscripts as they proceeded.

Right at the back, and through another door, were two further areas, which Annabel pointed out to them.

"On the right is the workshop for our bookbinder, Mr Ladbroke. He lives in Ryde and comes in when we have any work for him. He is a celebrated craftsman and, having lived in Islington, North London, he has known the Calafifis for many years."

"When was Mr Ladbroke last in the office?"

"Just on Monday, the 27th, the day before yesterday," Annabel said. "He uses the right-hand side room as his workshop. The left side office is kept locked because it's where we keep an antiquarian library. It's also where we package mail order sales. Finally, there is a sitting area, a toilet and a kitchen. This leads through to a rear door to the car park where we keep the bins. The security system control box is inside the back door, so we enter and exit through the back, and it leads to where Simeon and I park. He would set the alarm when he left, usually 15 to 30 minutes after me, I would think. You can also exit and lock up and put the alarm on at the front door, but we don't do that because we drive here, and our cars are at the back."

She showed them outside of the rear exit where Simeon's car was still parked, next to hers.

"Do people use the rear entrance?"

"No, only Simeon and me," she said. "We take all deliveries through the front because you can park outside on the wide pavement. And obviously our customers come through the shopfront."

"So, more likely, in your opinion, the killer would have entered through the front entrance?"

"I don't know," remarked Annabel, "but if they came to the back door, they would probably have been familiar with the building."

"And there are cameras front and back?" asked Andy.

"No, detectives, there are no cameras," she said.

"Do you know many of Mr Calafifi's friends or business acquaintances?" Andy asked, changing tack somewhat.

"I sometimes meet his clients, of course, and yes, I know some of them. In some cases, I'd need to look up names, because I don't know them all, nor do I know them personally. However, I do know most of the local people who come here to browse, to order books that we stock. Once or twice each week Simeon would meet a person by appointment and adjourn to the rear office to discuss their business. Sometimes I would attend to give information, or to take details, but not if the meeting was after closing hours. He regularly attended book sales and auctions on the mainland, where he bought and sold books. It was the main part of our business. I did not go with him to sales and auctions. I would stay here and hold the fort."

She continued with her explanation: "We keep books in the safe that have been sold and paid for, so they don't go astray. If a client comes to the shop and pays a considerable sum of money, by cash or cheque, then that plus the day's takings would be put in the safe, and I would go to the bank the next day with that."

"Who has the keys to the safe?" asked Andy.

"Both Simeon and I do. He seldom used his safe key. I say that because, if I'm in, he'll always ask me to open it."

"Can you explain why the safe is open and empty now?"

In the time Annabel had been in the shop she hadn't noticed that the safe was unlocked.

"I can't, Chief Inspector, because I locked it before I left yesterday, after putting in the day's takings."

She stood up and went to examine the safe, which had been left closed by the fingerprint detectives. She opened the safe, bent down and felt the two shelves. Andy had indicated that it was okay for her to do so.

"I went to the bank first thing on Monday, so the unbanked takings for Monday and Tuesday were there. I can look up the exact amount, but £500 would be roughly the figure for those two days. The books in the safe were the Talmud and the *Book of Mormon*. Simeon acquired the Talmud on behalf of Tel Aviv University for Professor Kazac in Israel, and the *Book of Mormon* for a client that I don't know."

"When the police arrived yesterday evening, the safe was closed – pushed to – but was unlocked and empty. There was no cash in it and the books you mentioned were not in the safe," said Bruno.

"So, they stole the Talmud and the *Book of Mormon*?" she said. "That's awful! What a terrible shame! Simeon was so excited to have bought that book on behalf of the University in Tel Aviv. It was a really big deal for him, that transaction. He was planning to deliver it next week, in person. Professor Kazac had invited Simeon to Israel to present the Talmud to him at the University. That's why the Talmud was still in our safe. Kazac wanted to make a ceremonial presentation of the occasion. That's why

Simeon was going over there to deliver it. That and because it is both rare and valuable."

"Might someone want to kill him for it?" asked Bruno. "One possibility is that the killer came for this Talmud book, and simply took the cash as well because it was there? But if the safe was locked by you on departure, perhaps it was opened by Simeon to show the Talmud or the *Book of Mormon*? Or maybe it was opened by the killer, after Simeon's murder, and the books and money taken."

"If I had the slightest idea what happened I would tell you, Chief Inspector, but I would think that the killer's mission was to steal the Talmud," she said. "Will you let me quickly search or check for the book and also see if anything else has been stolen? It's a special book and would interest very few people," she said. "I will check the stock just in case for any reason Simeon took it out of the safe and put it somewhere else. Unlikely but it's worth me checking, I think."

Annabel went to the case where the valuable editions were kept, turned her head to the side, making a quick scan of their spines and front covers where shown.

"Nothing seems out of place, and I can't see either of the two safe books, so I'd guess that they did target the Talmud, and succeeded," she said.

"So, if you locked the safe when you left, Simeon must have opened it to show the books to the killer," Bruno suggested.

"Yes, I suppose so," she said. "He would only have done that for a person whom he deemed properly interested in a religious book."

"So, that is one thing we can likely say about the killer.

They were credible enough for Simeon to open the safe and show it to him. He wouldn't do that for a stranger. Unless, of course, they opened the safe after Simeon had been killed."

Bruno stood facing the desk where Simeon had been knifed in the back, convinced that he must have been killed by someone he knew, and knew well enough to allow him to browse the contents of the shop while he was preoccupied sitting at his desk. Furthermore, he thought it likely that only Simeon could have opened the safe.

Bruno asked Annabel, "But seeing as the book was already sold, why would Simeon take it out of the safe to show someone else?"

After a lengthy pause she said, "I don't think Simeon thought that his evening visitor's intention was to steal the Talmud. I can think of no one I know who is like that. This business is extremely competitive and secretive, and in this environment perhaps you never know the true nature of people, so for him to have opened the safe, it might well have been to just show the Talmud. Maybe to show the quality of books that pass through our hands?" she said.

"Do you know of anyone in particular that Simeon might want to show the Talmud to?"

"No, I don't, the Talmud could have been of interest to many people. Furthermore, people who collect Jewish religious books are not necessarily Jewish."

"What about the other book you mentioned?"

Annabel was starting to get a bit overwhelmed. "I really don't know, Chief Inspector. The truth is, I have no idea what happened," Annabel said. "There are the dealers and the collectors who compete with each other for ancient manuscripts, first editions of books, music scores and original hand-drawn maps. At auction, you never know who you are up against. Simeon said they sometimes bid on the internet even though they are also physically present in the sale room just to maintain their anonymity. He does it too. Some clients do not want it known publicly what they buy, or they could become a target."

"But in this case, everyone knew that Simeon had bought the Talmud. So, in that way he could have become a target?" said Bruno.

"It seems that way, Chief Inspector," she said.

"Then it is a ruthless business!" said Bruno.

"Yes," she said.

"Among all the people he deals with, who would you classify as ruthless enough to commit this murder, just to steal two books?"

She grimaced and answered quickly.

"Capable of murder? I think one or two of them are capable of extremes, but I'm not sure about murder. Really, I don't know."

"Can you provide us with a list of all the dealers and collectors that Simeon has dealt with in the last six months?"

"I will," she said. "It will take me half an hour to email you a copy of our database."

"Miss Wilson, obviously you knew Mr Calafifi well. Do you know also know Mrs Calafifi? Can you please tell us about her?" said Bruno.

"I do know her, yes. I like her. She is a very elegant woman, sophisticated and beautiful, Chief Inspector. She is younger than Simeon, I would say about 45. She doesn't come to the shop much, but she often accompanies him to auctions, I think. She seems to really nurture her two boys. She comes across as a very loving mother, but ambitious and has already mapped out careers for them. She is an architect by profession and works for a London firm. She travels to London a couple of times a week and works from home the rest of the time. They are a really lovely family," she said.

Annabel's sadness was visible, as she realised she should have been speaking in the past tense. Her life would surely change now, surmised Bruno, as it would for everyone connected with the shop. He thanked her for her help, and she promised to be available any time the police needed her.

She did ask about re-opening the shop, and they asked her a few further questions about the day-to-day business. Before they left, Andy secured the office again, ensuring that nothing could be disturbed there, even if the shop reopened. Andy took several pictures of the position of Simeon's desk and the desktop with the bloodstains, for his own records. He and Bruno then drove back to Newport to establish the incident room and assign tasks to more junior members of their team. There was a lot to do, including the need to prepare a statement for the local press.

Before that, Bruno himself wanted to see two important people; first to see the cleaning lady who had discovered the body and to make his own judgement as to what might have happened by listening to her words first hand; then to see the victim's wife. He decided to see the cleaner first, in a reverse of usual protocol, so that he would not be hurried in talking to the victim's wife. He sensed, given what he had already learned about Simeon Calafifi, and from Annabel's comments, that Mrs Calafifi would be an interesting person with a lot to tell.

Bruno knew nothing about books. The book trade, in particular this high-end specialist business, was a mystery to him but brutal murders were not, and he was quietly confident that his police training and extensive experience would eventually help them discover the motive, and then the killer.

Everything connected with Simeon Calafifi's murder so far seemed to centre on the business, and yet he must now speak to Mrs Calafifi, in order to learn more about the man and his family life. In the meantime, Bruno reflected on what Annabel had told them.

"I am not entirely easy with what Annabel told us about her own departure last night," said Bruno to Andy. "Would she not offer to wait an extra fifteen minutes to greet Simeon's visitor, and perhaps offer to help or make a drink? And even stay until his visitor had collected the book and left? I am surprised, given how closely they worked, that she didn't ask who was coming, or just know anyway because of her involvement in the day-to-day work. As this visitor was supposedly coming to collect a book, she would at least know which book, I would have thought. Her role in Simeon's business was key to its success, which Simeon would have understood, so why would he conceal the details of a client visiting from her?"

"It doesn't make sense," agreed Andy, who was used to there being more questions than answers at this stage of an investigation. "Yes, she has offered us nothing of any use or help about the book the visitor was supposed to be collecting or about the identity of the visitor, which is strange given the type of person she is, her experience, knowledge, and so forth. I think that's a bit odd. If we examine the street camera though, it could show the time this visitor arrived, and who it was."

"If they came in through the front of the shop, that is," said Bruno.

Chapter 2

In any murder investigation, Bruno did not underestimate the importance and urgency of the statement from the person who discovered the body. They arrived to take Mrs Catchpole's formal statement around 4 p.m. at her home, at the end of a small close off Green Lane, a fifteen-minute walk to Simeon's Bookshop. She was dressed casually and looked like she hadn't slept since the events of the night before. Knowing how traumatic the experience would have been for her, they approached her in a calm, consoling manner, by asking her to describe simply what happened in the lead up to finding Simeon dead.

She said that when she arrived at 6:45 p.m. to clean the shop and offices, she did not discover the body of Simeon Calafifi immediately.

"I let myself in through the front entrance and locked the door behind me. I put the lights on in the shop, but I always start to clean from the back, where I clean the kitchen and toilet first, so I didn't light up the office which is in the centre. I didn't even go in there. When I'd finished all the back rooms, I did the shop and then went into the office and noticed Mr Simeon. Because everything was locked and there were no lights on when I arrived, I thought he had left. At first, I thought he'd gone to sleep on his desk, but when I got closer, I saw his face was down, his head turned slightly to one side, his shoulders slumped across the desk. I didn't know he was dead. When I spoke to him and got no answer, I went up and kind of nudged him," she shuddered and went quiet.

"What happened then, Mrs Catchpole?" Bruno asked.

"There was blood. Just a little bit, Chief Inspector, but he was bleeding from his mouth, and I just knew he was dead. I was so frightened they might still be there, the murderer, I mean, that I ran to the front of the shop. I unlocked the front door and ran out. Then, I dialled 999 from my mobile. I spoke to a girl and told her I thought Mr Simeon had been killed and gave her the shop address."

"Do you always carry your phone on you when you are working?"

"Yes, because if I put it down, I never remember where I put it. I have a zip-up side pocket in my work trousers. I spoke to a woman in the street, and she waited with me until the police car came. No one came out of the shop. We didn't see anything. Nothing at all."

The two detectives let her continue.

"After what seemed like hours, a police car arrived with two officers in it, and I told them what I had seen inside the shop. I think they were about to go inside when lots of other people arrived. An ambulance and another police car and a van."

Mrs Catchpole told them what had happened then outside the shop up to the time when Andy had sent her home: "And then you told me I had to go home, and you'd come and see me today and here you are."

So far, Mrs Catchpole's explanation had told them nothing new. Having listened to her hurried explanation of what happened, Bruno took her back to the beginning.

"Yes, that's why we're here," Bruno assured her. "And you are being immensely helpful, Mrs Catchpole. Now, when you first arrived at work, was the shop locked?"

"Yes, when I enter the shop, I unlock the mortice at the bottom and then I use the Yale to open the door; then when I am in, I close the door which shuts the Yale lock automatically and I lock the mortice behind me, leaving my keys in the lock."

"Was the mortice locked when you opened the door?"

"Yes, I think so. I think it was. Yes," she confirmed, although her tone suggested that this may or may not have been the case.

"Did everything seem normal when you came in?"

"Well, yes, completely. I mean the alarm wasn't on but that could be normal," she added.

Immediately interested, Bruno asked her to explain what she meant, and she told them that Simeon Calafifi and Annabel Wilson both usually entered and exited by the back door and used the burglar alarm keypad by that back door. There was an identical keypad at the front door meaning you could come in and out using either entrance and still manage to set an alarm.

"Did this mean that you expected to find someone inside?"

"No," Mrs Catchpole explained. "To be honest, they weren't always one hundred per cent reliable in locking up and setting the alarm. I think Annabel was better at it than Mr Simeon. He often shut the door behind him having forgotten to set the alarm. So, no, it didn't make me think anything in particular. Anyway, I called out and no-one replied, so I just assumed that I was on my own and everyone else had gone home as normal."

After thinking for a moment, Bruno ventured: "We believe the murderer may have left by the back door. It was dark, and they wouldn't be seen. Did you check the back door?"

"No, Chief Inspector, I may have glanced at it when I was down that way but, even though the alarm wasn't on, because of the Yale locks at the top of each door, the door is kind of locked when it is pulled shut, if you get what I mean."

"Do you have a key to the back door?"

"Yes, it's on my key ring. The bins are outside the back door. But I hadn't put the rubbish out yet. By the way, you've still got my keys, or someone must have, because I left them in the back of the front door."

"What did you touch while you were cleaning the kitchen and lavatory?"

"I always go straight to the kitchen and wash up the coffee cups. Then I clean the lavatory. I don't do the other back rooms unless I am specifically asked to, which is almost never. That part's for storage and book binding and the like. Anyway, after the kitchen and the lavatory, I get the hoover from the kitchen cupboard and get ready to do the shop and then the office in the middle, but last night I didn't get that far because – well, you know why."

"In Mr Calafifi's office, did you notice anything unusual?"

"Nothing. I don't remember anything. Apart from him, of course."

At this stage, Andy and Bruno asked a few more simple questions about routine and about her relationship with Simeon Calafifi. Everything seemed in order and very unremarkable.

"Well, that's all for today, and you have been very helpful, Mrs Catchpole," said Andy. "We will type up what you have told us, and you will be asked to read and sign it for our records. If you think of anything that maybe useful to us, however trivial, perhaps you would call us."

"Of course, I'll do that, Chief Inspector. Who do you think killed him?"

"At this moment we have no idea."

Even without confirmatory forensics, neither detective felt that Sheila Catchpole had had anything to do with Simeon Calafifi's murder. Having said that, their suspicion that something was missing from her account of her activities was confirmed when they got back to their desks an hour later and Bruno took a rather anxious call from Mrs Catchpole.

"Chief Inspector, I have remembered something. If the bin bag is full in the kitchen, I will put it out when I clean the kitchen, into the black bin outside the back door. If it's not full, I might use it to empty the shop and office bins into. It saves on black bags, that's all. Last night I remember doing that – putting the kitchen bin straight out, I mean. It was full. So I used a different, fresh one for the shop and the office. But here's the thing: the back door Yale lock was clicked open. It looked shut because the door was pulled to, but it wasn't. So I suppose anyone could have come in or out. I hope I haven't given you any trouble by forgetting that," she said.

"Absolutely not, Mrs Catchpole. And thank you for your call." This news was important. The back door was effectively open for anyone to enter or exit.

While Bruno was speaking to Mrs Catchpole, Andy had called Mrs Calafifi to warn her of their impending arrival. She asked them to come over the next morning, early, rather than straightaway, because it was already nearly 6 p.m. Andy explained that they really needed to see her that evening and so she reluctantly agreed. There seemed nothing strange about her reluctance, given that she must also have been in severe shock.

After he put down the phone, Andy said, "Mrs Calafifi is expecting us now, sir."

Bruno explained what Mrs Catchpole had told him. The information about the alarm not being on and the back door being open was filed, mentally, as useful and potentially important but, of course, suggested nothing concrete at this stage. As they were about to leave the office, Andy put the following to Bruno:

"So, if Annabel Wilson left at 6 p.m., let's say the killer didn't arrive until 6:05 p.m. at the earliest. That gave him or her forty minutes maximum to have committed the murder and to have left the shop before Mrs Catchpole arrived at 6:45 p.m. Do you think that Simeon let the murderer in – this supposed visitor – then, after the crime, the murderer left by the back door? Would they have left the door on the latch? Or was it already on the latch? And, either way, why? I would have thought that the murderer would have shut the door behind them firmly. Or maybe the door was already on the latch, and they didn't want to touch it?"

Bruno was pleased to see that Andy was thinking along these lines, and therefore he listened and nodded along to Andy's musings. He added:

"Of course, this is all assuming that Sheila Catchpole and Annabel Wilson are telling the truth, you know."

Andy chose not to reply, knowing that his boss was right.

Chapter 3

A first meeting with the surviving spouse of a deceased person is an occasion requiring tact and delicacy. Even more so, in the case of a murder.

Andy Bowen had met Mrs Calafifi late on the previous evening when he had been to inform her of her husband's death. A Support Officer had also made a preliminary visit to her on Wednesday morning to offer support and advice of a pastoral nature.

This third visit to Mrs Calafifi, almost 24 hours since the discovery of her husband's body, was a key interview in terms of the investigation. Armed with initial information gleaned from the scene and from Simeon's workplace, this was their opportunity to find out as much as possible about the victim from the person who probably knew him best.

They were greeted at the front door by a lady who lived up to Annabel Wilson's description of her. She was strikingly beautiful and gave the appearance of a well-educated, professional architect, just as she had been described. The house was silent, as if in mourning itself. They offered their condolences on her loss.

"Please sit down, detectives," she spoke softly, ushering them in to an elegantly decorated sitting room. There was no television in this room but, as they might have expected, the walls were covered with bookcases.

Almost as if in prayer, the detectives took their lead from Mrs Calafifi, and sat silently and mindfully, for a period of no longer than a minute, calmed by the room itself and her presence in it. It was almost as if they could hear her thinking, trying to understand the reason for the evil act and its effect on her life going forward.

"Mrs Calafifi, we can come back if you would prefer," said Andy. Bruno looked at him slightly reproachfully and was relieved when Mrs Calafifi demurred:

"No, thank you. If I can help you in your investigation, I will. I think we can start, gentlemen." Without waiting to be asked a question, she continued, "I visited my husband in the mortuary at St. Mary's Hospital last night at midnight to identify him. I didn't see his injury, just his head and shoulders. Detective Chief Inspector, I know it may not be allowed, but I really would like to bury him as soon as possible. Today is Wednesday, so tomorrow, Thursday, would be ideal. Otherwise it will be Friday and that is difficult because funerals can be prohibited on that day. It is quite difficult to strictly follow religious protocol from here on the Island, so I need to put arrangements in place as soon as possible."

Realising the significance to Mrs Calafifi of an immediate burial, Bruno agreed to do his best, at the same time knowing that police procedure would certainly prevent the police releasing the body immediately. In the case of a murder, regardless of the faith of the victim, it was often a month or so before a funeral could take place.

"Mrs Calafifi, what can you tell us that might help us understand your husband and his business and his life?"

"Well, apart from his work, which was his passion and was all-absorbing, he had various interests. Our London life was vastly different to the life we have here. There my husband was involved in various charities; we went to the theatre, the opera, the ballet and the cinema, and he sat on an antiquarian book committee at the British Museum. He had many friends. Here our life has changed dramatically; we know almost nobody. Island culture is different, as you surely know."

"Why did you move here?"

"Lots of reasons. Simeon wanted the boys to have a different life, to be by the sea. He wanted to buy a boat and go sailing, but he never did, of course. He was searching for some kind of peace. Although we loved it, he found the pace of life in London too much."

"Mrs Calafifi, I sense moving to the Island must have been difficult for you and your family. How did you feel about it? Was it a joint decision?"

"It was Simeon's idea. He felt under threat in London."

"Under threat? From whom or what?"

"I don't know, Chief Inspector. I think he felt that stretch of water was protective." Bruno noted Mrs Calafifi's careful choice of words.

"Was Simeon worried about anything?"

"He was a worrier, for sure. He worried about anything and everything, but there was nothing specific he was worrying about that I am aware of. The shop was doing well and travelling to the mainland, both for sales and purchases, was not a problem. He retained his contacts after our move from North London and the internet mail order business was doing very well. There was no competition to speak of on the Island for ancient books. If you wanted something special, you asked Simeon to source it for you."

"What about further afield?" asked Bruno.

"As I said, sales online were doing well both from the UK and from Europe and beyond. You can find British books of the kind Simeon specialised in at antiquarian bookshops in Paris, for example. The market is good. Simeon knew many dealers there and across Europe. Remember that he had a business in London for many years until we came to the Island."

"So you would say he has done well here?"

"Very well in maintaining the business he had in and from London. Portsmouth and Southampton are easy to travel to and from, and many customers actually like to come to the Island. This part of Southern England, close to London, has offered up incredible back stories, artefacts, ancient maps and books. I also wonder if the slight difficulty and long journey makes the acquisition of a special book seem even more of an achievement."

"On the Island, who were your husband's friends?" asked Andy.

"Specific Island friends? As I said, there weren't so many. His contact list will be in his phone, which he took to the office. I assume that you have it. Annabel can tell you more than I can about business contacts. The bulk of his business was international, with dealers in New York, Los Angeles and Paris. The Americans are terrific book collectors. Books that were written about the American Civil War, the American War of Independence, are greatly sought after, as are original documents from the American

Civil War. All books from the Middle Eastern countries on religion are keenly bought and collected. You occasionally find the most extraordinary books far away from home."

Miriam Calafifi continued. She spoke very fluently. "Our friends socially were mostly parents whose children go to Ryde School. You would probably call them social acquaintances rather than true friends. Like his father was, Simeon was a Freemason and had joined the Royal Vectis Lodge, which meets in Cowes, and he was a member of the Grand Lodge in London. I don't think many of his Masonic friends were in the book trade."

"Anyone you know, friends or acquaintances that he knew well, who might visit him after hours in his bookshop? On a one-off basis, or regularly?"

"I can't think of anyone. It is not a time-critical business." She paused to reflect. "I have to say that I always thought that some people in the book business are a bit," she paused as she looked for the right word, "well, a bit shifty, the kind of people who creep around in the shadows," she said. "Perhaps I'm being naïve, and all businesses show the same face to the uninitiated. At book auctions, they often stand together in corners, two or three of them whispering, as if what they are buying or selling is a secret. Maybe that's just the nature of the auction world."

"Did you often go to book auction sales with him?"

"Not often – I went with him occasionally, but only if it fitted in well with the boys and my own work. To be honest, it was an excuse to get off the Island. While Simeon was at the sale, I might see a local client of my own or just go shopping. Simeon knew many people in the book business who all wanted to speak to him, so I left it to him. I never specifically met any dealers or buyers. Simeon's comments gave me the impression that buyers are either very rich, with plenty of money to spend on books as a kind of luxury, or conversely didn't have a penny to bless themselves with and were just interested in the idea of buying and selling, rather than actually being able to do it. Without experience of doing business with them, you couldn't really tell the difference. With respect to the dealers, there are good ones and bad ones. By good, I mean successful. Successful dealers are those that make big profits from sales because they are clever and know what book to buy and who to sell it on to. They really are experts in their specialist subjects."

"We have reason to believe that two books have gone missing from the bookshop at the same time as your husband's murder. One of these was a Talmud. Has your husband told you about that specific book? It is high value and rare and, as I said, it is missing," said Bruno.

"Of course I know what a Talmud is, but I don't know about this specific one or the transactions surrounding it. You'd need to ask Annabel."

Bruno thought this was odd, given Annabel's comments that Simeon was planning to deliver the book to Tel Aviv in just a few days.

"Mrs Calafifi, what time did your husband normally get home from work?"

"He always got home around 6:30 in the evening, in time for us to eat together at 7."

"Mrs Calafifi, yesterday evening, we understand your husband had an appointment after closing time in his office, hence he was working late. Did he tell you who this appointment was with?"

"I didn't know he had an appointment yesterday evening after the bookshop shut, and if he had set one up during the day, he would have rung and told me."

"So, you expected him as per usual?"

"Certainly, or he would have called me."

"Could you sketch out for us your movements yesterday evening?"

"I was home when the police arrived with the news of Simeon's death," Miriam stated remarkably calmly.

"Does that mean you were home all evening?"

"On Tuesdays my sons have violin and piano lessons after school, so I pick them up from the school site when their lessons finish at 6 o'clock. We come straight home and then Simeon would usually arrive around 6:30. I had prepared supper for 7 as normal. I wasn't unduly worried when he had not arrived home by 7 but I called his mobile 'phone. There was no answer, which I thought strange. I texted and called him a few more times. The boys and I ate, and I put them to bed. I texted him again and was beginning to wonder whether I should contact someone or go and look for him when you came to the door," she nodded in Andy's direction referring to his arrival on the previous evening to inform her of her husband's death.

Bruno spoke next: "Annabel Wilson in the shop told us that Simeon was expecting a visitor after normal hours, and he omitted to tell her who it was."

"I find that extremely hard to believe, Chief Inspector. She would know, I'm sure, in fact, wouldn't she do most of that kind of organising? I'm not saying that I don't believe her, but she must be getting muddled."

"We will go back to her on that point," said Andy. "What are your plans over the next couple of days?"

"I need to have Simeon's body so that I can organise a proper Jewish funeral and burial. That will be on the mainland. My preference would be to return to the mainland, to London, as soon as possible. I mean permanently. I need to focus on my sons. They are just boys, who now have to come to terms with their father's murder. That is why I would like to take them home to be near family as soon as possible – to protect them. If I could, I would leave tomorrow morning, but I will leave as soon as reasonably possible."

Bruno said: "Mrs Calafifi, I have to ask: do you know of anyone who might have had a grudge against your husband? Personally or professionally? Do you know anyone who would want to kill him?" Bruno always felt that such questions were a bit inappropriate, but it was important to ask this, if only to gauge the reaction of the deceased's nearest and dearest.

"I don't know who would want to kill Simeon. I don't know where this person would be from, Chief Inspector. I can't even guess," she said.

Bruno asked, "Do you have anything else that can help the police with our investigation, Mrs Calafifi?"

She paused slightly before continuing.

"There is just one thing that I believe I should tell you, Chief Inspector. It's about the business. Since Simeon and I moved to the Island, I have continued to work for a London-based architectural practice, which I visit each week. Occasionally – perhaps every six weeks – my work takes me to Paris. This has placed a strain on the whole family, mainly because of the additional travel time. When we were in London, I could get off the Eurostar and be home in half an hour. And we have lots of family in London who could step in and help out with the boys, and they did. Here we don't have that help and it has been difficult. Simeon decided, some time ago, that we should move to Bournemouth, and he would sell the business here and re-establish himself on the mainland. He suggested Bournemouth because it was still by the sea and was not London, as it were, but it does have an airport, from where I could fly not only to Paris but also to London City airport. It was to be an exciting change, Chief Inspector, and I was all for it. He found a buyer on the Island, to purchase the shop and the stock and the goodwill that he had established here. Contracts were signed just two days ago – on Monday. We won't move to Bournemouth now, but it is a blessing – perhaps the only small blessing in this – that I do not have to worry about the business. It's sold."

This was important news to the detectives.

"Mrs Calafifi, does anyone else know about the sale of the business?"

"No one. Not even Annabel. I have spoken to the purchaser today. He confirmed that contracts were indeed exchanged on Monday. Completion was supposed to happen in a month, during the Easter holidays for the boys. The completion was delayed to allow for all the stock work that would need to be done and also because the new buyer wanted to take the opportunity to have a holiday before the business became his. We were going to enjoy the summer term all together here and then re-locate physically in July and August. The purchaser is happy to take over when your investigation is complete. I suppose you will want to speak to him. However, I would appreciate if you could keep the sale quiet for the immediate future. I don't want anyone to know."

"Can you tell us who the buyer is?" asked Bruno, noting that she had called the purchaser already, clearly able to still focus on business despite her husband's murder.

"On the condition that it remains between us," said Mrs Calafifi. "Until we, that is the buyer and I, are ready to announce the sale. It is Nathan Philips, who owns the Bembridge Bookshop. I understand he has borrowed money from the bank, and I know that he and Simeon were going to continue in some form of reciprocal agreement, but I don't know what form that was to take."

"Our investigations are always confidential. Not a word of this conversation will be divulged to anyone," said Bruno.

"Thank you, Chief Inspector. I want to avoid any press publicity which might upset the boys and affect their schooling, or any intrusion into our private life. The Head-master of Ryde School has already been in touch today to offer financial help with school fees and other support for the boys. They haven't gone in to school today – they're upstairs with our housekeeper watching television. I'll give them supper on trays tonight in front of the TV."

Bruno offered some condolences and agreed how everyone, especially the school, would doubtless be keen to help if she were to stay on the Island, choosing the continuity of school life there for the boys.

Miriam Calafifi shook her head. "Sadly, I must conclude that for us, the Isle of Wight experience is over. I'm sure you can understand that as soon as possible we want to return to the safety and security of friends and family in North London. My mother-in-law is coming from London this evening. She is distressed. She only lost her husband a few years ago. Now her son. She wants to see Simeon. She could hardly speak on the 'phone to me. But she is also a level-headed woman, and she said she wants to bring some normality and to help me with the boys in the wake of their father's death."

"One last thing, Mrs Calafifi. You mentioned that Simeon was a member of a Masonic lodge here and in London. You also said that you didn't think that many of his lodge connections were involved in the book trade. We'd like to look into that ourselves. Who were his particular friends at the lodge? Any names you could give us could be helpful. Furthermore, what was stolen is of such high value and is of such symbolic significance that I suspect we will need to look beyond the Island, to the mainland and possibly beyond. I may need to ask you about your life in London too at some stage and in more detail."

"I don't know if any of Simeon's Masonic friends come into the category of the type of people you are referring to. You should speak to the lodge secretary. I know his number because he tends to contact Simeon at home rather than at work and by telephone rather than email or text," Miriam stood up and walked to the desk. She wrote a number from a book onto a piece of paper and handed it to Bruno. She did not sit back down, and her manner suggested that the interview was over.

It was time to leave. Both Bruno and Andy were separately struck by her composure. Was this strange or simply indicative of the kind of woman that she was?

"Mrs Calafifi, I would like to thank you for your help. We are sorry to have intruded at this time but to find your husband's killer we need to act quickly and investigate all avenues. I note formally your request for the release of your husband's body, but I do have to inform you that, even after the post-mortem has been completed, there will be a delay. You have been very helpful in the midst of an extremely traumatic time. You have both my and Andy's direct mobile numbers. Please tell us immediately if you remember or notice something you think we should know about. Furthermore, your family's safety is important to us," said Bruno, "So for the next few nights, we will leave an officer and a police car outside of your home."

"Thank you. That is very reassuring," said Mrs Calafifi.

With that the detectives terminated their interview and left.

"Interesting," said Andy whilst they sat in his car. "If her sons have music on Tuesdays then she could have been away from the house during the late afternoon period. Do you suppose that she could have gone to see Simeon at the shop straight after Annabel's departure, argued with him about something, murdered Simeon and then hotfooted it back to collect the boys?" Bruno agreed that the timings would indeed have been tight, almost impossible, but that those timings should be checked independently, including who actually saw her collect the boys from school and at what time, etc.

"We should never discount anyone without hard facts

and evidence," said Bruno thoughtfully. "Having said that, at this stage, I don't want her to believe that we think she might be involved in any way in her husband's murder. We'll get back to that if something develops. Her composure is remarkable, yes, and she seems particularly keen to move back to London as quickly as she can. Let's just keep a gentle, protective watch on her movements."

Chapter 4

On Thursday morning, Andy and Bruno returned to Simeon's Bookshop. It was the second day of March but still felt cold and wintery. A thorough search of the premises had not found Simeon's mobile. The two men wanted to look for themselves. Simeon seemed to have two dynamic women in his life – his wife, Miriam, and his work colleague, Annabel. Both were educated, professional and accomplished. That did not make them trustworthy.

The story of the late caller to the shop after hours, not being known about by either his wife or his co-worker, did not quite add up.

"We only have Annabel's word that he was waiting to see a late caller, a late caller that she did not know about, and that she was not there when the caller arrived."

"Do you think she made a mistake, sir? In the way that Miriam Calafifi suggested."

"Annabel make a mistake? No. I don't think that she is that kind of woman," said Bruno. "But I think you should call her and ask her to come in again now. I'd like to hear her speak a bit more, so that we can get a clearer picture of Simeon and his work but also get more of a feel about her."

"What do we need specifically from Annabel?" asked Andy, "What should I ask her for?"

"A clearer picture of him from his daily activities," said

Bruno. "She must know more about him than she is letting on."

*

Forty minutes later, Annabel had arrived at the shop. She seemed pleased to have the opportunity to come to her usual place of work. In fact, she seemed very upbeat for someone whose boss had just been murdered. They thanked her for the customer and supplier contact details which she had emailed them the day before.

Annabel sat down with the two detectives in the front of the shop, which was closed. She offered to make coffee and, because the SOCOs main work was complete, and they were able to enter and exit the scene of the crime, they accepted. Bruno hoped that, on home territory, with a relaxing coffee, Annabel might let her guard down and tell them something useful or helpful. Simeon's Bookshop was an attractive place to be in, recently decorated, well-lit, and inviting. It was easy to forget that a man had been brutally murdered there, less than 48 hours ago.

Annabel told them more about her late employer. "Simeon had a formidable reputation as an antiquarian bookseller. He told me that the decision to move to the Isle of Wight had been prompted by the hope it would afford his family healthy outdoor freedoms and a calmer pace of life than they had enjoyed in North London."

They asked her about Simeon's background and whether she knew how he had got into the book trade. She was a noticeably confident storyteller: "Simeon loved the antiquarian book trade. He had worked alongside his father, David, who died a year or so before the move to the Island, in his eighties – eighty-four, I think. I never met his father, of course, but he had clearly been a massive influence on Simeon. I wondered whether the loss of his father was actually what prompted the move here – whether working in London without his dad was simply too painful. Everything that Simeon bought and sold he wanted to be precious and intellectually stimulating, a mantra he said he had learned from his father."

Without them needing to ask further questions, Annabel continued:

"David Calafifi was very well known in the antiquarian book trade as an expert in religious books printed in the early Middle Ages. I knew of him for some years before I met Simeon, and of his excellent reputation. He was known for finding and being able to buy early printed editions of the Torah, the Jewish bible, and of the Talmud, which, as you now know, is a written record of ancient rabbinical teachings. He was also able to locate special editions of the King James Bible, which he bought and sold on to collectors and fellow dealers. Simeon told me that his father wasn't just active in the field of books relating to Judaism, but in all European and world religions. As a friend of theologians of all the principal religions, he had visited holy places throughout the Middle East, in Turkey, Greece and Russia. What is more, he introduced Simeon to every one of his European and Middle Eastern contacts, I believe."

"Simeon Calafifi, and his father before him, were clearly successful and well known in their field. I have to say that it does feel quite incongruous to me that Mr Calafifi should have found his way to Shanklin. I still would have thought that he would have needed and wanted to be in London," Bruno said, hoping to get even more comment from Annabel. He also thought, but did not utter out loud, that the same applied to Annabel herself.

"I have just explained to you why Simeon said he came to the Island, together with my additional feelings on why they moved here. And when on the Island, although Simeon's first choice might have been a bookshop in Ryde, an opportunity to acquire this shop came up. It was recently refurbished and fully shelved, for a very reasonable rent compared to Ryde, and certainly to North London. I do think Simeon recognised that moving to the Island was something of a gamble, but he was confident that his local reputation would spread throughout the book-collecting residents on the Island and that his international reputation would not suffer, especially as so much of his business these days was carried out via the internet, as opposed to walk-in trade."

Annabel explained the book business to them, outlining the roles of the many people involved: authors, agents, publishers, booksellers, readers and collectors. Her experience was of course in antiquarian booksellers, who acquired books of a rare intellectual quality and served the academic and library demand. "Then there are scholars, men and women with an encyclopaedic knowledge of literature, who spend their days visiting every conceivable place a book might be found. They understand the value of every book ever printed and have good memories and are as much collectors as dealers. Then there are those we call 'runners' – similar people but on a lower level, who barely make a living and do not collect books. Somehow, they often come up with gems, including adulterated stolen books, which are to be strictly avoided. I would say book collectors and dealers are not the type to be murderers," Annabel added, her conclusion seeming casual and unsubstantiated.

To Bruno, at this stage, Simeon's murder could have been unplanned. He was not convinced that the motive for the murder was to steal two books, particularly as there was no proof yet, other than the absence of the books themselves, that it was even committed by a person or persons in the book business. Was it simply in a fit of anger resulting from a disagreement that the killer or killers lost their head and murdered Simeon?

"It is hard to imagine a murderer amongst the kind of people I am describing," said Annabel.

Andy and Bruno again ignored Annabel's comment. The notion that book dealers and collectors were too cultured and well educated to be murderers was ridiculous. In their experience it was just such a person who would kill, driven by a passionate interest in a subject and by greed.

Annabel produced records of Simeon's visits to book auctions, the books purchased by him for particular customers and a complete record of sales and purchases for the previous six months, including his last auction visit, where he purchased the Talmud. Simeon bought books in several categories, and he was a recognised expert in the field of Judaica and Hebraica, the ancient history of the Jewish faith, as well as in the Near East and Islamic volumes. Such rare books always attracted worldwide interest among the same collectors, some of whom attended in person, others being represented by dealers present at each sale.

Andy asked, "We would like you to tell us as much as possible about the books that were in the safe and which are now missing, starting with the Talmud."

"The Talmud was purchased at Wheelers Antiquarian Book Sales. You can see it in the records there," Annabel gestured to the piles of paperwork and ledgers she had just put in front of them. The figure that she went on to tell them made both Andy and Bruno fall silent: "Simeon paid £50,500 for the Talmud on behalf of his client, Professor Maurice Kazac at the University of Tel Aviv. The thing is, detectives, I don't think a stolen book could be acquired by any academic institution secretly. Knowing its value and rarity, and even though it is stolen, there are collectors who would pay an acceptable sum, but much lower than £50,500, to acquire it for themselves personally."

Consulting the bookshop records, Annabel confirmed that the bookshop had been paid £55,550, which included Simeon's 10% commission for the ancient Talmud, by bank transfer the day after the auction, so it was not out of funds on this transaction and the Talmud was, effectively, the property of Tel Aviv University at the time of its theft, although until handed over it did remain the bookshop's responsibility and therefore its theft would be their problem. Tel Aviv University maintained a huge library of historical Jewish literature and this particular Talmud would add to its already impressive collection. The price paid for the book was not considered excessive by them for such a unique record of scripture.

"The value of the Talmud lends a great deal of weight to the theft of it being a motive for Mr Calafifi's murder," ventured Andy.

"Yes, but everyone would know it was stolen. It's like a stolen painting, in a way. Only a questionable individual would buy a stolen book or painting of that value. At auctions, the highest bidder wins the prize. At Wheelers auctions, it was often Simeon. Considering an underbidder as a suspect would be a waste of time in my opinion. In this particular tussle between two bidders, everyone knows that the underbidder was Ben Hirshman, who is a well-known London dealer." Andy took note of the name.

From the paperwork Annabel had presented, they were able to see all of Simeon's rare book purchases and the auctions he had attended during the previous six months. She indicated which of his purchases had so far been sold, to whom, and the amounts paid and received from the buyers.

"Do you think that any of these people would murder to acquire the Talmud?" asked Andy.

She contemplated her answer thoughtfully before her reply.

"I can give you two answers. The first is, I don't think any of them *would* murder for the Talmud. However, I think most of them *could*, for something they really wanted."

"Would anyone on your list regularly come and see Simeon after normal business hours?"

"If they had, I would have known about it. Sometimes, yes; regularly, no."

"The missing books fall into particular genres," said

Andy. "So, could you indicate who on the list would be interested in buying these two books?"

She studied the list for a while and marked five names.

"Professor Kazac is the person Simeon acquired the Talmud for, and he intended to deliver it in person shortly. The others have an academic interest in the book."

The other four names were Professor Ian Farrell, of the Bodleian Library at the University of Oxford; Simon Woolf, of the *Jewish Chronicle*; Mersh Lebran, of the Manchester Institute of Religious Studies; and Gregory Lilton-Thomas, a historian, based in London.

"These four gentlemen would definitely have had an interest in the Talmud, as it was written by one of the greatest Jewish scholars. Of these names I have met only Ian Farrell at the Bodleian, but not the others. Everyone gets our newsletter, which Simeon and I wrote together."

"Auction catalogues detail the provenance of rare editions," Annabel continued, picking up a leather-bound book and an auction catalogue which lay on her desk. As an example, she read details of a volume from the library of the late Sir John Gielgud, detailing the number of pages, the exact size of the book, and its condition, together with any singular facts about the book and its owner.

At Wheelers Antiquarian Book Sales two weeks previously, Simeon had bought the two religious volumes which, according to Annabel, had been in the safe at the time of his murder. Wheelers were located in Chichester and were the largest book auction house in the south-east of England. Given the size of the purchase, they would certainly know Simeon and might be able to shed some light on the activities that Annabel could not.

The first purchase had been the copy of the original *Book of Mormon* by Joseph Smith, circa 1829. The auction catalogue described its condition with a section on its provenance, which proved that the parchment on which it was handwritten had been available from a local paper merchant at that date and that the signature on the final page was that of Joseph Smith, which compared favourably to other signatures of his on other documents of that time. It had remained in the archives of the State of Utah Mormon University library until 1895 when it was bought by Walter Constance, a New York banker, a Mormon and a major contributor to the new Mormon cathedral in Salt Lake City. He had placed it into the New York City Mormon Tabernacle, where it remained until 2018, when the Mormon congregation in New York City wanted to gather funds to build a new Tabernacle. It was then sold to a religious bookshop in Manhattan called Miracle Books, who have a financial investment in Wheelers Antiquarian Book Sales, from where it was purchased by Simeon Calafifi for £42,000.

The Talmud came up several lots later and was described as follows:

> *An original first copy of the Vilna Shas edition of the Babylonian Talmud, printed in Vilna (Vilnius) Lithuania in 1834. The Talmud, a book of Jewish Law, is a compilation of ancient teachings regarded as sacred and based on rabbinical debates between the second and fifth centuries.*
>
> *The Vilna Shas edition is derived from the teachings of Rabbi Eliyahu Ben Shlomo Zalman, considered one*

of the greatest Talmudic minds. It contains facts integral to Jewish life i.e. Shabbat, laws of Niddah, blessings, fasting etc., and is written in Hebrew, the holy tongue used specifically to discuss holy matters. The Talmud is written as conversation, regarded as hundreds of years of knowledge packed into one place. As a bridge between the word of God and Jewish observance, it is the basis of everyday life to be cherished and taken seriously.

A coloured drawing of the Venerable Rabbi, clothed in traditional robes, features on the cover of the Vilna Shas edition, which has been carefully preserved, although it shows signs of diligent use.

The catalogue stated the number of pages as 470 and it being of special interest. The page size of the Talmud was stated as 41 cm high by 30 cm wide.

Significantly for the detectives, the bloodstains were on documents and the blotter that lay underneath Simeon's corpse when it was discovered. Bruno's conclusion was that Simeon was not studying the Talmud when the killer stabbed him in the back through his heart. The small pool of blood from Simeon's body would not have covered the documents and desk blotter in the way it had, if the Talmud had also been on his desk, so he concluded that it must still have been in the safe.

Choosing to visit the experts who resided in the academic world could only improve the police understanding of the stolen books, as none of those identified by Annabel, she claimed, could be involved in murder.

The shop telephone rang, and Annabel went to answer it. This gave the detectives a few moments to reflect. So far, they had extraordinarily little to go on. They had only finger-marks, which could be matched against a suspect or person of interest, but which were clearly of more limited use in a shop, frequented by many people, including the general public, than in a closed environment.

"I know that Annabel said that the visitor was coming to collect a book. That suggests a purchase. However, if the caller had come to *sell* something, it might explain the open safe. In which case Annabel would not have known about it," said Andy. "This widens our net to potential suspects, when we find them."

"Let's deal with what we have so far," said Bruno. "It wasn't normal for Simeon to work late. He said to Annabel that he was expecting a visitor at 6 p.m. She left at 5:45 p.m. If the killer had been watching her departure from the rear exit, then he or she could have entered the shop very soon after 5:45 p.m. That's actually a full hour before Mrs Catchpole's arrival."

Annabel returned and Bruno decided to probe a little further into the people who would sell to, rather than buy from, Simeon Calafifi.

"Apart from auctions, such as Wheelers, who did Mr Calafifi normally buy books from?"

"Anyone really, strangers used to ring him all the time. People would also turn up with all kinds of books. I suppose Simeon would buy about one-tenth of what he was offered, if it was his line of business, but if it wasn't and it could be of interest to another dealer, he'd try to introduce the seller to that dealer."

It was another avenue for the detectives to explore – strangers on the knocker hawking valuable books for sale.

It had been a long and somewhat fruitful morning, and it was time to take a break. They thanked Annabel for providing them with information and told her that they would doubtless see her soon.

Over a sandwich at the Corner Café, Bruno said to Andy, "We have not learned as much from Annabel as we need to know. We need to find out who came to see Simeon and whether they were selling or buying. And, of course, if that encounter ended up in a murder."

During their lunch, Andy received a call from Shanklin Police Station. A close examination of the CCTV footage had focused upon the two street cameras which included the front of Simeon's Bookshop from several angles. No one had entered or approached the front entrance to the bookshop from 5 p.m. until the cleaner, Mrs Catchpole, arrived at 6:45 p.m.

"This confirms two things. First, Annabel definitely left from the rear entrance, her usual practice. Second, the visitor must have also entered through the rear entrance," said Bruno.

"In which case, it does seem that the visit was pre-arranged, as Annabel said, and the visitor known to Simeon," surmised Andy.

"Not necessarily known – the visitor may just have been coming by car, and it was sensible to park at the back and come in that way. If the visitor had been known to Simeon, I rather think that he would have referred to him or her by name, when telling Annabel about the imminent visit. Unless, of course, he clearly didn't want her to know who was coming. It's tricky but the longer I think about this murder, the more I think it is not just about books," mused Bruno. "I know valuable books were stolen and a small amount of money, but let's concentrate on the people."

"I agree," nodded Andy. "So, let me just confirm this: we have established that the killer entered through the rear of the shop. I agree that that is unnecessarily secretive for a bona fide visitor, for Calafifi to insist on them coming in the back unless, as you say, it was to park there. I've looked in the car park. It takes four cars. I think we should take a quick look. Let's wander round there now."

Although it was only 2 p.m., the car park was gloomy and in shadows. As a result, the sensor-controlled lights came on and the parking area was clearly illuminated. It occurred to Bruno that it would be difficult for anyone to slip through the back door in darkness.

There were two cars parked there: Annabel's was the first car, which she had presumably driven in by that morning. The second car was Simeon's: never to be driven by him again and awaiting collection by Mrs Calafifi. The car had been searched by the SOCOs, revealing nothing remarkable.

Both Bruno and Andy agreed that Simeon Calafifi's murderer had certainly entered from the rear and most likely on foot, affording the least likelihood of being detected by his or her car. There was a certain safety in the darkness – for a murderer.

*

Annabel Wilson made time for the detectives on Friday morning to go through Simeon's appointment records before she reopened the shop for business for the weekend.

No trace of Simeon meeting anyone on Tuesday night could be found.

"Did you notice anything unusual about Mr Calafifi's behaviour when you left the shop that evening? Did anything give you cause for concern?" asked Bruno. At this stage in an investigation, asking the same or related questions was both usual and useful. Interviewees often ventured information that they didn't think important the first time around, or simply didn't remember. Sometimes they contradicted themselves.

"Well, just that he was waiting for someone calling in to collect a book in the next half hour. As I have said, he didn't say what book or who was calling."

"Mrs Calafifi said that he would have called her if he was meeting clients in the evening."

"I have never known him do that. I left at 5:45 p.m. We said good night, as usual."

"Tell me more about the shop's regular and repeat clients," said Bruno.

"I know some of them. And of those, I know some more than others. For example, John Beynon, who lives in Ryde, is a collector of twentieth-century American playwrights – Arthur Miller, Eugene O'Neill, David Mamet and others – but his interests don't extend to religious books. Richard Boot lives in Ryde, he collects old cookery books – Mrs Beeton's, first editions and others. Penelope Norton collects Agatha Christie first editions. I speak to her occasionally, if we have a Christie first. Mid-nineteenth-century European maps are rare and are collected by a person whose name is Simpson, who lives in Yarmouth. There is always somebody who collects something specific in the shop."

"And you've already told us that, after you left the shop at 5:45 p.m. on that evening, you went straight home."

"Yes, I did, to prepare a meal for myself and a friend. His name is Sam Trent. We've been friends for a while. He's a Classics master at Ryde School, and we are researching and drafting a book together. Alexander the Great's mother – that's who the book is about. Anyway, he came before 7 p.m. and left at 11 p.m., or thereabouts. He lives at school, you see."

"Can we contact him to complete our file?"

"Of course, I'll give you his mobile number. Remember that he won't answer during school hours. I wish I could be more helpful, Chief Inspector; with hindsight, I'd have paid more attention to what Simeon was doing and who he was expecting on that night."

Annabel had provided some scant details of local persons with a day-to-day connection with Simeon, and yet no one stood out as a particular person of interest. Bruno's hunch was that the murder was not just about books, however, the Talmud and the *Book of Mormon* could not possibly be ignored, given their disappearance, and so neither could anyone who Simeon had had professional dealings with be ignored because of what they might know about the Island book business and, possibly, about Simeon's murder.

"Did you lock the back door when you left at 5:45 p.m.?"

"Definitely," she said.

"Have many customers contacted you specifically about Simeon?" said Andy, trying to find out if anyone had been particularly or unusually interested.

"Some quietly say to me how sorry they are to hear

such terrible news, but only a few of the regulars. I think they don't know what to say."

"That is very usual in the case of a violent death. I think that's everything for today, Miss Wilson. We are grateful for your continued co-operation."

On their return journey to Newport, Andy asked Bruno, "Was that satisfactory, sir?"

"I think so," Bruno replied. "It revealed a formal, rather than an overly friendly relationship between them. I would have expected greater warmth and a better understanding of what he did for the business. Undoubtedly, she knows the book trade, but there is something very hard about her. I'd have thought the opposite would have been the right basis on which to run a bookshop, but it's clearly a rather serious business."

Bruno had firm instructions from his wife Janet to be home for lunch and to take the afternoon off to complete his recovery from the flu, so he gave instruction to Andy for Monday morning when they would continue their investigatory work.

*

At home, Janet told Bruno that they had been reporting the murder at the Shanklin bookshop on Radio Solent. She knew Simeon's Bookshop very well.

This was always the stage of an investigation when Bruno felt he was at the bottom of a mountain, with a very steep slope to climb.

"The only real clue we have is the two missing volumes," he said to Janet. "These point us in the direction of learned specialists who may be untouchable or merely irrelevant, but who could have an interest in the two books stolen from the dead bookseller's office. If the killer is a bibliophile, the volumes might not see the light of day and could secretly be added to a private collection. We must hope the killer is not such a collector, and that they surface for sale, and when that happens, we'll make progress. The problem for the thief is that although their value commands a high resale price, they appeal to a limited market. They are rare properties, and no reputable dealer would touch them," he reflected.

It made sense to Bruno that they should give consideration to the auction attendees and find out who had a genuine interest in those two items. The place to begin was at Wheelers, the Chichester based auctioneers, who had sold the books to Simeon. Like any sales organisation they would know a great deal about their clients so as to guarantee the right people turn up to their auctions. They would know who they were, where they lived, their likely budget. They would not have put a special rare item in this sale unless they had been certain that the antiquarian booksellers and the private collectors would turn up and bid for these two books up to their true value. The group would have been sent information by email and catalogues by first-class post containing all they required to evaluate the items, which at this auction sale would feature the Talmud and the *Book of Mormon*. So, the next step was to visit Wheelers to obtain the names of the attendees at the auction where the books were bought by Calafifi.

It was Janet's opinion that, from their client history, Wheelers could produce a list of potential buyers, and therefore, persons of interest. She took the view that the killer could be one of the attendees at the auction: perhaps a dealer who was unsuccessful in acquiring either or both volumes for a client? Janet discounted the Island people although Bruno was reluctant to do so.

"Find out where people who deal in valuable books are. They can't live on the Island," she said.

Chapter 5

On Monday morning Andy phoned Sam Trent and left a message. He called back between lessons and explained that he regularly visited Annabel on Tuesday evenings. He confirmed that he had indeed seen her on Tuesday 28th February, and that they had spent the evening together.

"When she is too tired to cook, we'll have a drink, while she takes a bath, and I order a delivery from one of the local restaurants. Often a pizza or an Indian takeaway. I usually cycle from school to her home, and I'll take a shower at hers, before we eat and then we will work on the book we are writing until late. Last week, on Tuesday 28th, Annabel cooked – fresh pasta from the small Co-op on Regent Street in Shanklin, with chilli, tomato and prawns."

"What's it about?" said Andy.

"The book? It's about Alexander the Great's mother, Olympias, and the control she exerted over her husband and Alexander. She drove him to be the great conqueror."

Having spent a relaxing weekend at home with Janet, and now feeling fully recovered and ready for the week ahead, Bruno asked Andy, soon after he got off the telephone:

"What kind of person is Trent, then?"

"I'm trying to figure that out, sir. We obviously need to see him. He's writing a book with Annabel, just like she said. It's about Alexander the Great's mother. I've just looked her up, sir, her name was Olympias, and she played an important role in the power struggle that followed Alexander's death. Women were very powerful in Greek history, it seems. Anyway, back to Sam Trent. We've met Annabel. She is an attractive woman, and I suspect from how close they seem to be, that they are in a relationship."

Bruno and Andy agreed to visit Sam Trent in the next day or so. Then Andy phoned Alan Mosely, the secretary of the Vectis Masonic Lodge. He lived in Newport and said he'd call in to the police station for a chat after 2 p.m.

"So, we have several persons of interest, including Trent and Mosely," said Andy. "And a selection of customers whose hobbies are collecting books. Calafifi had few personal friends, but he was a Freemason. Mosely will give us a rundown on the members of his Lodge."

Bruno sat at his desk, deep in thought. He took a look at the list of names Mrs Calafifi had emailed and left it to Andy to speak to those he considered of interest. It was a list of names of parents of school friends without any connection with the book trade.

*

Alan Mosely came as promised to the station at 2 p.m. with personal details of the Lodge membership. There were twenty-five members, all Island residents, averagely aged in their sixties, retired, but none of whom were connected with the book trade. Mosely said that Simeon was not a regular attender and still maintained his London Masonic connections.

It was good of Mosely to come in, but he was of no help to them. After he left, Bruno and Andy tried to recreate the killer's activity on the Tuesday evening.

"As Simeon was the only antiquarian book dealer on the Island, or indeed across the South of England, who specialised in religious books, it is possible that the killer or killers could have come from the mainland, in search of the Talmud or the Mormon book," said Andy.

Bruno nodded gently. "Yes, he or she could have travelled by car and ferry, Cowes–Southampton, Portsmouth–Fishbourne or Yarmouth–Lymington, and selected a different route to return. Might even have stayed in a bed and breakfast overnight."

Andy thought that unlikely, because the thief, if from the mainland, might fear a manhunt the following day. "We have no idea whether we are looking for a man or a woman, young or old."

On reflection, Bruno thought that a person who had just committed a murder and stolen valuable books would not jump on the nearest transport to the mainland to depart the Island and expose themself to numerous CCTV cameras, thereby risking a permanent record of their departure.

They were considering the idea that the murderer had stolen the books for a dealer – and not a reputable one – who was himself obtaining the Talmud for a buyer or organisation who would not sell it on: a religious organisation, maybe? Whoever it was for, it could be hidden from the rest of the world for the foreseeable future and make the job of finding the killer ever more difficult. This advanced the theory that whoever had killed Simeon knew that he had bought the books at Wheelers and, more importantly, that they were still in Simeon's Bookshop, not having been delivered to the ultimate buyer yet.

"How would the thief have known that, after two weeks, the books were still in Simeon's shop?" asked Andy.

"Only someone with knowledge of the bookshop activities, which it had to be assumed had come from Simeon himself. Or from Annabel. Other people seemed to know that he was going to deliver the Talmud in person to the buyer who lived in Israel. If we can answer that question, it could be a positive lead towards finding the killer. Or was the killer just lucky to find the Talmud still on the buyer's premises?"

No, they concluded. To have found the Talmud by chance and to have stolen it did not add up, also there was no evidence yet to confirm the visitor was known to Simeon. He had told Annabel that he was expecting a visitor, who could have been a stranger.

"Annabel has already given us the names of collectors who regularly visit the shop," said Andy.

"They are people she had dealings with. We want to know who has bought a religious book from him, whom she may not have met. Let's go and have another look."

*

At the bookshop, their search amongst the sales invoices for the previous three years revealed that several religious books had been sold to Island residents; on the mainland, there were seven sales of religious books from Simeon during the past six months. Annabel said there was a continuing interest in religious books, with buyers regularly visiting and searching for a book to complete a set.

Professor Aaron Henderson, whose address was Bournemouth University in Dorset, was the most recent buyer. Henderson had purchased Volumes I and II of *The History of the Jewish Church* by Dr Arthur Stanley, the nineteenth-century Dean of Westminster, published in 1863 and 1865. The other buyer's name was Eustace Black, whose address was in Petersfield, Hampshire. Black had bought a first edition of the first English translation of *The book of religion, ceremonies, and prayers of the Jews as practised in their synagogues and families* translated from the Hebrew by Abraham Mears, printed in London, dated 1738. The value of these invoices was £650 for Henderson and £2,000 for Black. Interestingly, both purchases were of books about aspects of the Jewish faith.

The next names were of the Island residents who had purchased religious books from Simeon during the previous three years. Mrs Morrison of High Down Manor in Bonchurch had died two years previously. John Murray, aged sixty, was a retired publisher who had moved to live on the Island in an old house with a thatched roof opposite Godshill Parish Church, which was nicely preserved and beautifully modernised inside, and full of books. He knew Simeon well, who he had tasked to find old religious books published by his family business, which had existed in London since the mid-nineteenth century, under the name of John Murray of Albemarle Street.

By a stroke of good fortune, on a surprise passing-by afternoon visit to John Murray in Godshill, he was at home and happy to talk.

When Bruno told John Murray about Calafifi's murder, he had a story to tell.

"Chief Inspector, towards the end of January I received a phone call from an antiquarian book dealer in Petersfield. His name is Michael Turner. I know him from my working days in London. Whenever I drive back from London, if the time is right, I call into his shop and look at what he has got. Anyway, he asked if I wanted to buy a Talmud, a pretty unique edition, which he said was in the auction at Wheelers in early February. He said it was a very valuable edition and would sell for a figure in the tens of thousands, to which I said, 'Beyond my budget, Michael.' He called me right after the auction and told me that Simeon had bought it on behalf of a University in Israel for £50,500. I wasn't surprised that Simeon had acquired it, after all he is the religious books go-to guy in the south. So, I called Simeon and asked if I could see it and one afternoon, probably only two or three days after he'd bought it, he showed it to me in the shop. It is a beautiful book, nicely bound."

"Worth what he paid for it?" asked Andy.

"Definitely, I thought, probably a lot more. I called Michael Turner, told him I'd seen it, and we both thought £50,500 was a very good price. It might be worth your while talking to Michael Turner about the book. He might know a lot more than I do about possible interested parties, I was just one of the people he called."

"Thank you, sir," said Andy. "That's very helpful, we will go and see if he can help us."

Bruno and Andy were of the opinion that Michael Turner in Petersfield should be visited immediately, as he was actively trying to sell the Talmud prior to its auction, and he had tracked its journey after the sale.

Andy had a question for Annabel, so gave her a call to ask who knew of Simeon's intention to visit Israel to deliver the Talmud in person to Professor Kazac in Tel Aviv.

"It wasn't a secret," she said. "And he could have mentioned it to his friends. He was very open about his plans with some people."

"Anyone in particular?" said Andy.

"It is likely that Professor Kazac in Tel Aviv might have spoken to somebody about his success in buying the Talmud, and its imminent arrival in Israel. Many of the Jewish citizens of Israel have originally come from Europe or the United States, and altogether they are a very strong Jewish fraternity, so it would have been in order for Professor Kazac to tell his friends and colleagues that he had acquired a most sought-after Jewish record. Simeon Calafifi is well known in academic Jewish circles. I'd be surprised if Kazac did not tell his inner circle that Simeon had agreed to deliver the Talmud in person and when."

"It's time to visit Wheelers and get their take on the day they sold the books to Calafifi," said Bruno. "The auctioneer might tell us something useful. On the way we will visit Michael Turner in Petersfield."

Driving back to the station, Andy phoned and made an appointment with Michael Turner the next morning.

Chapter 6

On Tuesday, a week to the day since the murder, the two detectives arrived at Michael Turner's busy bookshop in Petersfield promptly at 9:30 a.m. The shop was situated in a prominent High Street position, at the highest footfall section of the High Street.

Inside the shop they were greeted by a charming lady with an easy manner and a pleasant voice. She was probably in her late thirties and was courteously attentive. She led the detectives up a flight of stairs to the first-floor café, serving coffee and tea, croissants and toast.

Mr Turner was seated in the front bay window, over-looking the High Street, and it was confirmed that the lady who had greeted them was Mrs Turner when she put her hand on his shoulder, and they were formally introduced.

Turner was dressed smart casually, as you would expect a bookshop owner who throughout a day would become engaged in the physical activities in the shop, but in a fashion to show respect to a Detective Chief Inspector arriving for a serious meeting.

"Chief Inspector, how can I help you today?"

While Andy Bowen explained the situation in brief, Mrs Turner went to bring them coffee.

Bruno got straight to the point: "We understand from John Murray that you offered to bid for him at Wheelers? In the auction of the Talmud?"

"Yes, I know John very well. I used to work with him in London before he sold up. I saw the Talmud in the catalogue, so I called him about it. It was out of his price range, and he wasn't interested in buying it. I attended Wheelers on auction day and saw it sold to Calafifi for £50,500. Before the Talmud he bought a handwritten copy of the *Book of Mormon*, signed by Joseph Smith. There is some doubt that it is his handwriting, however, apparently there is sufficient provenance to say that the signature is genuine. When I heard about Calafifi's murder, I cast my mind back to that day and to the dealers who were present. None of them would have killed Calafifi to get their hands on the Talmud. If they had wanted it that badly they'd have bid for it," said Turner. "And if any of them get as much as a sniff of the killer I think that they would tell the police straight away."

It was clear that Michael Turner had prepared mentally for the meeting with the detectives and that he was an active, rather than passive, helpful sort of person. He continued:

"I heard about Calafifi's murder early on Thursday morning, which would have been, what, 36 hours after he was killed? Anyway, on Friday morning, not 24 hours after I heard the news myself, I received a call from a withheld number. It was a man. Speaking with a broad and heavy Hampshire accent. He asked if I wanted to buy a copy of the Talmud. I clicked immediately that it was the stolen copy. I said 'Okay, but I must see it first,' hoping to lure him into the shop. He said he could come to the shop and would call back with a time. I don't know whether my enthusiasm put him off, but he has not called me back. I am really sorry, because I planned to trap him in the shop, and apprehend him somehow."

"How exactly would you have done that, Mr Turner?" asked Bruno. It was a genuine question, but Andy knew Bruno well enough to detect a hint of scepticism in the enquiry.

"Well, look out the window," Turner stood up in his seat and pointed to the market stalls in the street. "I know those guys really well, the stall which says 'Scarmoor Fruit and Veg' on it. I've known Tom Scarmoor for years and his son, Tom Junior."

Bruno peered out of the window too and saw two men, similar looking but one clearly older than the other. Both were at least 6 foot 4 inches tall.

"I have spoken to Tom and Tom about a visitor to this shop that I might want to, er, detain, shall we say, until police arrive. I didn't need to give them any more explanation than that."

Bruno explained clearly that he could not condone any individual taking the law into their own hands, particularly in the case of a potentially dangerous thief and murderer. Michael Turner seemed to accept this and agreed to call the local police and Bruno if he was contacted again by this individual. At the moment, the person had not called back so this was all, thankfully, academic. Having said that, Bruno was hopeful that the person would get in touch again as it seemed to be a proper lead in the disappearance of the Talmud and the associated murder. It was then time to leave for Wheelers.

*

When Andy called Mr Wheeler, the boss of Wheelers Antiquarian Book Sales, to arrange a visit to discuss the day Wheelers sold the books to Calafifi, he seemed happy to speak on the phone but resisted a face-to-face meeting with the police. When Andy reminded him that they were investigating the murder of one of their clients and even the smallest piece of information about Calafifi's competitors could lead to a development in the case, he reluctantly agreed to Andy's suggested late morning visit.

Wheelers Antiquarian Book Sales was located on the edge of Chichester on a purpose-built industrial estate. It had grown rapidly since a substantial interest in the business had been acquired by Princetown Publishing of Madison Avenue, New York City.

Princetown had a very experienced marketing division and had acquired their UK auction house interest, because they understood that the USA and UK were two complementary markets. Titles acquired in the US could sell for substantially more in the UK and certain European authors were likewise more valuable in the US than in the UK, Europe or connected English speaking countries, such as Australia, South Africa and the British Commonwealth countries. This was confirmed with the prices obtained in the February sale of the two volumes bought by Calafifi.

Robert Wheeler, the son of the founder, still retained day-to-day management of the business, ensuring that Wheelers Antiquarian Book Sales retained its pre-eminent position in the sale of valuable books from all parts of the world.

Although he was present at the auction when the Talmud had been sold to Calafifi, it was as an observer.

His colleague, twenty-eight-year-old Bob Mayne, was the impressive, young auctioneer with the gavel who sold the books.

Bob Mayne remembered the sale well. It had made good money for the sellers, the company and the staff, who shared the sales commission.

"It was our biggest sale of the year so far. Our winter sale in February always is. We send out our catalogue after Christmas and the response is excellent. There was a large attendance, antiquarian booksellers, collectors and 'runners' acting for overseas buyers. On the internet we had a number of known clients who registered before the sale, and we had a fine collection of books."

Bruno explained that they had come to Wheelers because they believed that Simeon Calafifi, one of the auction house's clients, could have been murdered by a person who stole the Talmud and the *Book of Mormon* which he had purchased at their February sale. Bruno passed to Mayne the note on which was written a description of the book which Mayne would have studied before the sale in order to provide the history to the bidders from the lectern. He remembered the books well.

"There was a lot of interest in both books bought by Calafifi and both far exceeded our printed catalogue guide price. There were many bidders for each title, and they were the same people for each lot. The early bidders were many, but the bids increased quickly and substantially."

"Do you recall any of the bidders in each case?"

"The auction room was crowded. The cards, used to identify buyers when bidding, were being shown from all quarters, so it was only when the bidders thinned out that

I began to recognise the usual faces I knew," said Mayne, "including those on the phone. What I can do is tell you who actually bought books at our February sale, and any other bidders I can remember, if you think that might be of interest?"

"That's precisely what we are looking for. We're interested in every attendee who was bidding for the Talmud. Perhaps you can talk through the names with us?" said Bruno.

"I'll try," he said. "I will just go and look at our contract sales ledger to make sure I don't forget anyone."

Bruno noticed that Wheelers were busy setting up for another book auction the following day. Young assistants wearing leather aprons and gloves were carrying book collections from private libraries and prized first editions which they placed behind glass-fronted cabinets for examination by prospective purchasers under supervision.

Mayne returned with a file containing details of the February sales business.

"We offered 156 lots for sale, of which 140 exceeded their reserve and 16 items were unsold."

"What can you remember about the sale of the two lots to Simeon Calafifi, lots 61 and 72?"

Mayne studied the two contracts and his handwritten notes for a minute or two.

"For the Talmud, lot 72, the bidding started at £20,000, with several bidders, until it reached £40,000, after which two bidders remained – Calafifi and Ben Hirshman from London. The bidding continued in increments of £1,000, until it reached £50,000. That bid was made by Hirshman. Simeon then dropped to just a £500 increment and bid £50,500, and Hirshman withdrew. He told me later that

£50,000 was his client's limit." Mayne paused and then continued:

"Lot 61 was the handwritten *Book of Mormon* by Joseph Smith, the founder of the Mormon religion. Simeon secured this book for £42,000. There were an assortment of persons bidding for this lot, none I could recall now. These two lots exceeded our catalogue estimates substantially, because they are both unique. The *Book of Mormon*: we had valued it at about £28,000; and the Talmud we had estimated about £30,000. The reserves were set higher. There was no in-fighting between Mr Calafifi and Mr Hirshman. Both lots were sent from our New York store, expecting them to sell for more than in a New York sale, and they read the market correctly. We achieved those prices because we followed Princetown's marketing strategy to dealers and collectors. We don't necessarily know all underbidders, particularly if they haven't dealt with us before, although the regular dealers we do know well. In order to bid at auction you have to register with your personal and business details – which we check and verify – and provide you with a bidding number. As the bidding increased, the sale room was buzzing. We expected the *Book of Mormon* to sell to the Mormon church in England, but oddly the Mormon church bids were from members of the Mormon church in the USA. The underbidder for the *Book of Mormon* was Herbert Rickler, who has a business in East Grinstead in Sussex, where the headquarters of the Mormon church in England is located. Mr Rickler is a rare book dealer, and he is a University Professor in Theology. At £41,000 he gave up, so Calafifi's bid at £42,000 was the successful final bid."

"Did Mr Rickler bid for the Talmud?"

"No, he didn't. He is a regular visitor to our rare book auctions and, as far as I know, deals in a variety of subjects. We know that he buys for private collectors worldwide. Both books found what everyone who sells at auction hopes for, that is at least two willing buyers who want them passionately."

The word *passionately* raised Bruno's interest.

"Could one be so passionately interested in a book to kill for it?" said Bruno.

"Chief Inspector, I don't know anyone who has ever done that because, to be honest, I don't know anyone who has ever killed someone," replied Mayne. "However, in answer to your question, I believe that none of our clients would kill to obtain a precious book. They are scholars, as well as dealers, but not murderers. The Talmud is a controversial interpretation of the 'Word of God' by scholars at particular times in history and has been debated since the days of Moses. It's studied by Jewish Theologians all over the world and its meaning can change depending on which branch of Judaism you belong to, the country you live in, and the century you live in."

"You said there were other interested bidders?"

"Several of our regular clients were interested but seeing the determined heavyweights doing battle at such a high level they clearly decided that they were not the books for them. I make little notes on the sales sheet when I am working, so I will look back on my notes for that day and see if I made any comments, which I will gladly email to you when I have time and the names of attendees who were present. As you see, we have a sale tomorrow. I shall be busy studying the lots later today, so it won't be for a day or two. I will leave the science to you. That's not my job. I hope I have helped you, detectives," he said.

"We will look forward to hearing from you and thank you for your help so far," said Bruno, accepting that he'd run out of time, and they departed in the friendliest way.

Bruno thought their visits to Michael Turner and Wheelers had been helpful, providing them with a better understanding of the book business, and giving them something to work on.

Turner's keen interest in the Talmud, his wish to involve Murray, the withheld number call from the thief and/or murderer, and his repeated desire to help and be involved, were all too much of a co-incidence for Bruno not to hypothesise that Turner might be more involved in this case than he had indicated. In which case, their meeting with him might dissuade him from reporting any further contact from the withheld number caller, if indeed he even existed. It was even possible that Turner was a recognised dealer in stolen books. Bruno resolved to keep Michael Turner on the list of persons of interest. At this stage, no one could be ruled out for sure.

"So far," said Bruno, "we haven't focused on Calafifi's purchase of the *Book of Mormon*."

"Is the copy genuine?" said Andy.

"Calafifi thought so. Wheelers guaranteed its provenance, so yes, I think it is, but who did Simeon have in mind to sell it to, and why was it still in his possession when he was murdered? I can understand him wanting to deliver the Talmud personally, but not the *Book of Mormon*. Maybe he saw value in it that no one else did and wanted it in stock? Call Professor Herbert Rickler in East Grinstead and ask if we can go and see him this afternoon. How long will it take us to get there from Chichester?"

Andy looked at the map on his phone. "About an hour. It's 1 o'clock now, so I'll ask if he's available to see us at 2:30."

*

Thankfully, Professor Rickler was at home and amenable to seeing the detectives, so their drive from Chichester to East Grinstead was worth it.

Rickler greeted them warmly. He explained that he combined the role of being a visiting professor lecturing in Theology at Sussex University, with that of being the chairman at Rickler Press, a publisher of theological textbooks and degree-course books on science subjects. The chief executive of Rickler Press was his younger brother, Melville Rickler.

Rickler looked and behaved like the successful company chairman that he was, combined with a learned, academic air.

"So, detectives, you have come to see me about John Smith's handwritten *Book of Mormon*. I understand it was bought by Simeon Calafifi. My brother told me that Calafifi bought it at Wheelers – he was at the auction, you see – but that Calafifi has now been murdered. Are the two situations connected? I imagine so, because you are here, now, talking to me."

Bruno took control of the question asking: "You weren't interested in buying it?"

"No. I wasn't. Nor would I be now. I am not convinced

it is genuine. John Smith's handwritten original was superseded almost before his ink was dry by a bigger, complete, printed version. I say complete because the *Book of Mormon* was being added to continually by new prophets, from the Church of Jesus Christ of Latter-day Saints."

"Let's assume – as others did – that it was genuine. To where or for whom do you think this book was destined?"

"I don't know. It entirely depends on who stole them," said Rickler. "They could be of little or no value on the open market, maybe, given their individuality and recent public sales, but to the private sector collectors the volumes, despite being stolen, have real value. There are more secret collectors in the book world than the art world. Think about it. With a painting you can put it on show and secretly admire it, show it to your trusted fellow collectors. With a book, it's hidden on a bookshelf, to pull out to read and admire, and hide away."

Bruno listened intently.

"What is more difficult to understand, is why the thief murdered Calafifi," said Rickler. "He wouldn't have let a thief just walk out with the books, so I'm sure that there would have been a fight. Obviously, you can't tell me anything about the shop and how he was found. Can I ask you, though, is there something you have found out about Calafifi that suggests there is a motive, besides stealing the books?"

"Even if we could comment on that, which we can't, we really don't know enough yet about his personal or professional life to give an informed answer."

"I think you might consider the books incidental and concentrate on something more personal, Chief Inspector."

"Well, we are just gathering information at this stage, as I said."

"There is an expression for what I am doing, Chief Inspector – telling you how to do your job. I can't think what it is now, but please forgive me."

"We welcome any help solving crime from everyone," said Bruno, trying to be as amiable as possible.

"Let me make a suggestion. The John Smith manuscript is of interest to a small number of people who have a connection with the Mormon church. Whoever has it can probably only sell it to one of those persons who, when they discover that it has been stolen and the thief has committed murder to obtain it, will surely tell the police. I can introduce you to a leader in the Mormon church, a High Priest, who has responsibility for seeing that the correct financial contributions are made by each member. In that respect he is aware of those who would be wealthy enough to buy it, and who might be persuaded to. To some person, it is as valuable as if Jesus had personally written the New Testament," said Rickler. "These are not people I know of, but it is from this group that the buyer of the Mormon bible will come, unless the thief already has a buyer. I think to the thief the Mormon bible was an afterthought. Chief Inspector, leave this with me until I have met with the High Priest and briefed him. Then, hopefully, I will arrange a meeting. That's the best I can do for you."

"You have been very helpful, sir," said Andy. "And maybe your introduction will help us in our investigation."

"If the members of the Mormon Church can help you, I know they will."

Andy and Bruno thanked Rickler for his time, conscious that they had a long drive back to the Island ferry.

*

As they were getting back into Bruno's car, Andy said, "With the list from Wheelers and an introduction from Rickler, that's some progress, sir."

"Yes, it is," said Bruno. "But just because we feel like avenues are opening up off the Island, we must not rule out the possibility that this murder was committed by a person Simeon Calafifi knew and that could well be a person from the Island."

During their journey back to the Isle of Wight ferry, Bruno expressed the view that the theft of the *Book of Mormon* was potentially an error on the part of the killer, and their effort to sell the Mormon Bible could expose them. There had been considerable interest in the Talmud, nationally and internationally. It had already been sold to the University of Tel Aviv. Many other potential buyers and bidders had been interested in it. In other words, there was a relatively easy market for it. It did not seem to be similar for the *Book of Mormon*. However, from what Rickler said, Calafifi would not have speculated in buying the *Book of Mormon* without an onward buyer. Yet there was no indication from his records or from Annabel that he had any connection with the Mormon church.

"Maybe the High Priest in East Grinstead can help us with that?" said Andy. "Rickler's contacts may lead us somewhere."

Bruno agreed. "He is a wealthy man, with considerable

status as an academic and as a publisher and understands this murky business."

"What about Ben Hirshman, sir, who buys expensive books as an agent and sells collectors' items from his London bookshop? He had a £50,000 ceiling for the Talmud. So, he must have a disappointed client somewhere."

*

A call to Bob Mayne at Wheelers gave them Ben Hirshman's London business address: Hirshman's Antiquarian Booksellers, 22 Curzon Street, W1, just off Park Lane.

Andy called Ben Hirshman at his London office to introduce himself and to arrange a meeting. Andy did not mention the Talmud and avoided saying that they were coming from the Isle of Wight; however, Hirshman would have been naïve not to connect them with Calafifi.

So far, Bruno's meetings with Michael Turner, Wheelers and Rickler, had left him unsure if they had achieved anything concrete, other than to sketch out a map of the direction they should be travelling.

*

After an early start and an exhausting day, a relaxing, recuperative Tuesday evening lay ahead for Bruno and Janet. She had made a special effort for this evening. There was a log fire ablaze when he arrived home. It was miserable, cold and wet outside and it was a treat to relax in the warm, with a glass of wine in front of the fire. Bruno felt that he had at last shed the infection that had dogged him for three weeks and was properly prepared for the challenge of finding Calafifi's killer.

"Tell me more about the new case," she said.

In a relaxed mood Bruno explained to her the puzzle that would preoccupy his vacant moments until he resumed with Andy the following morning.

He explained their visit to Michael Turner's, to Wheelers, and to Herbert Rickler – three visits in one day. He mentioned the upcoming antiquarian book sale the following day, which she encouraged him and Andy to attend.

"That is where this case begins and you might see something that triggers a line of thought that leads you somewhere," she said, "and you will see how it works and how the dealers operate. Apart from a couple of auctioneers you've already met, no one will recognise you, and you'll be able to spot any unusual behaviour. You don't think these people turn up at auctions and just bid against each other, do you?" she said. "Think about it, forget about the value of what is being sold, concentrate on the bidders. You two should be able to spot anything suspicious going on. The religious book market is a closed shop, which must be dominated by a Mister Big, and he must be your target."

Their discussion opened a new line of thought for Bruno, which Janet developed further by bringing up Wheelers' online catalogue for the book sale due the following day.

"Before you meet Andy, read about some of the lots for sale and who the buyers and sellers are. It's possible that this murder could have been done by someone there, who would not expect the detective investigating Calafifi's murder to be present."

It was an impressive catalogue running to 90 pages, identical in appearance to that from which the Talmud had been sold. Four categories were listed in the sale. The last two, Judaica and Hebraica, and Middle East and Islamic, were where the interest lay.

In the past, whenever Janet had asked her husband if he had a gut feel who he thought the murderer might be, usually he had some idea. This time he had none.

"Take a look at the buyers of those eighteen lots and tell Wheelers you want them to supply their contact details after the auction," she suggested to Bruno.

"So far, we've interviewed the ladies close to him: Mrs Calafifi, Mrs Catchpole, the cleaner, and Annabel Wilson, his colleague. The retired publisher John Murray in Godshill and an antiquarian bookseller Michael Turner in Petersfield," he said. "We haven't yet found a person in the book trade who has a passionate interest in antiquarian religious books. They were stolen by someone who is confident they can sell them for a lot of money, because of their unique value."

"So, you are looking for a thief who is a book person?" asked Janet.

"There are several names we have yet to interview and then we might get a better idea," said Bruno. "I am convinced that from this group we will find the murderer, not necessarily one of them, but through them."

Janet had printed out a copy of the auction catalogue, put it into his carrying case, and said, "That's for you to discuss with Andy on your journey back to Chichester tomorrow."

With difficulty Bruno switched off from his police job to enjoy the rest of the evening with Janet who, as Head of a local junior school, had been snowed under with clerical work recently, as a result of school inspections.

Chapter 7

Bright and early the next morning, Bruno was raring to go and ready to travel back to Chichester with Andy to see for themselves how people behave at rare book auctions. They caught the Wednesday 7:05 a.m. hovercraft from Ryde Pier and their train from Portsmouth and Southsea arrived in Chichester before quarter to nine. It was a short walk to the premises of Wheelers Antiquarian Book Sales.

Unknown to any of the significant dealers, Bruno and Andy were anonymous among some fifty people who had come to buy and sell. They were able to watch the action and to mingle with different groups.

One dealer from Bournemouth remarked to Andy that this was a pretty normal crowd and that the auctioneer would anticipate selling the majority of the catalogue.

"It's not the size of the audience, it's the quality of the lots on offer and the affluence of buyers in attendance," he added, which on this occasion the dealer from Bournemouth thought above average.

The auction opened with Lot 1, a classic of American author Samuel Clemens, better known by his pseudonym, Mark Twain. The *Adventures of Huckleberry Finn* in its first US edition, printed in 1885, was described as in good condition. It sold for £17,200.

The detectives stood at the back and surveyed the

room before Lot 6 came under the hammer. Bruno was interested in the behaviour of the attendees, who chatted away about their business and could be overheard whilst seated quietly studying the catalogue. When interesting lots came up, the bidders would vanish into the auction room, make their bids, and return to the office to pay and collect and, following a successful purchase, disappear.

When a fine miniature Qur'an, copied by the royal Qajar scribe Abdullah al-Ranani and with a price estimate of £30,000, came up, most of the dealers returned to the sale room to see this item sold. The bids for the miniature Qur'an were thoughtful and restricted to three persons plus an internet bidder. At £25,000, only two bidders remained. The bids were lifted twice until the auctioneer said, 'fair warning', slammed his gavel for the third time on the block, and ended with 'sold to Mr Hirshman for £28,000'. At that, the detectives turned their attention towards the very man they had next on their list of persons of interest, who had agreed to meet them the following day in London.

"Shall we introduce ourselves?" said Andy.

"No," said Bruno emphatically. "We want to see where he operates from. Letting him see us here won't help us at all."

The refreshments provided at the auction sale were generous – free coffee, tea, sandwiches and biscuits – and kept the detectives going throughout the sale. They watched the strange world inhabited by the buyers, sellers and collectors of valuable books. Without a learned appreciation of antiquarian religious books that developed into an obsession, the business could seem as mundane as any other hobby to the uninitiated, although Bruno admitted they had learned something about the book business, and how it operated. Bob Mayne, the auctioneer, promised to email the contact details of the purchases in the Section 3 category, Judaica and Hebraica, in a day or two.

Before the final few lots were sold, the detectives left to walk back to the station to catch the early afternoon train back to Portsmouth. Something about the immersive experience of the morning made them feel – rightly or wrongly – considerably more confident of the type of person they were looking for.

*

The appointment with Ben Hirshman at his Curzon Street office in Mayfair was at 11 a.m. on Thursday morning. His bookshop was similar in size to Calafifi's in Shanklin, but was more opulent, and his rent was probably ten times as much. It surprised Bruno that whenever he ventured into an upmarket shop, there never seemed to be much business going on. Well laid-out, expensively decorated, and staffed by attractive men and women, but no actual sales seemed to be happening. Behind locked, glass-fronted cabinets lay a collection of leather-bound books on every learned subject.

A well-attired lady showed the detectives into a back office and left them to tell Mr Hirshman they had arrived.

Ben Hirshman was a tall, middle-aged man. He was well spoken, came across as very well educated and was clearly a bibliophile. After an introduction and an exchange of business cards, they sat down. Bruno explained the lead up to their visit.

"Mr Mayne at Wheelers in Chichester, who conducted the sale of two rare books at a recent auction, informed us that you had been the underbidder for a Talmud that was sold to Simeon Calafifi. That Talmud has since disappeared, and Mr Calafifi has been murdered."

Bruno paused to allow Hirshman to respond, but he remained silent, and his expression was inscrutable, so Bruno continued.

"We believe the Talmud, about which there was considerable interest on the day of the auction, may have been stolen by a person trying to satisfy a request from a collector or a book dealer. To us this book is a complete mystery, of course, so we are asking anyone even remotely connected with such a treasure to help us. We are trying to piece together any circumstances or information relating to Mr Calafifi's activities that could be connected to these crimes."

Hirshman replied, "It is true, Chief Inspector, that I attended the auction to buy the Talmud on behalf of a client. Since many who were present know me, they would know of my interest. If I can help you, I will. I knew Simeon very well. And I knew his father David, a respectable, highly regarded man. I met Simeon's wife, Miriam, at a book show a couple of years ago. I am very sad, distressed actually, to hear of his death."

"Could you tell us why you were interested in the Talmud?"

"I know a great deal about this Talmud, and why it's so sought after, and my client was disappointed not to win the book. I was asked to buy it by a person in London, for whom I sometimes find special books. We expected to get it for something like the catalogue guide price. However, my client had set a limit, and Simeon was able to exceed it. Simple as that. I suspected Simeon was able to go much higher, so I was relieved to exit the bidding when I did.

Do you know, and can I ask you, why Simeon still had the book in his possession two weeks after the auction?" asked Hirshman.

"We were told that he wanted to deliver the Talmud in person and that the delivery was imminent."

"My guess is that something was wrong," said Hirshman. "Perhaps the person he was acting for hadn't put him in funds before the auction, and he relied on him to pay later. You should be able to find that out from his records."

Bruno did not disclose that funds had already been paid to Calafifi by Professor Kazac in Tel Aviv and therefore that his guess was not correct. Nor did he elaborate on the fact that personal delivery to an international client would clearly increase the time between purchase and delivery.

"Chief Inspector, the value of this book should not be underestimated. It was written in Hebrew by one of the greatest Talmudic minds of the eighteenth century. I'd imagine that from the moment Calafifi tabled his winning bid, he became a target."

"A target? For whom? And of what?" asked Andy.

"A purchase of that value indicates significant wealth and will attract the attention of potential thieves, especially those who already have some contact with the under-bidders. Security and discretion are important."

"Why would the client not have come to the auction?" asked Bruno.

"Well, they may have been present at the auction. This edition has surfaced into the public domain having been sent from New York by a seller who wanted to escape the attention it could have created in the USA."

"Surely the vendor is only interested in getting the highest price?"

"Yes," he acknowledged. "But European auction houses regularly achieve record prices for this type of book. I understand that Simeon also bought a historic Mormon Bible, presumably for another client, which had also not been delivered. I believe that, as with the Talmud, he would have planned to deliver it personally, probably back to America from whence it came. The thief will have the same difficulty with both books. It's obvious to me that you might need an introduction into this exclusive business," said Hirshman, evidencing that news travelled fast, particularly when theft and murder were involved.

Bruno and Andy listened, while Hirshman continued:

"If you share with me what you have so far discovered, I may be able to explain its relevance. Don't be misled into thinking this is an entirely Jewish activity. I myself am not Jewish, despite my name. My mother was a Catholic and she saw that my father's three boys were christened into her faith. My dad was a great man, and I often went to Friday evening prayers with him in the synagogue and my mother ensured that we also celebrated every Jewish festival as part of family tradition," Hirshman explained. "I truly believe that no Jewish person would commit murder to obtain a Jewish prayer book, or even consider buying a stolen copy, so that could be an advantage at the start in your quest to find your killer. You could be looking for a gentile, like me, or a person with another religion who collects religious scripture. They will surface, take my word for it, and then you will get your man."

Although Bruno did not agree with Hirshman and his many assumptions, he decided that he was being helpful and had given them some further ideas upon which to further their investigations, so Bruno decided to ask him the question that he expected Hirshman would avoid answering.

"Mr Hirshman, would it be possible to speak to the person on whose behalf you were bidding at the auction?"

After considering, Hirshman replied, "I cannot give you that information without asking him first. I will let you know if he is happy to speak to you, but I am not optimistic that he will agree or that he would be of any help to you. Have you thought of offering a reward for information leading to the arrest of the thieves?"

"That is not standard police procedure, particularly not at this early stage."

"Ask the insurance company, who I suspect will ultimately bear this loss. They could advertise a cash reward for information leading to the discovery of the books. You never know."

*

Bruno had switched his mobile to silent during the meeting but checked it as they departed from him. A voicemail was waiting from Professor Rickler, who said that he had spoken to the most senior elder of the Mormon Church in England, who had agreed to speak to them if they could be there at 2 p.m.

Andy checked the railway timetable on his smartphone. They could get to East Grinstead by 2 p.m. and later return to Portsmouth via East Croydon. It was an invitation they could not turn down. Bruno phoned Rickler and confirmed the appointment.

Rickler met the detectives at the East Grinstead mainline railway station and drove them to the Mormon temple on the outskirts of East Grinstead. The central feature was the Mormon Tabernacle, constructed of white marble, beautifully maintained, standing in the centre of well-tended gardens.

Rickler had arranged for them to meet Ronald J. Arnica, the senior Elder of the Mormon Church in the United Kingdom, who was waiting in a reception room built specially to receive visitors, some distance from the temple itself. It was an interesting room designed to introduce curious visitors to the Latter-day Saints' theology.

After a proper introduction, Arnica spoke first by saying that Professor Rickler had briefed him and asked if he could help the police to find the thief.

Arnica began, "Let me explain some background. It has always been accepted that Smith wrote the *Book of Mormon* himself, rather than translated it from an ancient biblical record by an early Christian scribe. The book that was sold to Calafifi at auction had been authenticated as an original *Book of Mormon*. It would have been a collection of his interpretation of some of the chapters of the Latter-day Saints, of which there are fifteen, whereas in the King James Bible, the Acts of the Apostles has twenty-eight chapters."

He continued his explanation. "In the archives of the church in Salt Lake City we have originals of most Mormon writings and literature. I am sure the buyer, convinced of the authenticity of the book, acquired it for a member of our church, but at this stage I have no idea who or where that person might be. The murder of Simeon Calafifi, who bought the *Book of Mormon*, is a crime of immense horror and I will do everything I can to help you find the killer. I will inform the church at all levels. Should any member be approached with an offer of the book, they should contact me, and I will introduce you to them."

Bruno thanked Ronald Arnica for his contributions and with keen anticipation hoped to hear from him soon. It was more than he could have expected from the leader of the Mormon Church in England. He hoped that by seeing Ronald Arnica they had not cut off a potential route for the thief trying to raise cash, and that any contact by the thief with any prominent member of the Mormon Church would be reported to them.

Professor Rickler emphasised as he drove them back to the train station, "For this volume there is a very restricted market. The thief will soon discover that it is potentially worthless, even a trap, so I fear it could be filed away or, worse, destroyed, or just lost on the shelves of a second-hand bookshop."

They returned to the Island having made good progress with Hirshman and the Mormon Church, which might generate leads. On the train, they considered other persons of interest who might shed light onto their quest, including the three local Ryde residents: Boot, Simpson and Norton, all customers of Calafifi, and also Sam Trent, Annabel Wilson's friend, all yet to be interviewed.

Chapter 8

By Friday, 10th March, Annabel had conveyed the news of Calafifi's murder and the theft of the Talmud to Professor Kazac. She reported to Bruno their conversation, that she had assured Professor Kazac that the book was insured for the full amount of the loss. It was of little consolation to him. He had known Simeon for many years, and they had often done business together. He was a friend with whom he shared knowledge and scholarship; that he died during their dealings hurt him and would do so for a long time.

Later that morning, Bruno himself followed up with a call to Professor Kazac at home in Haifa to ask if he could shed any light as to who might have an interest in the Talmud and might commit murder to get their hands on it. Kazac had a new development to report.

"I have received a call from a London antiquarian bookseller called Walter Spens. He had heard, although he did not say from whom, that I had purchased Ben Shlomo Zalman's Talmud. He was aware of the auction sale price of £50,500 that Calafifi had paid and was prepared to pay a substantial premium if I would sell it to him. I explained that it was purchased by the University of Tel Aviv, not by me personally, and that it was not for sale. I did not inform him of Simeon Calafifi's death, but I think he was aware of it," said Kazac. "I asked him for whom he was acting.

He would not give me the name but said that his client was a benefactor of the Culture Synagogue in Vilnius in Lithuania, who wished to return Rabbi Eliyahu Ben Shlomo Zalman's Talmud to where it had been written over two hundred years ago. He spoke about the suffering of the Jews in Lithuania in 1942 and how the population of Vilnius had fallen to just a few thousand from a peak of a quarter of a million, and how the return of the Talmud to its birthplace would have a huge impact on the Jews in this ancient city."

Professor Kazac spoke softly and eloquently. Bruno thanked him for the information and promised to get back to him once he had established its relevance to Calafifi's murder. It was an important lead that he would follow up confidentially.

Kazac had provided contact information for Walter Spens. Bruno decided he should be investigated, so he set Andy that task.

When Andy telephoned, Spens was friendly. Andy did not disclose or discuss the murder and theft of the Talmud, only that he'd like a meeting to discuss the theft of some old religious books. However, he gathered from their conversation that Spens knew a lot more about the Talmud and its theft than he had led Kazac to believe. Andy arranged a meeting with him for the following Monday, 13th March.

*

In the days since the murder of Simeon, Annabel Wilson appeared to have replaced grief with a determination to ensure the business continued to thrive without him.

That Friday afternoon she phoned the Police Station and asked to speak to Bruno. He took the call and brought in Andy on the speaker phone. During the conversation, she described to them how the book trade on the Island worked.

"There are two major book dealers apart from Simeon. Max Carter owns the West Wight Bookshop in Cowes and has a half interest in a Southampton book business; and Nathan Philips in Bembridge, who specialises in first editions of the winners of the Noble Prize for Literature. Max and Nathan are both highly regarded locally. Max Carter is on the committee of the Island Literary Festival, an October event held at Northwood House, which attracts an international set of writers and an audience from the mainland. Island writers attend and act as volunteers on site during the four-day festival and help set it up. It is a fantastic opportunity for local authors to learn from the well-known, established authors' presentations and to show and sell their books."

"Do you think that either of these two booksellers might know anything about the stolen books? Could they have been offered to them? Or be involved in any other way?" asked Andy.

Annabel didn't answer until she'd given his questions serious consideration, seemingly not wishing to point the finger or make even the remotest accusation. She eventually said, "I don't know. I don't think anyone here would be really interested in the Talmud, nor to have the kind of money needed to buy it. Both Max and Nathan have suffered since Simeon became established. To any book collector Simeon had become the first point of call.

Could this have led to one of them killing Simeon to get their hands on the Talmud? Or on his business? I don't know."

She was silent for a few seconds; clearly not prepared to exonerate or excuse either man, she moved the conversation along.

"The specialist niche that Simeon created here was very forward-thinking. He hoped that the Island could become like Hay-on-Wye, a mecca for bibliophiles. I try to go to the Hay-on-Wye Literary Festival every year, and in my opinion the Island is a superb location with facilities that Hay cannot match. More accommodation for visitors, for sure. And, of course, the coast."

"Do you think that Simeon could have met someone at the Literary Festival who might have been interested in the Talmud or the *Book of Mormon*?" asked Bruno.

She replied, "Maybe, but as far as anyone being considered capable of murder, I'd never considered the possibility. I mean, you don't think about such a dreadful thing until it happens."

Pausing for breath, Annabel continued, "You never know what new businesses are being run via the internet. The Talmud could show up any day. Simeon's business was international, with clients in America, South Africa, at home, and in Europe. All that he did in North London he did here. He didn't travel like he used to in London, except when he went to book buying auctions in the South of England. His promise to deliver the Talmud to Professor Kazac at a ceremonial presentation and discuss other requests on behalf of the University was to cement his relationship. If you talk to Nathan in Bembridge and

Max in Cowes, you will learn more about the Island book trade and the people involved. They have been in business on the Island for many years."

"Did they regard Simeon as a competitor?" asked Andy.

"Yes, although they addressed different sectors of the market, of course. Actually, I reckon they saw him as the forerunner in developing the Island as a book centre. In spite of his demise, I think that will eventually happen, because of what Simeon started."

"Thank you, Annabel, for calling. We will keep in touch," said Bruno, and ended the phone call.

"These two booksellers become obvious persons of immediate interest," Bruno said to Andy. "A visit to Max Carter's West Wight Bookshop in Cowes is our next move, and, after that, to the Bembridge Bookshop owned by Nathan Philips."

Andy phoned to make appointments.

Bruno accepted that Annabel Wilson's call could be interpreted in two ways. That she was genuinely trying to help the police with information that was new to them, or that her real reason was to deflect attention from herself, and present two new suspects to be investigated.

Chapter 9

Max Carter agreed to meet the detectives the following morning. It was Saturday and a busy morning in Cowes. As someone involved with the organisation of the annual Isle of Wight Literary Festival, Max should know many people with an interest in the book business, and especially this kind of book.

Max lived in an elegant fully restored Victorian house on the Esplanade facing the sea near to the Royal Cowes Yacht Club. His business was located in the busiest part of Cowes with a shopfront on the High Street including a small warehouse full of books, maps, pictures and a collection of sixty-year-old portable typewriters adjoining the rear of the shop. He displayed a gregarious personality, garrulous even.

"The thing about the book business is that you have to love books to be in it," he said enthusiastically. "Each book has a story behind it. Each author is totally driven to write, has conceived the book in their imagination, sweated to write it, and believes sufficiently in their book to take it to a publisher and to repeatedly overcome the rejection of what is sometimes their life's work."

"So, you deal in old books?" said Andy, cutting off Carter in mid-flow.

"We're a recognised antiquarian bookseller, but some might call us a second-hand bookseller. We sell both kinds of books – old and new. If you browse around the shop, you'll find all the latest titles as well as the classics – every kind of book you'd expect to find in a decent bookshop. We sell a lot of sailing books and charts of famous voyages of discovery. Our clients for these historical works are principally sailors and seafarers. They come from the places that have been discovered by adventurous travellers, whose names you probably know from history…"

"Did you know Simeon Calafifi?" interrupted Bruno.

"I did, and I also know Annabel who runs the shop."

"When did you last see him?"

"Recently," said Max. "About a month ago but I can give you no idea about his killer," he advanced before Bruno could even ask him.

"Do you know anything about the books that were stolen?"

"Books? I have heard about one. It's a Jewish prayer book, a Talmud, is that correct?"

"Yes, it is. How did you find out?"

"That it was stolen? Or that Simeon had bought it in the first place? It was in the Wheelers catalogue, which I examined before the auction. I think Nathan Philips told me about it all."

"Did you attend the saleroom?"

"Yes, for a bit," he replied vaguely. "The Talmud was bought for a lot of money in the sale. There were lots of people there on the day and many interested parties, I would say. The killer has to be connected to one of them."

"So do you think that it was stolen because it was valuable, and the killer hopes to sell it on to make money?" said Bruno.

"No, Chief Inspector, it's highly unlikely. That kind of book? Definitely not," said Carter.

"How would they know who bought the book?"

"It was sold at a public auction. Everybody would have known who bought it. I mean, I did, didn't I? Among the book collectors on the Island only one or two would be interested in that book, but not at that kind of money. Definitely out of their league. The market for valuable books about every subject under the sun is not exclusive to one group. It's an international business."

"Can you tell us who in your opinion would be specifically interested in that book?"

"I can't do that off the top of my head, because I don't know. But I will give you the contact details of my clients who might be interested, without saying that I know of a reason why. I'll get them for you now," he said, and disappeared out of view.

A minute later he returned with details printed on a sheet of paper.

"There are several names, Chief Inspector, including some antiquarian booksellers. Let me add that I don't think any of them would mind being contacted by you. You can tell them that I gave you their details. I can't think that the individual buyers will be much help. The booksellers might be of more use – they could be interested in the Talmud, or they might not be. Either way, they might provide some input into your investigation."

Bruno and Andy asked Max if he knew Nathan Philips well and explained that they were going to see him next.

"Of course I know him. He's a contemporary of mine. He will help you. Furthermore, he's Jewish and so might have an insight that I don't. He is well-respected and liked by everyone who knows him – including me. I'll be interested to know how you get on. He's always got plenty to say."

"Mr Carter, is there any other information that you think might be helpful to us. Are there any other persons you know, maybe not in the book trade, even people who do not live on the Island, who could be interested?"

"There are one or two London dealers who come to book auctions on the South Coast. You never know when a first edition might show up, or a batch of books from a well-known person's library," said Max.

"Who are they?"

"The person I see at every auction is Ben Hirshman. He has a business in Central London. He's international and pretty big." Neither detective mentioned that they had already seen and interviewed him.

"Just one final thing, sir, can you tell us where you were on the evening of Tuesday 28th February?" Andy asked.

"That's easy to answer, actually. I was at the Royal Cowes Yacht Club with some friends. We meet on the last Tuesday evening of the month at 7:30 p.m.," he replied.

"Can anyone confirm that, sir?"

"The Secretary will confirm my attendance. In fact, anyone else who was there can." He didn't voice the Secretary's contact details; instead he took a business card from his desk and wrote them on the back.

"Shall I call Nathan for you and let him know you are going to see him?"

Bruno declined the offer. He liked to make his own approach when speaking to a person of interest, although he suspected that the moment they left Cowes, Max Carter would call Nathan anyway and tell him about their visit and brief him.

As they were about to leave, Carter offered to show them round his warehouse behind the shop, which contained much more than antiquarian books. It was crammed full of paintings, garden sculpture, a vintage E-Type Jaguar, and a couple of motorbikes.

On their way back at the station, Andy said: "My wife thinks that Cowes is full of second-hand junk shops. Carter's warehouse is certainly full up with things."

"His stuff is not junk," said Bruno. "He said he was an antiquarian bookseller, but I think he's a shrewd dealer who recognises the value of everything and if something is a bargain, he will buy it. Why else would a self-appointed antiquarian bookseller, who specialised in marine charts, have two vintage motorbikes and an E-Type Jaguar in his showroom?"

"One of those bikes was a BSA 500 Gold Star, sir," said Andy.

Bruno looked at his colleague who had just revealed a knowledge of classic motorcycles.

"And it said on a label that the other was a Royal Enfield replica," said Bruno. "He's a dealer in anything valuable that he thinks somebody, somewhere could want, so we should pay attention to him and follow up every lead he gives us."

"Okay," said Andy. "Before we leave Cowes, let's look at the addresses of the names Carter gave to us."

"Four collectors are on Carter's list, and three dealers who he knows from Wheelers," said Bruno. "The dealers are Bobby Kilroy from Knutsford in Cheshire, Angus Smithson from Edinburgh, and Carl Bullivent from Bournemouth. From pure distance we should exclude Kilroy and Smithson. We cannot justify a nationwide search at this stage, but we will keep them in reserve. Let's plan to interview Bullivent but leave him until we find something else apart from his saleroom attendance. It should not take more than half a day to speak to the four local collectors. I don't expect them to be involved in the murder, but they could lead us somewhere."

*

The first of the collectors, Mr Arnold King, lived in Queens Road, Cowes. When Andy phoned, he was in and available to speak to them in person.

After an explanation as to why they were visiting, Andy's first question to Mr King was, "Have you been offered the ancient Talmud by any dealer or runner, or received any phone calls about this book?" Andy described the book to him in such detail that he sounded like an expert.

Arnold King spoke very softly but clearly. "Although I collect rare books, I do not collect religious books. My specialist subjects are naval: the design of nineteenth-century warships, marine charts from famous ships on momentous voyages, and maritime history."

"Do you have any dealings with other Island booksellers?"

"I know them, and I visit them whenever I'm in their area. There is a bookseller in St. Helen's from whom I always buy something. Max Carter in the High Street is my prime source of naval history books. He sells everything:

flags, naval instruments, he even had an old diving suit when I last went into his shop. He does sell other kinds of antiquarian books and some of them are quite old, but seldom of interest to me."

"What about Simeon Calafifi in Shanklin?"

"I wondered when you were going to mention him specifically," he said. "Have you found his killer?"

"That is why we came to see you. We are working on the case, gathering as much information as possible. Is there anything you can tell us that might be helpful to our investigation?"

"It's a very hard business at the present time. Many of these so-called 'antiquarian' booksellers don't make a good living. They just get by. It's small margins, I imagine, unless you get lucky with big sales. Yes, most of them just get by, I would say," he added.

"Max Carter gave us your name as one of a number of book collectors who live on the Island who might be able to help us in our search."

"No one has come to me with anything that could help you. I haven't asked anyone either. Perhaps I should? Ask questions, I mean. Ask around. Who are the other collectors?"

Bruno saw no reason not to tell him. He might even make an informative comment.

"There are three others. The nearest person to you by location is someone called Stanley Ridge."

"He lives in Northwood," said Arnold immediately. "On Love Lane, opposite the sports ground. He collects everything to do with Queen Victoria, old photographs, memorabilia, and books about her. He used to be a tour guide at Osborne House in the summer. He has also written books, self-published ones, about her life on the Island. He's worth a visit if you want to learn something about his special subject, but I don't think he will be of much use to you in the finding Calafifi's killer."

"The second name on the list is Robert Peel."

"Ah, sadly, he died three months ago. He was in his eighties, lived at Calbourne. A very nice man who collected post-First-World-War literature – Eliot, Woolf, and Lawrence, etc."

"Finally," said Andy Bowen, "a lady called Penelope Norton, who lives in Yarmouth."

"Big house in Arreton, see her every year at the Literary Festival. She collects first editions of Agatha Christie, P.D. James, that kind of thing. She likes Josephine Tay, Daphne Du Maurier, Dorothy L. Sayers, and also many other twentieth-century detective writers like Val McDermid. She has written a couple of books, herself, you know. One on Agatha Christie and she even appeared on television talking about Christie's life. I'd say you would be wasting your time with Stanley and Penelope. On the other hand, if you told Penelope your story, she might come up with a clue or two," he added, as kind of a joke.

"Is there anyone else on the Island who you think it would be worthwhile speaking to?"

"I can't name anyone, Chief Inspector, but I would say that the murderer has to be a person in the business. Not necessarily from the Island but definitely within easy travelling distance. To a common thief a valuable religious book would be worthless, wouldn't it? They might not even know its value. So I think it must be someone after the very valuable Talmud and something went wrong." After reflecting, he concluded, "I have been of little help, Chief Inspector, but I will keep my eyes and ears open."

On their way back to Newport, Bruno said, "It's been a morning of covering the ground and eliminating names, by which I mean the four collectors on the Island named by Max Carter. I don't think we should bother with Penelope Norton this time. Arnold King seemed to have a handle on the Island bibliophiles and if he suspected anyone that could help us, he'd have told us. Let's look at the three mainland dealers Max Carter gave to us."

"Okay, sir, but I'd like to change your mind over Penelope Norton. If we cautiously lay out what we have got, an experienced sleuth could put it all together in a different way revealing something painfully obvious, like all Agatha Christie crime stories."

"All right, Andy, I take your point. We'll include her in our plans for next week. On Monday, our next visit is to Walter Spens in North London, the chap who contacted Kazac. We can think about Carl Bullivent in Bournemouth, and we still need to visit Nathan Philips back on the Island. Oh, and Sam Trent."

Chapter 10

Walter Spens had agreed to see the detectives at his home, The Grange, at Spaniards End, on Hampstead Heath in London. Spaniards End is situated behind The Spaniards Inn, a historic highwayman's bolthole in the eighteenth century, reportedly used by Dick Turpin. The Grange was an impressive house, worth a fortune today, with views across the Heath as far as Hampstead High Street, a mile away.

Walter Spens was in his mid-eighties, but gave no indication, physically or mentally, that he was limited by his age. He had been a successful publisher for most of his working life with several famous authors amongst his clients when he had retired fifteen years ago. At The Grange he had a substantial library. He was a collector of authors on subjects that interested him, particularly astronomy, and of course he had every book his company had edited and published during his ownership. He had worked hard to promote and publicise the authors under contract to Spens Publishing; their book sales, as a result of astute marketing, had made him, and them, wealthy.

Since selling his publishing empire, he had acted as a consultant to the Greenwich Observatory and to theological institutions searching for ancient manuscripts, maps, books and sometimes early postage stamps. He was often contacted to find things that were frequently buried in the archives of museums which had long ago forgotten them, and which were usually open to fair offers to purchase them. He was almost always successful finding a sought-after target and was generously rewarded by his clients. It was his vast knowledge and special skill at finding long-lost treasures, combined with a photographic memory, which had led to him being consulted about the Talmud by a collector with a special interest in Jewish literature.

A lady who introduced herself as his housekeeper greeted them at the door, with Spens not far behind.

"You've had a long journey, detectives. Please do come in," he said, by way of a friendly welcome.

Spens was a widower whose wife Sandra had died fifteen years previously. Her death left him free to travel and indulge himself with friends at the Athenæum Club in Central London a couple of days a week, during which he would lunch and afterwards play backgammon. The members, many of whom were prominent in the arts and science, knew of his skill in discovering lost treasure. Scarcely did a visit to the club occur without a member approaching him.

Spens explained that, on a recent visit, one member who knew of his interest in ancient theological books questioned him about the Eliyahu Ben Shlomo Zalman's Talmud and asked him to explain its origin and significance. Spens responded to the limit of his knowledge, adding that he had never seen it, but he knew that it had been sold recently at auction. When Spens had enquired of his fellow member what had prompted his interest in the Talmud, the member had replied that a wealthy friend, who was not a member of the club, would pay a large sum to acquire it.

"Did he mention to you the name of this person?" asked Bruno.

"He didn't, but I said if I came across the Talmud, I would tell him. We then discussed its origin and why his friend was keen to purchase it. He said he was eager to return it to where it had been written. Apparently, the importance of this particular Talmud is the fact that has been written by one of the most revered rabbis in the history of Judaism. Furthermore, it's the definitive interpretation of the Ten Commandments revealed to Moses at Mount Sinai. I took the finding of this book as a challenge and telephoned my good friends in the business," said Spens.

"What did you find out from your friends?" asked Andy.

Bruno had already explained the reason for their urgent visit was to progress their investigation into the murder of Simeon Calafifi.

"I found out that Simeon Calafifi bought the Talmud at Wheelers auction, where it was sold after a bidding war. My friend also told me about the murder of Simeon Calafifi, and the identity of the underbidder for the Talmud on that day, namely Ben Hirshman. I know Ben, he's a splendid fellow. I didn't expect my friend to tell me for whom Calafifi was acting, but he did in fact tell me that the lot had been purchased on behalf of Professor Kazac in Tel Aviv."

"How would he have known that?" asked Bruno, keen to capitalise on Spens' personal investigative work. "Perhaps Simeon Calafifi himself told him? What do you think?"

"At their level, the antiquarian book business is a fraternity, close-knit, secretive. No surprise really, I suppose, that a dealer could be murdered by a book thief," said Spens. "Kazac told me he had been expecting delivery of the Talmud any day, but he had not yet received it."

"Perhaps you can tell us how you are progressing with finding the stolen book?" asked Andy.

"I started at the auction," Spens replied.

"I am curious to know why you called Kazac?"

"Exactly that. Curiosity, detective, for a chat and to confirm that he had not received the book. Is there any actual evidence that the book has been stolen?" asked Spens. "Apart from the fact that it is not in the shop?"

"The manager of the bookshop confirms that it was in the safe when she left the premises the evening of the murder," Bruno replied, content that he was giving away information only to potentially receive more.

Spens' face exhibited some doubt, as if he didn't quite get it or perhaps didn't agree, but he let the matter pass.

"It could have left the safe before the murder of Simeon," suggested Spens.

"How do you mean?" said Bruno, still keen to explore another person's line of thinking.

"Unless you witness a crime, you cannot be sure. The safe could have been empty for days."

That thought would require further examination with Annabel, who possessed a key to the safe, and who had attested to the book's presence the day before the murder.

Spens continued, "Valuable items like this Talmud do not come to auction often. The Americans who decided to sell the book in England were looking to European and possibly Israeli buyers to reach the highest price. I'm sure it didn't reach their expectations. From the discussions I have had, the sale price was substantially below what they had expected in the USA."

"If it was meant to attract bids from Europe and Israel, the auction could have been conducted online from the USA. Why was the book brought to England to go to auction at all?" asked Andy.

Spens replied quietly, as if sharing a secret. "The idea being put about is that there was an agreement between the bidders to conduct a second auction between the representatives of those interested parties immediately following the auction, and that second auction would have been more easily undertaken in the UK in person."

"Is that normal practice?" said Bruno.

"No," said Spens. "Certainly not for a very valuable book. If the bidding reaches the reserve, the item is sold to the highest bidder. What happens following that is entirely between the successful bidder, in this case Calafifi, and other interested parties. There may well have been some skullduggery after the bidding. But that's hypothetical and for you to fathom, detectives," he said in an authoritative but slightly cheeky manner.

"In your opinion, what is the Talmud really worth?" said Andy.

"A great deal more than Calafifi paid for it," said Spens. "It is a great work of Jewish literature. It crystalises the meaning of Jewish faith."

"So, you believe that at £50,500 it was undersold?"

"Yes," said Spens. "And the argument that Calafifi could have been murdered because he bought it for

£50,500, might seem to support that. You place a valuable item in an auction to sell it as the highest price. You set a reserve to widen interest, but also so you don't give it away. But you must attract the right attendees and that is the responsibility of the auctioneer. I wonder if this book was sufficiently marketed to the European market. It should have been. Hirshman withdrew from the bidding at £50k. Calafifi remained the one man standing, so he got a bargain, in my opinion. The other potential buyers, if any, did not enter the bidding. Maybe one or two of them are kicking themselves now at their lack of boldness, allowing a competitor to grab a bargain. At an auction you are skating on thin ice. You can easily pay too much and sometimes, although rarely in my opinion, you get a bargain. Go and speak to Ben Hirshman. I think he will tell you that £50,000 was his client's limit, so he had to pull out. I think that was also the reserve, but you'll need to check that."

"Who would have set the reserve?" wondered Andy.

"The seller. I would think that as the Americans decided to sell it in the UK, they probably set the reserve."

"Perhaps they did?"

"Could they have gone against advice given by Wheelers?"

"Maybe, but Wheelers' interest is in turnover and on their commission on the sale, so their advice benefits both of them."

"It seems that way from the way the bidding developed."

"You can't assume that," said Spens.

"The gentleman who approached you at your club would be of interest to us," said Bruno.

"When it does surface, if it ever does, my buyer would be keen to bid for the Talmud, for the reasons I have explained. Its value to the purchaser would lie in its historical and religious significance," said Spens.

"Can you tell us who that person is?"

"No, Chief Inspector, I cannot reveal a private conversation with another member to a third party, especially not the police, or I could be expelled from the Club, and that would destroy my reputation. What I will do is ask him if he could tell me any more about who would pay a large sum for the Talmud. If it could help your investigation, I will ask him if I can divulge his personal details to you."

"At this stage in our investigation that could be extremely helpful," replied Bruno. "How would he have found out that Simeon Calafifi had bought the Talmud?"

"He had his ear to the ground. Naturally, I did not ask him, though again I think Hirshman might have told him," he said. "There were other bidders at the auction on the internet. There was a Dutch bookseller, Thomas Untender from Amsterdam, and a Parisian bookseller from Les Enluminures, who deals in manuscripts from the Middle Ages. Thomas Untender specialises in Judaica Russian books. You can ignore the internet bidders. They are highly reputable established international businesses, not dissimilar to Simeon Calafifi's, with the same professional way of doing business, many of which sell more expensive, rarer books. The rare book business is difficult to understand, and it seems to me that you will find this murderer sooner or later," said Spens.

Spens added as an afterthought: "I think fashion can

play a huge part in this business. One year a dealer can make a fortune, and the following year can come the famine. That's why you buy in the belief that next year the market will favour your special subject, so you need stock."

"What kind of market are you in this year?" said Bruno.

"We are on the edge of a surge in value of antiquarian books. Next year will be a bumper year for everyone. That is my guess," he added.

Spens had accommodated their questioning and had provided useful background information. They parted in the friendliest manner with his promise that he would be available should they seek his advice in the future and to contact them immediately if he discovered the name of his friend's contact seeking to buy the Talmud and whether his friend was happy to talk to them himself.

To Bruno, however, something about Spens' story did not add up. There was definitely something important that he was not telling them. It was possible, likely even, that he knew who was trying to buy the Talmud. He might even know who may already be in possession of it, and who might try to acquire it by any means.

From what Bruno had learned from Spens, he was inclined to agree that Hirshman was the man who understood this sale and knew all those interested in the Talmud. After all, he was the underbidder, prepared to pay £50,000 for the book. As his Mayfair office was on the way home, Bruno considered the possibility of them paying him a surprise visit.

Bruno and Andy chose to walk in the sunny, but cold, midday sun back to Hampstead Underground station. Bruno wanted to re-assess what they had achieved from

113

their visit to Spens and think hard about how what they had learned could be of help to them.

*

On the rail journey to Portsmouth en route back to the Island, Bruno expanded his thoughts on where they were in their investigation after speaking with Spens.

"It was Professor Kazac who said he'd taken a call from Walter Spens. Spens had learned that he, Kazac, had purchased Ben Shlomo Zalman's Talmud for £50,500. Spens said that he was prepared to pay a large premium if Kazac would sell it to him. Kazac said no because it was now the property of the Tel Aviv University. Spens told Kazac that his client was a benefactor of the Culture Synagogue in Vilnius, but he would not tell him who his client was," reflected Bruno. "Kazac may know or be able to find out who it is. How did Spens discover that Calafifi acted for Kazac at the auction?"

"Presumably from Hirshman? He clearly knows him well and likes him. Hirshman was the underbidder. If Calafifi was acting for Kazac, we have to assume that he couldn't have been part of any auction consortium, but that he was potentially a target for any member of that so-called consortium who wanted to get their hands on the Talmud," said Andy.

Chapter 11

Tuesday 14th March was a day working in Newport Police Station. Bruno was conscious that two weeks had passed since Simeon Calafifi's murder, and they still had not seen Sam Trent. He wasn't necessarily important, but Bruno wanted some complete information for their files about Sam Trent's interface with Annabel Wilson on the evening of 28th February. It wasn't that he was Annabel Wilson's alibi, but more because he could provide some background and additional information to expand the picture they had of Annabel.

Bruno called Ryde School to find out that Sam Trent was away. It was nothing untoward – a Classics tour to Italy taking in the sights of Rome and Naples. The lady in the school office confirmed that the trip had been booked for months, and that Sam Trent was leading the trip. He had left yesterday and wouldn't be back for ten days. "Annoying," said Bruno, who made a note to call on in Sam Trent on his return.

Andy appeared with two coffees and some information that proved to be relevant but did not immediately seem useful.

"I was reading the Wheelers auction catalogue again last night and discovered that Lot 40 consisted of two letters written by Lady Hamilton to Admiral Horatio Nelson. They're genuine love letters expressing her love for Nelson and praying for his safe return. The estimate for these two letters was £12,000. But of interest to us is that the seller was Max Carter. When we visited him last week, he didn't mention that on the day Calafifi bought the Talmud he was present at Wheelers selling the letters. Unusual, don't you think? He did say he was there, but he didn't elaborate further. His presence on that particular day indicates something to me, but what it indicates, I'm not sure," said Andy.

"Does it?" said Bruno.

"Yes, I can't think what," said Andy. "He just makes me feel like, well, like he's hiding something."

"Spens made a valid point yesterday when he questioned whether the Talmud had been stolen on that evening, suggesting that perhaps it wasn't in the safe when the killer arrived," Bruno replied. "It's the kind of observation that people make to show how smart they are. They could be 'blind alley' suggestions to lead you up the garden path, but it is a possibility we have not yet fully explored. Annabel indicated that both books were in the safe on the evening of the murder."

"Which she would know because she was in the habit of checking the contents of the safe on a regular basis. She said two days' takings were put in the safe, so she must have done that before she left, so she would have seen the books were there," said Andy.

"We know the Talmud was stolen for money. We just have to keep to our present line of thinking," said Bruno.

"Can you think of any reason, sir, why Calafifi didn't deliver the Talmud straight to Professor Kazac?"

"Because Kazac wanted to make the ceremonial presentation of the occasion. Those things take a while to organise. And Calafifi had to make arrangements to travel to Israel from the Island."

The question had not been raised before, but it was possible that it had disappeared from Simeon's safe soon after it was purchased by Calafifi.

"You mean that Kazac knew it had been stolen?"

"Yes."

"That's what Spens was insinuating, but I don't think Calafifi would have been careless with the Talmud. Even so, perhaps he could have been already looking for it and was meeting this mysterious caller about its whereabouts?"

"Let's stay with the books being stolen by the out-of-hours caller and see if Kazac can name this unknown benefactor that Spens spoke about."

*

The list of persons of interest had increased, to include those the book trade referred to as runners, mostly unknown, coming from various locations on the Island.

"Without names and addresses, we have to discount them," he said, "and concentrate on what and who we know. The Island book collectors have been eliminated, which leaves the dealers, and the people they work for: the buyers of valuable books, either for themselves or others like Kazac at the University of Tel Aviv."

Whilst they continued to examine the information to date, Ben Hirshman called Bruno from London.

"Chief Inspector Peach, I promised to call you when I learned of anything that might help you find the killer of Simeon Calafifi. Rather than speak to you on the phone, can we meet in my office? I want to introduce you to my client, who could help in your investigation."

"That would be excellent, thank you. My colleague here can set up a Zoom call today, so as not to waste any time. Can we do that? We can send you an invitation by email and can host the call today if your client is amenable to joining the call."

Since their foray to the mainland Bruno believed that Hirshman consciously or unconsciously held the secret to solving this crime and so, without delay, they arranged a 4 p.m. Zoom meeting and emailed it to Hirshman's office.

*

Once they were all logged on at 4 o'clock, Hirshman introduced them to one of his clients. Mr Peter Rose announced himself as the Chief Executive Officer of the Commonwealth Bank in the City of London.

"I am pleased to meet you, detectives, and to help in any way I can. It is a very sad situation. I know the Calafifi family well, and I was a friend of Simeon's for many years. It seems that we both had an interest in acquiring the Vilnius Talmud, although I did not know that until Ben told me. My recent interest came from my friendship with Rabbi David Samuel from the Wood Green Synagogue, who told me that this rare Talmud was being sold at auction and could I help the members to buy it. I instructed Ben to act for me at the auction with a limit of £50,000. That was Rabbi Samuel's limit. When the bidding reached £50,000, Ben withdrew."

"We believe that the Talmud remained with Simeon until it was stolen by the killer," said Bruno. "We do hope, of course, to recover it. Are you aware of any organisation, group or individual who would murder to get hold of it?

"That's a tall order," said Peter Rose. "Apart from my connection with Wood Green Synagogue, I can't think of any persons or organisation that could buy it. Ben has acquainted me with the facts, Chief Inspector, but no reputable setup or individual would become involved in this book, however important it is. If it has been stolen by a thief for cash, there is no market for it. Whoever they may be, I hope they make a mistake and give you a chance of identifying the murderer. I'm sure this will happen, Chief Inspector," he concluded.

Peter Rose promised to make direct contact if anything of interest came his way and left the Zoom call.

Hirshman concluded the meeting by saying that he had spoken to many of the people in the antiquarian book trade who were on the alert for any approach to sell the Talmud. They all knew they must immediately contact Detective Chief Inspector Bruno Peach on the Isle of Wight.

Having thanked Hirshman for his time, Bruno and Andy closed the Zoom meeting. They were glad they had not taken a five hour train journey for such a short meeting, and proceeded to discuss the meeting with Hirshman and Rose.

"Hirshman and Rose are friends, and Rose is some kind of collector?" said Bruno. "Who apart from Peter Rose knew that Hirshman was bidding on behalf of the Wood Green Synagogue? We should confirm that the Wood Green Synagogue wanted to buy the Talmud, and that Peter Rose was asked to negotiate a deal," observed

Bruno. "The Rabbi David Samuel at the Wood Green Synagogue is the person to ask, and we will only find out if we visit him and use our police presence to solicit an answer."

"A polite phone call might do that, sir?" said Andy. "I will try that tomorrow."

*

Later Bruno called Professor Kazac again with some further questions.

"Can you tell us more about Walter Spens?"

"He wanted me to know about the Lithuanian who was keen to buy the Talmud from me if it were for sale. Spens didn't reveal the name of his contact, he just wanted to know if I would sell the Talmud. He gave me just enough information for me to find out for myself who it was." Then, changing tack, the Professor asked Bruno, "Do you know anything about Lithuania?"

Bruno admitted that he knew very little, or in truth, nothing at all.

Kazac proceeded to give some background. "Vilnius is the capital and was once regarded by Jews as the Jerusalem of the north. Lithuanian Jews were called Litvaks and are descended from Ashkenazi Jews. Bear with me while I give you a brief history lesson, Chief Inspector. In 1940, a quarter of a million Jews lived in Lithuania, of which 200,000 were murdered by the Nazis in the Holocaust. The rest were wise enough to leave. Now there are only 3,000 living in Vilnius. The golden age of Polish Lithuanian Jewry was in the early nineteenth century when the Talmud was written in Vilnius in 1807. The 3,000 Jewish citizens who now live there are trying to re-establish the Jewish community which was once prosperous and brought much wealth to the country and is now growing exponentially. Many returned from America or Israel once the country gained its independence from the USSR in 1990."

Kazac went on: "In Israel we have close ties with Jewish communities all over the world, and as part of our heritage we help them thrive. We are active in helping the 3,000 Lithuanian Jews build the social fabric, including faith schools and hospitals to attract Jewish people to go and live there. These projects are to ensure the traditions of our faith are established."

"That's tremendous, but I'm not sure how that relates to our murder," was Bruno's comment, prompting Kazac to continue.

"When I finished speaking to Walter Spens, I decided to speak to Rabbi Barry in Lithuania. Barry is an American who moved to Vilnius from Chicago. He is responsible for the Culture Centre in Vilnius and is writing the history of the Jews in Vilnius. He said that he speaks with former Lithuanian Jews, some of whom live in the USA, some in the UK, all of whom generously contribute to any initiative for which Rabbi Barry is seeking financial support. Naturally, to acquire the Talmud, and to return it to its seat of origin, would be an enormous boost to Rabbi Barry and the community. He said that he was contacted by a prominent Lithuanian Jew living in Britain who discussed the impact of the return of the Talmud to its city of origin, and he agreed that, if possible, he would try to acquire it for Rabbi Barry."

"Did he give the name of the British person?"

"Rabbi Barry said the name of the benefactor of the Vilnius Synagogue is Wladimir Pivotkin. Mr Pivotkin manufactures components for electric cars. His business, which he established in the UK, has grown rapidly since he left his home in Vilnius for England forty years ago and has earned him something of a fortune. With his wealth he wants to help his fellow Litvaks recreate their home as it used to be before the Nazi invasion and he is prepared to rebuild the Synagogue as it was in the time of Rabbi Ben Shlomo in the late eighteenth century. I cannot tell you anything more, as I did not contact Pivotkin, but it's possible, Chief Inspector Peach, that you might obtain something useful from him," he said.

Bruno was pleased with his conversation with Professor Kazac. It clarified the position regarding persons they knew for certain who were interested in the Talmud, apart from the Professor himself and Simeon Calafifi; namely Ben Hirshman's client, Peter Rose, and now, Wladimir Pivotkin.

*

Bruno decided to speak again to Walter Spens now that he knew he was acting for Wladimir Pivotkin to confirm how Spens knew that Kazac had bought the Talmud through Calafifi.

Spens' response was what it had been when they met: that the information that Calafifi had sold the Talmud to Kazac had come from Ben Hirshman. He also added something interesting to their conversation, which Bruno thought relevant, but was not sure why.

"The market for significant religious publications

is very small, so it's natural for those who deal in these valuable books, manuscripts, and ancient writings, to share information about each other's dealings. Each dealer has a specific niche in this market with collectors and organisations that employ them to start or complete collections. They make the market and determine the value of everything."

"Have you ever undertaken any other work for Mr Pivotkin?"

"Not for some time, but on this occasion, he knew who had bought the Talmud from Calafifi."

"He didn't ask Ben Hirshman?"

"No, because he didn't want his quest for the Talmud to become common knowledge."

Bruno's conversation with Spens concluded any further discussion about the Talmud with him, but the knowledge that Pivotkin wanted to acquire it made him a person of interest and someone who should be interviewed. Spens would not help with Pivotkin's contact details, so Bruno passed the task of locating him to Andy Bowen, who obtained it from public company records.

*

When Bruno located and called Wladimir Pivotkin, his response to Bruno's introduction, namely that he was investigating the murder of Simeon Calafifi, an antiquarian bookseller from the Isle of Wight, was positive.

"Can we come and see you to discuss the circumstances surrounding his death?" asked Bruno.

"Of course you can, but I cannot contribute anything of use to your investigation, Chief Inspector. Not wishing to waste your time or mine I'd prefer if you would put your questions to me on the telephone, or preferably by email."

Bruno jumped straight in. "I understand that Ben Hirshman told you about the sale of the Talmud."

"I know Ben Hirshman, but no, he did not tell me about the book sale to Simeon Calafifi. It was a man called Max Carter who told me that the Talmud had been sold to Calafifi. He was at the auction, but he didn't tell me it had been bought for Professor Kazac at Tel Aviv University. I called Calafifi to ask if the book was for sale and he told me it had already been sold to Professor Kazac. That was our entire conversation. So, I spoke to Walter Spens and left it to him. But I don't suppose we will ever see the Talmud again, will we?"

"I don't know, sir, but I do hope so," said Bruno.

"If you do find the Talmud, and Kazac can lay a legitimate claim to it, which I am sure he will, I think he will sell it to me because he is also interested in its return to its native land. I am purely interested in the Talmud. None of this is connected with Calafifi's murder, Chief Inspector," said Pivotkin. "If it ever returns, there are 3,000 Jews living left in Lithuania now who would find great inspiration from it."

To Bruno, Pivotkin's motivation was sincere and infectious. In a peculiar way, he felt that he too was on a mission to find the Talmud.

Andy had listened to Bruno's phone conversation and was curious that Max Carter, who they had interviewed in Cowes recently, should have a direct contact with Pivotkin.

"I don't understand why he should have conveyed the information that Simeon had bought the Talmud. Carter must have known of Pivotkin's interest, which nobody was representing at the auction, it seems, unless it was a member of the consortium that was not bidding."

"I agree," said Bruno. "But what role do you think Max Carter is playing in this?"

Andy thought about it for a while.

"None," said Andy. "Max is an opportunist, but I don't think he is a murderer. We can soon find out by going to Cowes and asking him about his relationship with Pivotkin."

Having dabbled with Israel, Lithuania, London, and Wheelers on the mainland, it was time to follow up the curious connection between Max Carter and the wealthy billionaire in London.

Andy called him and requested a meeting, to which he was hesitant.

"I told you everything I know when you came recently, and since then I have thought of nothing to help you."

"We'd like to talk about the Wheelers auction at which Simeon Calafifi bought the Talmud, and at which you were present. You told us when we first met that you knew your fellow Island bookseller had made the purchase. Perhaps you can elaborate and tell us more about how things work at these auctions?"

"They are quite straightforward; just ask me the questions and I can clarify anything with you now."

Carter's reluctance to meet the police again suggested that he possibly had something to hide, which made them determined to visit him at his shop in Cowes.

"We have a couple of tricky questions to put to you concerning the attendees at the auction, which we would prefer to do face to face. Would first thing tomorrow, Wednesday, be convenient, before you start your day?" said Bruno.

"Tomorrow?" he repeated. After a lengthy pause, Carter said, "Okay, what time?"

"To suit you," said Bruno.

"How about 9:30? I will be here, at the shop," he said and ended the call.

"What is he frightened of?" said Andy as Bruno replaced the receiver.

"We'll find out in the morning and hopefully persuade him to open up on this auction game. Get your notebook out and go over what we spoke about when we last saw him," said Bruno. "I remember he was friendly, casual and a bit of a smart alec , and had an alibi for the night Calafifi was murdered. We'll take the opportunity while we are in Cowes to check that out."

Chapter 12

Andy was fully prepared when he and Bruno met Max Carter at his High Street bookshop on Wednesday morning. He had read his notes and highlighted the inconsistencies with what they had since discovered about Max Carter. Max had provided the names and contact details of four Island collectors: three men and one woman. They had yet to speak to the woman, Penelope Norton, who Andy had been keen for them to meet.

After the initial pleasantries, Andy Bowen cut straight to the quick.

"Max, when we last met you said that you had learned about the Talmud from Nathan Philips. Yet you were present at the auction and witnessed the Talmud being purchased by Simeon Calafifi."

"That's correct, Chief Inspector. I did say that, but what I meant was that I had talked about the purchase of the Talmud with Nathan. I also told you that I was at the auction."

"Is it a book you might have bid for?" said Andy.

"Not unless I was bidding on behalf of a client."

"Although there were several potential buyers and dealers who witnessed the sale of this lot, only two bidders were interested."

"Yes, when the bidding reached £50,500, I guess everybody was frightened off," said Max.

"Can you tell us the dealers who were present on that day? And about interest in the book in general."

"There were several I do not know, but there are three who I believe would be interested in the Talmud. They are Bobby Kilroy whose business is in Knutsford, Angus Smithson from Edinburgh, and Carl Bullivent from Bournemouth. I told you that last time we met."

"Just those three? Okay. Can we now discuss your contact with Wladimir Pivotkin?" said Bruno.

That sudden question and the mention of Pivotkin's name surprised Carter.

"He called me about ten days ago, and said he was interested in buying the Talmud if I knew who had it. I asked him how he got my contact details. He said Walter Spens had told him that I was his Isle of Wight contact and that I might know the whereabouts of the stolen book. I said Simeon Calafifi had bought it, but it had been stolen when he had been murdered. He said that if it had been stolen on the Island it might surface here, and he would pay a handsome premium for it. I've no doubt he would have called the other booksellers on the Island with the same approach."

"You know Walter Spens?"

"He calls me on maritime matters occasionally. He called me about the authenticity of the Hamilton letters. He might even have bought them, for all I know." This throwaway comment served to undermine much of what Carter had already said.

"Can we look around your warehouse before we go?"

"Of course, Chief Inspector, be my guest. Do have a good look around and call me if you find something you want to buy; I'm sure I can arrange a decent discount for you," Max smiled.

"What are you after, sir?" Andy said to Bruno as they wandered amongst the antique furniture, cabinets of porcelain, paintings, a penny-farthing bicycle, maps, and the rows of leather-bound books in glass-fronted bookcases.

"Nothing in particular," said Bruno. "I am trying to understand Max Carter. He is quite a collector, isn't he? He has every kind of antique here in this place. He is different to the others. They are dealers, they buy and sell. This man seems to mainly collect and, occasionally, if he has anything of real value, he sells at auctions. His net worth is here in this place, jam packed with unsaleable items. How does he make a living?"

It was an interesting observation by Bruno.

"I have the card he gave me the last time we were here, with the Secretary's contact details. Shall I call him while we are here in Cowes, sir?"

"Yes. If he can see us, the Royal Cowes Yacht Club is very near."

Freddie Fraser answered his mobile number immediately. When Andy Bowen asked him if he had a few minutes to spare as they were in Cowes, he said he wasn't in the club but was in his shop; indeed he was the only person in the shop and couldn't leave.

"I am the High Street butcher, you see, so mid-mornings are not a good time, I'm afraid," he said.

Andy understood and was in no mood to bully the shopkeeper, especially the local butcher. But as he was about to suggest an alternative time, Fraser's wife showed up in the shop.

"It's the police, love," he could be heard to say to her.

"Better speak to them," she said. "I'll look after the shop if anyone comes in."

The detectives located his shop at the end of the High Street. Fraser's shop was in fact empty when they arrived, but his wife stood in behind the counter so he could step into the back office.

Bruno explained that the police were looking for Simeon Calafifi's murderer and were speaking to everyone who had a connection with him. As Max Carter was in antiquarian bookselling, the same business as Calafifi, they were confirming his whereabouts at the time of the murder.

"Mr Carter said that on the evening of Tuesday 28th February he attended a meeting with you at the Royal Cowes Yacht Club."

"That's correct," said Freddie. "I'm the secretary of the Cowes Chamber of Commerce. Almost all of the small businesses in the town belong to the Chamber, including Max Carter's. We meet on the last Tuesday of every month at 8 p.m. Max was on time, as far as I remember. We sat down at about 8:15 or thereabouts, once everyone had bought a drink at the bar. Max is a regular, unlike some, and always has good ideas about improving the High Street. Is that all you wanted to know, Chief Inspector?"

"Yes, Mr Fraser, you've confirmed our information."

"In which case, I'll go back to work and let the missus get back to the bookkeeping," he said, then shook hands and returned to his meat counter.

"Are you happy with that, sir?" asked Andy.

"Not really," said Bruno. "An alibi at 8 p.m. or thereabouts does not rule out Max as a person of interest, especially as the last time we met he said they met at 7:30 p.m. If Calafifi had been murdered by Max at any time up to 6:45 p.m., he could still have travelled to the meeting in Cowes by the time they were about to start. Before we leave, I might just take a look at the butcher's counter. Good, old fashioned butchers are hard to find these days."

Bruno soon found two pork chops with kidneys and bought them to take home to Janet. He also asked for two rib-eye steaks, watching Fraser slice them with his butcher's knives.

"That's my supper for two nights this week," he said and smiled all the way back to his car.

"Is Max Carter a suspect?" said Andy.

"He is of interest to us, yes," said Bruno. "Lots of what he says doesn't add up. Did he actually witness the sale of the Talmud? Does it matter? He said he was at the meeting in Cowes at 7:30 p.m., when it was actually later than that. However, we can't question him again without a piece of concrete evidence."

Andy said, "Did you see all the knives in that shop? It made me think. I wonder what happened to the one that killed Simeon Calafifi? That has to be somewhere."

*

Back at Newport Police Station, Bruno took a call from Annabel at Simeon's Bookshop. She had a few updates to share.

"The shop has settled down somewhat and, in spite of a feeling of immense sadness at the turn of events, I have agreed with Mrs Calafifi that I will continue to manage the shop. She has agreed for me to interview applicants for the newly advertised job of assistant. I was surprised at how many people liked the idea of working in a bookshop. I am confident that even without the contribution from Simeon's antiquarian book sales I can still run the business profitably."

Mrs Calafifi had told Annabel that she had recovered from the initial shock of Simeon's death and, in an immensely practical way, had explained to Annabel the reasons for moving back to London, principally by saying that Shanklin had such awful memories for them now, so they had to leave, and that her boys wanted to return to their more familiar communities and traditions. She had given notice to Ryde School, and Haberdashers' Aske's school in North London had agreed to take the boys into their relevant classes whenever they could be moved.

"I think she is wise. How will she ever get over this?" said Annabel.

Miriam Calafifi had not shared with Annabel the momentous news that the shop was sold and that she was contractually bound to sell the business to Nathan Philips. This was probably because she was afraid of Annabel's reaction at what could be the end of her reign as the queen bee of Simeon's Bookshop. To avoid any aggravation, Mrs Calafifi had decided to wait until she had already made her exit for London.

Thinking about Mrs Calafifi's decision to leave the Island so soon after her husband's murder and abandoning the life they had started as a family did not sit right with Bruno. He had tried unsuccessfully to expedite the release of Simeon's body to her and the anxiety she had shown earlier to bury him had subsided.

Andy felt she should wait until the police investigation was completed and the murderer arrested before she hastened away. He could not see any reason for her to up sticks so quickly. Perhaps she was genuinely afraid of something – or someone? If so, Bruno wanted to know about it.

*

Over delicately pan-fried rib-eye steaks, Bruno and Janet sat down to supper. Bruno wanted to learn what Janet thought about Mrs Calafifi's decision to quit Ryde quite so quickly before any real progress had been made by the police investigation.

"What does the police investigation mean to her?" said Janet, in her usual matter of fact and confident manner. "If you catch the person who killed her husband, the murder trial will surely be too painful for her to attend. She won't be one of those victims who come to court every day to eyeball the killer, and see justice done. Once she has left the Island, you won't see her again. Simeon and she had already planned a life away from the Island, so her decision to leave was made a long time ago. The Island has been her home for three years and it doesn't feel from what you have told me that she has ever settled here. She's got a job and a life on the mainland. It's something that she doesn't want to be questioned about, and her decision to move was certainly made before the murder."

Bruno had no reason to believe that Mrs Calafifi had anything to do with her husband's murder and, yes, Janet was right. The intended move had been planned long before Simeon's death.

Chapter 13

B runo had asked the support desk to work out a travel plan and make an appointment to visit Carl Bullivent in Bournemouth. In the meantime, on Thursday morning they had arranged to visit Penelope Norton.

He knew that Andy had a particular gift when dealing with ladies of a certain age. They would engage him in conversation about every subject under the sun and he would banish their loneliness by giving them just a little of his time. This almost always enabled him to get valuable snippets of information and news that sometimes developed into problem-solving clues. As his reward, Bruno always asked him to make the first contact. Today it was Penelope Norton, the book collector whose name had been supplied by Max Carter. She was a widow in her early sixties who had been married to an Island solicitor. She lived in a cottage which was actually a rather grand house in Arreton Village.

To speak to a real-life detective who had asked to visit her to discuss the murder of Simeon Calafifi, Penelope Norton considered a well-deserved accolade. Furthermore, she believed she could be of valuable assistance to the police following the teachings and methods of the queen of detective fiction, Dame Agatha Christie. Penelope was well known on the Island as an authority and raconteur and a much-sought-after criminology speaker on the Agatha Christie detective stories. Sometimes she adopted the persona of one of Christie's detectives, Miss Jane Marple, an elderly spinster with an uncanny knack of providing the police with vital clues, as a result of closely observed character traits in suspects. Miss Marple believed that in a murder investigation nobody was above suspicion, and that a detective could not afford to believe everything that people told them.

"Good morning, detectives," she said as she opened the front door of Arreton Cottage in the principal part of Arreton Village. The house stood in its own well-tended garden within a stone's throw of St George's church. It was a house and garden that the villagers stopped and admired in the early summer when the roses were in full bloom. To a visitor the interior of the house was a complete surprise. It had been modernised to a high standard, and although the small leaded light windows at the front of the house suggested a dark old-fashioned interior, the inside had been completely rebuilt, with a modern lounge and kitchen. The ceiling had been raised to incorporate an atrium, which gave light to the entire ground floor. The floor-to-ceiling windows flooded the study with light and provided a beautiful view of the well-tended rear garden.

Crossing the threshold of her immaculate house, the two men faced an oil painting of a young, beautiful Penelope Norton, probably forty years ago, hung on the opposing wall to the entrance.

"Come through and please sit down," she said in an inviting manner. "And, please, call me Penny."

They sat in comfortable armchairs, facing her. She sat upright in front of them, expensively and elegantly dressed in pearls and a huge diamond solitaire ring.

"Well, Chief Inspector Peach, how can I help you?"

"We are speaking to all the book collectors we can identify on the Island to see if they can tell us anything that might help us to find Simeon Calafifi's killer."

"Yes, how sad," she said. "I have visited his bookshop on several occasions. Well laid out, a good selection. Such a tragedy, though! Now, would you mind telling me the circumstances of the murder, Chief Inspector?" she added in true Jane Marple style.

Bruno saw no reason not to share some details with her: "The bookshop closed at about 5:45 p.m. when the manager left the shop, by its rear entrance. Simeon Calafifi remained in the shop waiting to meet somebody by appointment who was due to arrive at or soon after 6 p.m." He added a brief summary of the situation regarding the safe and the missing books, and the discovery of his body.

"Did he know the caller?"

"We are told by the bookshop manager that she thought he did. But that she, the bookshop manager, did not know who it was."

"So, an unknown person arrived, killed Simeon, stole the money from the safe, the Talmud and another religious book. Did you say that the manager gave the day's takings to Simeon as she left?"

"No, we understand that she was the custodian of the second safe key and normally put the daily cash takings into the safe," Bruno explained.

Bruno continued: "The victim was killed with a thin-bladed knife driven through from the back. The blade pierced his heart, and he most likely died instantly."

"So, the victim was alone with the killer?" she said thoughtfully.

"As far as we can tell. The killer or killers got away with everything from the safe, which was open at the time."

"When you say 'open', Chief Inspector, you mean it was unlocked when the murder was discovered. So, was it opened by Simeon Calafifi? And if so, why would he do that?"

"I presume to put the takings for the day into the safe," said Andy, who realised he could not truthfully answer her question. They didn't know whether the safe was unlocked before or after Simeon's murder.

"If the victim was stabbed in the back and Simeon's attention was absorbed by something or somebody in front of him, it could suggest that there were at least two people present at the killing, doesn't it?" she noted. "But let's say the murderer was one person who knew Simeon well enough to wander about the shop looking at books while Simeon concentrated on something on his desk, that person would have had ample opportunity to kill him unseen from behind," the amateur detective continued.

Penelope's observations were, of course, correct and she had plenty of questions.

"What about those closest to him – his assistant, the cleaner who found him and, of course, his wife – is there anything unusual about them? Anyone is capable of murder, Chief Inspector, as a man in your profession would know. And by getting to know your suspects, you find clues you never expect." She was clearly enjoying giving them the benefit of her powers of analysis. Her telephone rang in another room.

"Gentlemen, excuse me for a few minutes while I answer that. I'm expecting a call."

Her departure to her study gave the detectives a moment to reflect on what she had so far observed.

"Perhaps if we let her continue, she could give us a different angle?" said Andy.

"I think she has already slotted us into one of Agatha Christie's crime novels," said Bruno, smiling.

"I read a few of them," said Andy, "when I was at school. Full of people with names like Sir Joseph Hoggin. I remember a Colonel Terence Melchett and a young woman called Ruby."

Penelope Norton returned from her study a few moments later.

"Now, do you want to show me the crime scene, Chief Inspector?"

Bruno did not know how to answer that question.

"I'll come back to you on that, Penny, when we have time." Bruno then asked her if any of the book dealers she knew on the Island could possibly have been involved in this crime.

"I can't name anyone specifically without further information. Anyone can commit murder. Let's consider myself, Chief Inspector. I collect detective stories. First editions. If you turn around, on the far wall are a collection of books written by world-famous authors."

She walked the detectives across the lounge and indicated editions of Agatha Christie, Raymond Chandler, Arthur Conan Doyle, and several other famous authors with whom the detectives were less familiar.

She pulled out a copy of Christie's *The Thirteen Problems*.

"There you are, detectives: what you have to solve in order to find a killer." Replacing it carefully, she took up another volume. "Or perhaps this is nearer to what you are looking for? *The Body in The Library*, another Christie mystery. It's very similar, isn't it?" she said. "Calafifi was found dead in a bookshop, just like a library, isn't it? Get yourself a copy, all her books are still in print."

Bruno wondered to himself whether she was seriously suggesting that you could solve murder mysteries with the help of fictitious plot lines in books.

"Perhaps *The Body in The Library* will help with this case," said Andy in his naturally self-indulgent manner. "As a collector you must have booksellers ringing you often with books that interest you?"

"I do, Detective Sergeant, though almost always I already have a better copy than what they are offering."

"If your valuable books were ever stolen, from amongst the people that know of your collection, is there anyone who you would suspect immediately had taken them?"

"I'd have to investigate it carefully, examine the crime scene, note the access, doors, windows, and so on, hopefully before anyone has touched anything. I might come across a vital clue, but, like Agatha, no guessing. I would do what I am sure you have already done."

She continued dreamily, her growing enthusiasm animating her: "Imagine you are the murderer. Go back to Simeon's shop and re-enact the murder and see if one person can accomplish the killing. It might become obvious. Yes, it can or no, it cannot be done. Either way, you will know whether you are looking for one or two people. Just spending more time at the scene might trigger something helpful or lead you to someone important," she said, waving her heavily ringed fingers as if counting the suspects.

Bruno felt that Penelope had been of help to them. She certainly had given them a lesson in detection in the style of Agatha Christie, and he knew that one of the first things Andy would do would be to find a copy of *The Body in The Library*. But as far as providing information about individuals on the Island who might steal religious volumes, she had not been helpful, except to enable them to eliminate her from their list of persons of interest. She was dedicated to preserving the memory of Agatha Christie. She was definitely clever but also eccentric.

"Her observations," he told Andy on the way back to Newport, "I found them basic but also helpful as a good reminder. Concerning our knowledge of the three ladies who were closely connected to him, we should discover more about them. Miriam Calafifi, Annabel Wilson, Sheila Catchpole. Perhaps it's my age," said Bruno, "but in murder cases male suspects always jump to the front in my mind. And yet, there are just as many guilty females. Let's re-enact the murder as we think it happened in the shop this evening when it shuts, around 6 p.m. when it's quiet and the staff have gone home."

*

That evening, Andy Bowen arrived at Simeon's shop at 5:30 p.m. to request that Annabel lend him a set of keys.

"We have a police photographer coming to take some photos and we might be here for a couple of hours."

She offered to stay and help.

140

"As we don't know how long we shall be, I will bring the keys back in the morning," said Andy, to which she agreed, slightly reluctantly.

Bruno arrived as she was leaving at 6 p.m. and they exchanged greetings.

After she departed, they moved around the back office to reacquaint themselves with its layout. Everything was in place, as it had been on the night of the murder.

It was impossible not to feel sadness, tinged with discomfort, to be in the place where the ultimate crime had been committed at the same time that it had happened.

"Let's start at 5:45 p.m. on the day Simeon Calafifi was murdered. We are to assume the reason for his being in the office on a cold, dark evening was to meet somebody," said Bruno. "That is what our witness, Annabel Wilson, has told us. I still think it was strange that he didn't call his wife and tell her that he'd be late, and possibly why?"

"Maybe he thought the meeting would only take a few minutes?" replied Andy.

"Quite possibly."

"If the killer were coming from the mainland, would they arrange to visit the Island for a business meeting on a winter's evening?" said Andy.

"Most unlikely," said Bruno. "So, perhaps we must assume his visitor is from the Island, and that Simeon knew them. Our work so far has been an exercise in elimination, and suggests to me that some clue, as yet undiscovered, will point us in the direction of the killers."

Bruno continued with his previous line of thought: "So, Simeon opens the back door, greets the caller or callers, and admits him or her or them, then closes and shuts the door. I imagine he doesn't lock it because he and the visitor or visitors will soon be leaving the same way. They then come through to this office."

"The street cameras show that no one entered through the front door after the shop was closed by Annabel, so whoever it was had to come in the back door as you have just explained," said Andy. "Simeon resumes his seat, and one person sits on the chair in front of his desk, and the second person – if there was one – sits where I am," Andy hypothesised.

"Yes, that's if there is a second person," said Bruno. "If the killer is alone, he sits in one of these seats at the beginning of their meeting. At some time during the conversation, the visitor gets up and wanders around, maybe looking at the books in the bookcases that line the wall behind Simeon's desk, whose attention is focused on whatever business the visitor or visitors has called to see him about. Maybe it's the Talmud?"

"I doubt it," said Bruno, "because it's been sold awaiting despatch. But Simeon has opened the safe, which we'll assume was locked until his visitors arrived, so why would he do that? Normally if you open a safe to deposit something in it, you lock it straight away."

"Perhaps he opens the safe to pay for something? Maybe he is indeed buying a book rather than selling it," said Andy.

"With cash?" said Bruno. "He could be examining something on his desk, while the visitor studies – or pretends to study – the books in the cabinet behind Simeon, then he draws the knife and kills him," suggested Bruno.

"That is in the circumstance where one person killed him."

"It is the only way one person would have succeeded in the murder."

"They could have agreed a deal, and while Simeon was doing something at his desk, or signing a document while still in conversation, he could have walked to the bookcase behind him, produced a knife and killed him," Andy surmised.

"It seems too opportunistic for one person to be successful," said Bruno. "My theory is that two people killed Simeon after he'd opened the safe to show the Talmud. It had to have been the subject of the conversation for Simeon to open the safe. For the time being let's still keep an open mind. We'll analyse the report from prints. They should help us to recreate the murder scene further."

Andy added, "The killer would have had a short period of time to complete his deal. Realistically, I would give him or her a maximum of thirty minutes between 6 p.m. and 6:30 p.m., to avoid Annabel leaving at 5:45 p.m. and Mrs Catchpole arriving at 6:45 p.m."

"It's long enough, but it would have been straight down to business to finalise a deal that had already been agreed," said Bruno.

"Which confirms to me that he was not meeting a stranger, but someone he knew. We haven't found his phone and there could very well be helpful information on that," said Andy.

They sat in the semi-darkness of Simeon's office for quite a long time, thinking about the evening he was stabbed to death, turning over the possible scenarios that led up to his murder, until they decided to lock up and go. They retired to the pub two doors down for a pint and continued to analyse their visit to the crime scene.

"Let us examine the facts so far," said Bruno. "We know the killer was admitted and left by the back exit, where Calafifi parks his car. The Talmud was already in Simeon's possession, ready to be delivered in person while he pays a visit to Tel Aviv. If he made an appointment after regular business hours to see a client, he would have known the person. If the purpose of the appointment was not to talk about the Talmud, it had to be something else. If stealing the Talmud was the objective for someone, then the book was stolen for its sale value," said Bruno. "We need to think about the other old book – the *Book of Mormon*, and also the fact that some cash was taken. People have been murdered for less."

"So, we are looking for a thief who understands the significance of rare books, or perhaps just an opportunistic burglar?" Andy groaned as he sipped on his pint of beer.

"Before we traipse off to Bournemouth to see Carl Bullivent, let's take a leaf out of Penelope Norton's book and look more closely at the people on the doorstep. Let's speak again to Mrs Catchpole."

Chapter 14

An hour after arranging to visit Sheila Catchpole at her home on Friday morning, Bruno and Andy called at a tidy cottage in a neat Victorian terrace about a mile from Simeon's Bookshop. The front door opened directly into her small front room, which she had cleared of clutter for their visit. It was St. Patrick's Day, she reminded them, gesturing to a green tablecloth on a side table and a small vase of green and white flowers.

"Mrs Catchpole, we first saw you just over two weeks ago now, on the day after Mr Calafifi's murder. You were still in shock at finding him. It must have been the most awful experience for you, and you have our greatest sympathy. Now a little time has passed, perhaps you might be able to answer a few more questions about that evening?"

"I'll do my best, Chief Inspector. I still have the most vivid recollection of finding poor Mr Calafifi," she said.

"Most murders are committed by people who have a connection with the victim. In this case, the majority of his business connections were on the mainland because of the specialist nature of his antiquarian book trade. Where possible, we are urgently following up these leads. The theft of something so valuable here in Shanklin might suggest that it was intended for someone living on the Island. However, we can find nobody here who specialises in collecting or selling such a book. So, we have concluded the Talmud was destined for someone on the mainland. Regarding the Calafifis' social and personal connections, we are limited, because Mr Calafifi has not lived in Ryde for long and didn't have a local circle of friends, whereas his business contacts were based principally on the mainland. So, we need to build up a picture of Mr Calafifi in both spheres of his life to see if there is something that leads us to the killer. Can you tell us anything about his private life that might help us?"

She thought carefully for a moment or two before replying.

"Chief Inspector, as well as cleaning the office every day, I clean the Calafifis' house once a week. Also, when Mrs Calafifi is away or late back, she might ask me to collect the boys from school."

"When you say, 'Mrs Calafifi is away', when does she go away?"

"Every week, she is away for at least one night in London. Sometimes she is in Manchester, and she has flown to Paris twice in the past few months. She flies from Bournemouth airport. She is an architect and is working on projects. Everything is on her website and that laptop of hers, so she never carries any drawings. She is always smartly dressed for her work – very attractive, I would say," she added.

"What do you think she does when she goes to London?"

"Chief Inspector, I wouldn't like to gossip, I really wouldn't."

"How do you mean, Mrs Catchpole?" prompted Bruno.

Lowering her voice as if being overheard, she confided, "Well, I think she has a fancy man."

Bruno made no verbal response but may have raised his eyebrow, enough that Mrs Catchpole continued: "And I think Mr Simeon knew about it."

It was an important statement coming from her and Bruno was pleased she had not turned out to be someone who was afraid to gossip.

"I think he couldn't wait for her to go away and not come back."

A vitriolic Mrs Catchpole was beginning to emerge.

"I have her mobile number, which I use if I need something for the boys. She is away at the moment," she said, "arranging for her move to London."

"When is she returning?"

"Tomorrow afternoon."

"We understand that her mother-in-law came to stay?"

"That's right. Mrs Calafifi got rid of her after a couple of days."

"Mrs Catchpole, we are trying to build a true picture of what kind of man Simeon was, and any information you can give us about Miriam Calafifi would be useful."

Mrs Catchpole's face took on a bright intensity, and she had something to share with them.

"Well! One day she came back from London wearing a smart suit. She gets invited to lots of social events, you know. Her jacket had a buttonhole with some kind of printed badge hanging from a string, looped through it. A few days later, when I was cleaning her bedroom, I found this thing on the floor near her dressing table. I brought it home to have a look at it as I guessed it would not be missed."

She went to a box on her mantelpiece and found a badge that you put through a buttonhole. It was an owner's enclosure badge for Ascot racecourse for Wednesday 19th June, the previous summer. The ticket had a number but no name.

"May I borrow this from you, Mrs Catchpole?" Andy asked.

"Please, take it, Chief Inspector."

Andy knew that an enquiry of the course or the Jockey Club would reveal the name of the owner. From that, they would be able to create a picture of Mrs Calafifi's social life and any contacts. Their visit to Mrs Catchpole's cottage had not been fruitless and a slightly different Miriam Calafifi was beginning to emerge.

*

Sitting in the car in Green Lane outside Mrs Catchpole's, Andy called Ascot Racecourse to find out the name of the owner of badge no 8566 at the race meeting on 19th June some eight months previously. It seemed that Number 8566 had been allocated to one of the guests of a private box in the main stand. The debenture box was owned by the Commonwealth Bank in the City of London.

What a coincidence, Andy noted to Bruno sitting next to him: they had interviewed Peter Rose, the bank's Chief Executive, just a few days previously. The lady in the admin office at Ascot promised to send a guest list of invitees for that day, but needed confirmation of the police request in writing, which Andy agreed to send by email straight after the call, and said that she would or could only give it to the local police office in Ascot for transmission to Newport, which could take one or two days.

After their visit to Mrs Catchpole they decided to call in to the shop, which was just a few minutes' drive away, to drop off the set of keys that they had borrowed the evening before. They took the opportunity for a chat to try to understand the Calafifi family from Annabel's perspective, particularly in light of Mrs Catchpole's comments. Bruno wanted to ask her what she felt about the situation in which she now found herself.

Annabel had recruited a young sales assistant named Chloe, who enabled Annabel to sit with the detectives, uninterrupted, in what was now her office.

She told them proudly that one of the contracts she had secured recently because of her liaison with the Ryde School Classics teacher was to supply all academic and study books to the school. It was a very profitable part of the business, the more so because of her skill at sourcing the best educational books on the market at the keenest prices. She admitted that Simeon had accepted that he could never have run this successful business without her help, and that she undoubtedly ran the sales, purchasing and accounting.

"Were you sufficiently rewarded for your effort?"

"It was satisfactory," she said. "I had ambitions that one day I would become a director or partner."

"As you know, we are still trying to locate the name of the person who came to see Simeon on the evening of 28th February. No-one that we have interviewed has said it was them. So, as it was a person not from his regular contacts, I believe he would have kept a record of it. You yourself said it was by appointment, but we can find no trace of that anywhere. I'm sorry to ask again, but can you repeat when you heard about this evening appointment?"

Annabel sighed.

"I have answered this question previously, as you say. However, I was cashing up at about 5 and Simeon arrived in the shop, coming through the back door from where we park. He came through to the front, said hello, and told me he was expecting a client in an hour or so. 'Probably after you have left at about 6 p.m.,' I think he said. So, when I left at 5:45, we said goodnight. I locked the front door in my usual manner and left by the rear door – which I shut by pulling it closed – into the car park."

"So he was all alone. His visitor or visitors arrived soon after 6 p.m., and he let them in the back entrance," stated Bruno.

"I think he would have let them in the front, Chief Inspector. They wouldn't know about our rear access."

"There is no record on the street camera that anyone visited the shop after you left. Do you lock the back door when you leave?"

"Yes, it's kept locked."

"Sorry, you just said that you pulled the door closed?"

"I mean it's locked because of the Yale. What I mean is that you would need a key to get in the back door after I left or for it to be opened from the inside by Simeon. That's what I meant. And that's what happened. Yes?"

"And you already said that you placed the day's takings in the safe and locked it."

"Yes."

"Okay," said Bruno, noting her comment. "Within an hour of your departure, Mr Calafifi is stabbed to death, and the robbers have fled with two valuable books and the shop's unbanked takings. Stolen by somebody he knew, yet he didn't tell you who was calling to see him. Any guesses who that could have been?" he persisted.

The expression on her face tightened and she did not answer for a while.

"I didn't know most of his clients. I have told you this. When they phoned, I just put the caller through or took a message. He didn't discuss the deals with me."

"But you were such an integral part of the business?"

She didn't answer specifically.

"What other interests did he have?" Andy interjected, Bruno wishing that he hadn't.

"Books were his life. That is all I know."

"Do you think his meeting was with somebody from the Island?" said Bruno, returning the conversation to the night of the murder again.

"I have no idea. He did not give me a clue who was coming. Whoever it was had come on some pretext and stole the Talmud to sell it, but not to a collector or person on the Island, so I'd guess they were not local. It's worth a fortune, so somebody would make big money, not what it was worth, but I would guess in the thousands, but to sell it on they would have to be in the antiquarian book business and take risks, otherwise how would they capitalise on their crime?"

"How do you know that it was the Talmud that they wanted? What about the *Book of Mormon*?"

"Yes, yes, it could have been that too. I just know less about that book and so I keep thinking about the Talmud."

The detectives changed tack:

"Can you tell us anything about Miriam Calafifi that we might not know?"

"Did you know she is the boys' stepmother? The boys' mother died when they were very young of an aggressive form of breast cancer. Simeon married Miriam very soon afterwards, but instead of being a substitute for his first wife she carried on as before as a single woman, enjoying the security that her marriage to Simeon gave her, leaving him to look after his boys, which he did faultlessly. His move to Ryde was not simply to run his business, as he did in London but with lower overheads. It was to put a stop to Miriam behaving as a single woman. During a conversation I had with her when the bookshop first opened, she said that she thought she would miss the stimulation of working in a large international architects' practice and was exploring with Simeon how she might continue her career living on the Island."

A new picture of Miriam Calafifi was indeed emerging, completely at odds with the detectives' initial impressions gleaned and information gathered.

"Is that your opinion, Annabel?"

She paused to give her answer some thought, before replying, "Yes, but Simeon moving her to Ryde was unsuccessful in bringing her under his wing."

"What did he do about it?"

"She had made it clear to him that she did not want to live here. It was against her wishes, and as far as I know she carried on seeing her friends in London, staying away overnight when it suited her. She often stayed away in London. Having said all that, she was – she is, I mean – a great mother. You wouldn't know that the boys weren't her biological sons. She really loves them. In fact, I often wonder if they are the reason she married Simeon."

"Have you any idea where she stays in London?"

"No idea, I have told you everything I know. About Simeon, about Miriam, about the shop. Everything," she said emphatically.

"Thank you, Annabel. We appreciate that. I'm sure you have a lot to do on a Friday afternoon, so we will leave you now. Have a good weekend," and with that, they got up and left the shop.

The information Bruno and Andy had gathered from Annabel and Mrs Catchpole gave the detectives a different slant on the murder.

"As outrageous as it might seem, could Miriam Calafifi have a lover who could have conspired with her to end her husband's life, and free her to live as she wanted to?" asked Bruno as they drove back to Newport.

"It's a possibility," said Andy. "Miriam Calafifi is certainly a person of interest. I'll ask Data Division to probe into her background a bit more," said Andy.

"Andy, do you recall Annabel suggesting that Simeon's mystery visitor entered through the front door?"

"Yes. I noted that, but we know that did not happen, so why would she suggest that it did?"

"Well, if they entered through the back, and if it's always kept locked, or at least closed by the Yale lock, which is basically locked, they must have knocked at the door to get in."

"Agreed," said Andy. "It's food for thought, sir."

*

Back at the station, the fingerprint report confirmed they had identified Annabel and Mrs Catchpole's prints and were left with a dozen or so unknown that could be matched against suspects when identified. In the report it claimed that the only prints on the door of the safe were Annabel's and Simeon's, which was therefore inconclusive.

A positive email had been received from Ascot racecourse, via the Berkshire police, quicker than expected, with a list of those guests who attended the race meeting on 19th June, in private box number 8566.

Bruno asked, "Is Mrs Calafifi one of them?"

Andy replied, "Yes, she is on the list."

"Can you read out the list?"

"The host was Peter Rose. His guests were Colin Willis, Mrs Autumn Crofts, Mrs Miriam Calafifi, Keith Lomas, Dr Morris Walker, Sir Ralph Ockenden, Ben Hirshman, a Mrs Minter, and Jack Cooper. In all, ten names including the host, who is the Chief Executive of the Commonwealth Bank. So, now we have a connection between Miriam Calafifi, Ben Hirshman and Peter Rose," said Andy.

Bruno smiled and could see the case beginning to open up and possibly a whole new list of persons of interest.

"I think we can return to Hirshman on that basis, with some additional questions," said Bruno.

"Of course, their relationship might be casual, platonic," said Andy. "And even if it's more serious, it may be unconnected with the murder." Although this was a lead they needed to progress, was it connected with the Talmud? What did the fact they went racing together as guests of a bank chairman mean? How were Peter Rose, Ben Hirshman, and Miriam Calafifi connected?

"They make a handsome couple, sir," said Andy.

"Who?" said Bruno.

"Mrs Calafifi and Ben Hirshman."

"Hirshman said they're old friends," said Bruno. "He has known her for years."

"Peter Rose wanted to buy the Talmud for the Wood Green Synagogue. Isn't that another coincidence?"

"Thieves and murderers, that's who we are after," said Bruno.

*

So far, the police suspects in the hunt for Calafifi's killer were few. A number of persons of interest had been unearthed so Bruno spoke about them with Janet that evening over dinner, to see if a fresh mind could reveal something they hadn't unearthed so far. She was always a helpful sounding board.

Janet's take was that Annabel should be considered as a suspect because she knew everything about Simeon's business and the benefits that would accrue to her with his death. Sam Trent, whose intellectual and professional interests were similar, might also have something to gain from Simeon's death if, as Janet imagined, he really did have a close relationship with Annabel, and an interest in the antiquarian book trade by virtue of his job as a Classics master at Ryde School. His detailed whereabouts on the evening of the murder were as yet unconfirmed. They needed to see him in person. Bruno explained that he was away in Italy on a school trip, prompting Janet to say how much she felt like a European holiday.

Miriam Calafifi, given her reported relationship issues

with her husband, had a number of question marks against her which might soon be answered, hopefully before her impending move to London. Her absences from the Island and the suggestion by Mrs Catchpole that she had a "fancy man" in tow could open up their search for the killer. Janet did not necessarily believe that Mrs Calafifi was interested in the antiquarian book trade, or that a fancy man even existed.

"She seems to me to be too ambitious to play around like that. Distinction in her architectural career is surely more her line."

She did not consider Mrs Catchpole to be a person of interest. She thought she was fortunate to have avoided the killer and could well prove to have provided them with an important clue now the attendees at the Ascot races had been revealed.

Janet agreed that Max Carter's alibi at the time of Simeon's death needed confirming. As for motive, his closeness to the dealers at the Wheelers auction, and his knowledge of their background, enabled him to recognise a serious collector's keen interest and put him on to it, namely his call to the Lithuanian, Pivotkin, who it was reported would pay a great sum to obtain the Talmud. That made him, too, very much a person of interest. His contact with Pivotkin achieved no more than to tell him that the Vilnius Talmud had been sold. Max would also have told him that it had been stolen from Calafifi and might become available to purchase from the thief or murderer some time. Max Carter's contact with Pivotkin in fact qualified both him and Pivotkin as suspects, the latter because of his desire to obtain the Talmud.

Of the collectors' names given to Bruno by Carter, none qualified as a person of interest. One had died and of the three remaining all were interesting people but could never be considered murder suspects. That left the three dealers, only one of whom was local-ish.

"Tomorrow we will go and see Carl Bullivent in Bournemouth. As a dealer he could be a bibliophile interested in Jewish religious books," said Bruno. "When he attended Wheelers on the day of the Talmud sale, he could have observed any interest in the non-bidders, and he has a connection with Max."

The weekend was beginning but, on Monday, the two detectives had a ferry booking from Yarmouth to Lymington, and a drive to Bournemouth town centre was the plan, to arrive at 2 p.m. for their pre-arranged meeting with Carl Bullivent.

Chapter 15

Carl Bullivent lived in a large Victorian house appropriately called Victoria Villa. It had once been a very grand house in the best part of Bournemouth before, and for a number of years after, the Second World War. When Carl Bullivent received them, he was welcoming, dressed in a dark suit, as if he was between meetings. He looked to be in his early fifties.

"Detectives, over to you," he said as they sat in comfortable chairs in a large study lounge.

"We are investigating the murder of Simeon Calafifi on the evening of 28th February at his bookshop in Shanklin. Valuable editions of two books were stolen from the safe at his business premises. We know that you attended the auction at Wheelers recently when Mr Calafifi bid for and purchased the stolen books."

"Yes, I did, but there was nothing I was keen on. At auctions you can sometimes find the missing piece of the jigsaw. I have clients that have spent half a lifetime looking for items they know are out there, and which will come to the auction for sale when the present owner dies or has no further desire for them. If I know what they want, and it shows up in the catalogue, I attend and bid for it."

"Did anything show up on that day?" said Andy.

"Not in the sense I have just described, but I did buy some James Joyce poems that date from his early days at Dublin University. I know one collector who will buy them from me."

"We understand that if something valuable, really valuable, is being sold, the interested bidders will bid as a consortium to get it at the lowest price," said Bruno.

"Not a practice I am familiar with," said Bullivent.

"Do you think it happens?"

"I have no idea, Chief Inspector. It sounds pretty dodgy to me. What do you think? You're a policeman. Is it legal to do that kind of thing?"

"We thought that if that kind of activity took place at Wheelers, then the sale of the rare Talmud would be the opportunity for a consortium to work together. If you examine the bidding for the Talmud, it ended once the buyer had bid past the reserve, which leads us to think that it could have been one of those situations."

"Once a lot passes the reserve it's in the market and everyone knows it will go to the highest bidder, so I don't see your point, Chief Inspector. Regarding the Talmud, I had gone for a cup of tea when it came up. I don't deal in religious books, but I am interested, because I am Jewish, you see. It's true I knew Simeon, but I don't know of his enemies, for want of a better word."

Bruno and Andy asked Bullivent if he knew the two other dealers who Max Carter had mentioned to them.

"Hmm, Kilroy lives in Knutsford and Angus Smithson is from the Edinburgh area. Kilroy deals in sports paintings, and Smithson concentrates on Scottish authors mainly, I think. There was a very early volume of Robert Burns for sale. Smithson might well have bought that. Neither of them would get involved in a bidding swindle.

I know them well at a distance, if you know what I mean. If it happens, Chief Inspector, this consortium that you speak of, then I would certainly investigate the dealers and people involved, but I can't give you any help with that. I don't think it exists. Our trade can be a cut-throat business, but I've never heard of anyone getting their throat cut, or of dishonesty. I'd suggest that Simeon's murder wasn't to do with the stolen books. Really, I think that there must have been another motive."

Bullivent expostulated his theory further. "If I had to guess, I would say that Calafifi's killer stole the book, or rather the books, but that he is not in the book trade. He – let's call the killer a 'he' – might be on the edge and know of a potential buyer, but at this moment I think he is stuck with something that's unsaleable. I don't think you will ever trap him into trying to sell it. That's my opinion, Chief Inspector. Bournemouth has a large Jewish community. News that such a rare Talmud has been stolen from a Jewish antiquarian bookseller, who has been murdered by the thief is disturbing. Prayers will have been said by the Rabbi. The scholars in the congregation may have ideas, which I will pass on to you if they seem plausible. I don't think anyone will have the slightest interest in buying it, but news travels from one place of worship to another. Who knows what small revealing snippet might turn up? If anyone is approached with the Talmud for sale, every endeavour would be made to apprehend the thief and report them to the police. I am certain of that, as I am certain they will not let them slip through their fingers."

"Thank you very much, sir," said Andy, and they talked

for a further fifteen minutes or so, before they shook hands and left Victoria Villa.

"If anything can be found out from the Jewish community in Bournemouth, he will tell us," said Bruno, "but I don't think he had any involvement in either a dodgy auction or in the murder of Calafifi."

"What about the others, sir?"

"Bullivent is probably right, that neither Kilroy nor Smithson would get involved," Bruno said. "Let's take his word for it. They seem too remote."

Andy agreed, "I can't see a dealer from Knutsford who sells sporting prints, or a man from Scotland who buys books on Scottish poets, coming to the Isle of Wight to kill a dealer in religious literature to steal a book that he could not sell."

Bruno responded, "I can see how some people might regard Carl Bullivent to be a snob, who likes to be seen as a man at the top of his profession. He is certainly a man who takes pride in his reputation and doesn't want to be seen to be associated with any shady practice, like bidding scams."

"There is a common thread in the mentality of any dealer. How little can you pay for it, and how much can you sell it for? This always applies, whether to books, cars or antiques," said Andy.

After a few minutes silence, Bruno ventured:

"Moving back to Ascot Races on 19th June last year, and the ten people who attended the Commonwealth Bank's invitation. It is too great a coincidence to assume Miriam Calafifi attended with anyone other than Ben Hirshman, even though she was Peter Rose's guest. Some of the other guests could be in the book trade of course. My guess is they are not."

"How do we tackle it, sir, and what relevance is it to this case?"

"At this moment I don't know, but perhaps we should see Hirshman again. His connection with Miriam Calafifi means he could have known more about Simeon's business than we previously thought. For example, Simeon's intentions regarding the delivery of the Talmud to Professor Kazac in Tel Aviv meant that he knew it was being held in Simeon's Shanklin bookshop."

"That's true," said Andy, "but his relationship with Mrs Calafifi is nothing to do with us. He admitted he knew her, in fact he said he knew the family well, so even if he did go racing with her last June it does not imply a connection to the murder."

"For the moment, we must keep an open mind. We'll talk to him. There is not just Mrs Calafifi in the loop. Did his client, Peter Rose, their race-day host, who failed to secure the Talmud for £50,000, just give up?"

*

Ben Hirshman and Miriam Calafifi's connection had to be investigated, because both were intimately involved with Simeon and the family, but Bruno was not prepared at this time to put a sinister interpretation onto their relationship. They knew each other and as such he was a family friend supporting her at this distressing time.

Andy Bowen thought Annabel might reveal more about Simeon's private life than she had done so far. There was also Sam Trent, with whom she had some sort of relationship, and who seemed to be an innocent bystander but needed investigating. Was there more to be learned about the connection between Carl Bullivent and Max Carter? Bruno guessed they operated in different parts of the market: from his appearance and purchase history, Bullivent was at the top end.

Calafifi's business seemed to have been successful and now, assuming that she could raise the capital, Annabel could certainly be keen to acquire the business. However, according to the confidential information given to Bruno by Miriam Calafifi, the bookshop had been sold to Nathan Philips by Simeon before his death.

It really was time to take a closer look at Sam Trent. Andy phoned the school secretary, but got a different lady who didn't even know who Sam Trent was, nor that he was on a school trip. She promised to leave a message for him to call on his return, which Bruno expected to be in the next day or so, from the information he had been given the last time he called the school. Andy had tried Sam's mobile but it rang with a foreign ring tone and wasn't answered.

"Don't worry," said Bruno, "if he hasn't called by the end of the week, we will just drop in at the school and find him in person. We know he's genuinely away, so I don't think he's avoiding us."

*

Later that afternoon, what followed in a phone call from Carl Bullivent was an intriguing development and put all thoughts of Sam Trent out of the detectives' minds. He said that he had spoken to a prominent member of the Jewish community in Bournemouth, who was a supporter of the

Central Synagogue in Vilnius in Lithuania, a charity that had established a help centre to welcome and look after Jewish refugees from Lithuania during and after World War II. They had done so at the instigation of Benjamin Deutsch, who had fled Vilnius in 1942 when Lithuania was invaded by the German army.

Benjamin Deutsch was nineteen years old when he had arrived in England. He had escaped to Sweden before making his way to Scotland on a fishing boat. He then travelled to London and applied to join the British Royal Air Force. His English was good enough for him to be accepted for flying training as a rear gunner on Lancaster bombers.

Benjamin was awarded the Distinguished Flying Medal, or DFM, for bravery in action before being discharged as a flight sergeant gunner in 1945. He took advantage of the offer to all young wartime servicemen of a fully funded university education at the London School of Economics. As a student he excelled and, determined to repay the kindness of the British, he worked hard and became highly successful.

As a distinguished economist in the 1980s, Benjamin reconnected with his homeland and with the help of his son and grandson, George, raised a considerable sum from British Jews towards rebuilding Vilnius in Lithuania, from where the Deutsch family originated. Benjamin was a major benefactor, revered to this day.

George Deutsch had been invited to Vilnius to accept the imminent return of the famous Vilna Shas edition of the Babylonian Talmud, printed in Vilnius in 1800. Bullivent had said that he had checked its authenticity through George Deutsch. After discreet questions to the Rabbi at the Central Synagogue in Vilnius, George had been assured it was the edition that had been bought by Calafifi. This was big news.

How this could be so, neither Bullivent nor George Deutsch could offer any explanation. They had known each other since their school days at Bournemouth Grammar School and, without any prompting, George had volunteered the information to his friend that he was going on a trip to witness the occasion of the Babylonian Talmud being restored to the Vilnius Synagogue soon. No specific date was given for the return of the Talmud, but the invitation implied that it was either already, or was soon to be, in their possession.

George Deutsch had agreed to attend on behalf of his grandfather, the Deutsch family and the Bournemouth Central Synagogue. George's grandfather had passed away twenty years previously and his father, Abby, was not well enough to attend.

Bullivent provided contact details for George Deutsch but did not want to make a personal introduction, relying on the police to do that in their proper manner.

"I think it's now over to you, Chief Inspector."

The information was extremely welcome, if not hard to believe. It was the first trace of the stolen Talmud, but how could it be going to the Synagogue in Vilnius? Bruno did not think an interview with George Deutsch was necessary at this stage as there was no suggestion that George or the Bournemouth Synagogue were involved in the acquisition or procurement of the Talmud. It was their Lithuanian connection and the assistance they provided to the community in their homeland that had generated their invitation to celebrate the return of their sacred Talmud.

So far, the police investigation had revealed only one person whose ambition was to return the Talmud to its birthplace: that was the wealthy, evasive Wladimir Pivotkin, a one-time Lithuanian national who had been reluctant to meet the police on a previous occasion. He must now be contacted as he had become a definite person of interest, who could lead their investigation directly to the killer. If Pivotkin had acquired the Talmud, then he must have been in contact with the killer. However, he might deny being the benefactor who was now donating the Talmud to the Lithuanian Synagogue, so before he could be approached that had to be confirmed. One person who might confirm that would be Walter Spens.

Spens in Hampstead was acting as Pivotkin's agent, and he remained another person of interest. He could have brokered a deal with the murderer to acquire the Talmud.

*

Bruno phoned Professor Kazac in Tel Aviv regarding this latest news about the return of the Talmud to Vilnius.

"Professor Kazac, I want to update you regarding our pursuit of the Talmud. We have not succeeded in finding it or Calafifi's killer, but we have learned that a Jewish businessman, who resides in Bournemouth, has been invited to Vilnius as a guest of the Central Synagogue to witness the return of the Babylonian Talmud, printed in Vilnius in 1800. The same Vilna Shas edition that was stolen from Simeon Calafifi."

Bruno explained the background: "No date has been set for the return of the Talmud, but it seems that a promise has been made by a person, so far unknown, to the Rabbi at the Central Synagogue that it will be returned."

Professor Kazac was seemingly unaware of the Vilnius development and pleased that the police were advanced in their quest for the killer, while the Talmud was legally his property. That a Jewish philanthropist had chosen this opportunity to return the Vilnius Talmud to its birthplace was commendable, but illegitimate, until the complex ownership issue had been resolved and Calafifi's murderer captured.

Kazac confirmed his complete confidence in Bruno Peach and his colleagues to unravel this puzzle. "I feel assured that in due course the Talmud will be returned to me. If it proves to be the edition stolen from Calafifi, you detectives would have a lead to arrest the person who delivers the Talmud to the Vilnius Central Synagogue."

Chapter 16

On Tuesday, the next morning, Bruno and Andy returned to Bournemouth to meet George Deutsch in an enthusiastic state, because if the Talmud proved to be the stolen copy, it could lead to Calafifi's killer. They had decided, after all, to interview him in person.

When Bruno revealed the purpose of their visit to him, which was to acquaint him with the facts concerning the Talmud, George Deutsch understood immediately how his visit to Vilnius might help the British police to find Calafifi's killer.

"Carl Bullivent told me about the tragedy of Simeon Calafifi's murder. He is a friend, and he felt he had to tell me."

"Do you think you can find out how the Central Synagogue obtained the Talmud?" asked Bruno.

"I will do better than that, Chief Inspector. Clearly the dedication of the holy book cannot proceed under these circumstances, and Rabbi Barry would not allow this. His only aim would be to help you find the killer."

"When are you going to Vilnius?"

"The date and time of the dedication is confirmed for next weekend."

"The person who is referred to as the benefactor is our focus of interest," said Bruno, who realised now that the Talmud had actually been located and was either in

Vilnius, on its way there, or about to be. A date would not have been set for the handover and dedication otherwise. This was real progress.

"The word 'benefactor' could refer to a group, Chief Inspector. I will glean as much information as I can about the return of the Talmud. I am certain, however, that no one will be aware of the dreadful situation with the murder of Calafifi, and that until the ownership of the sacred volume is determined this planned dedication cannot proceed."

Bruno and Andy left George Deutsch confident that if he identified the benefactor who was promising to return the Talmud to Vilnius, he would tell them, although it would not necessarily reveal the identity of the murderer to them. It could be the breakthrough they were seeking and more important was the route by which the Talmud might be returned to Vilnius.

"Should we travel to Vilnius and directly investigate these new facts?" asked Andy, partly tongue-in-cheek.

Bruno considered it as a serious question. He knew they should go and investigate a positive lead.

"Let us examine the chronology of the entire investigation and decide whether this story holds water. Has there been time for the thief to negotiate the disposal of the Talmud to Rabbi Barry in Vilnius? Is there a connection between the thieves and the Vilnius benefactor?" said Bruno. "We won't know that unless we go and find out for ourselves."

*

Whilst painting a picture, from time to time an artist will retreat and study the image from a distance to get an overall view of perspective and detail. Bruno's equivalent was his periodic report to Chief Superintendent Barlow, who was always keen to understand the need for travel to the mainland as part of the investigation, so that he could defend his detectives' activities to the Chief Constable if they were found working in other policemen's territory. This time their range of travel was more extensive, with visits to Chichester, London, East Grinstead and Bournemouth, and this case involved an even greater geographic spread of contacts if you considered Professor Kazac in Tel Aviv and dealers and book buyers from other parts of England and, now, Vilnius in Lithuania.

Chief Superintendent Barlow would decide whether they would go to Vilnius. Despite what seemed a number of unconnected activities and people, Bruno believed that they were making real progress. He could feel it. That is what he reported to Chief Superintendent Barlow.

"I suppose you'll be off to Israel next?" said Barlow when they met that afternoon at Newport Police headquarters.

"Lithuania first, sir, please," said Bruno. He related the very reliable information they recently received from Vilnius. Bruno believed that they would only make further concrete progress if they could have a face-to-face meeting in person with Rabbi Barry.

While waiting for Barlow's decision, Bruno checked that a direct flight to Vilnius departed Gatwick at 9:30 a.m. the following morning, Wednesday 22nd March. A flight time of 2 hours and 55 minutes, then returning late on Thursday, should give them plenty of time to meet the leader of the Vilnius Synagogue and investigate the source of the information.

Barlow phoned as they were about to go home and told Bruno he agreed that the information demanded police action immediately and wished his two detectives well in their two-day visit to Lithuania, while reminding them of the rules of policing in a foreign country, principally that this was a tourist visit. Should they, by means of good fortune, find a genuine suspect, they would be obliged to enlist the support of the local police to arrest, caution or detain them.

"Wrap up well, I hear it is bloody cold at this time of the year. And good luck," said the boss. He knew that in any murder investigation a bit of luck was often what counted in the end.

Chapter 17

L anding at Vilnius airport on Wednesday afternoon,
Bruno and Andy were transported by taxi to the
Hilton hotel in the centre of the city.

Despite the ravages of war and occupation by the
most oppressive regimes in history during the twentieth
century, Vilnius had clearly recovered and regained its
former vibrancy and desirability as a place to live.

They set off on foot from the hotel. Exploring Vilnius
was an unexpected treat for two working detectives.
In the fifteenth century, Lithuania had been the largest
country in Europe. Its old town displayed a mixture of
architectural styles stretching across eight centuries. Many
buildings had been converted into gift shops, cafés, and
restaurants. It was an atmospheric old city, and Bruno and
Andy promised each other they would return with their
partners at a later date.

They had downloaded a map of the city centre, showing
the location of the principal places of interest to them.
On their way they passed the Vilnius Choral Synagogue,
a beautiful example of pre-World War II architecture,
which had survived the occupation of the Germans and
the Russians. A map of the Ghetto showed the Vilna Gaon
Monument to the eighteenth-century scholar and author
of glosses on the Babylonian Talmud.

Rabbi Barry had not been overly surprised to receive

a phone call from Detective Chief Inspector Bruno Peach the previous day from England to request an urgent meeting to discuss the return of the ancient book to Vilnius. Being busy with his religious duties until the evening he suggested they meet for dinner at 8 p.m. at the Nineteen18 Restaurant, where he could entertain them in proper Lithuanian style on their first visit to the beautiful city. Rabbi Barry was a short, stocky American man, with little about his manner or his appearance to distinguish him as a holy, Jewish man, apart from a discreet *yarmulke* on his head. Indeed, this wasn't even a kosher restaurant.

"Detectives, this restaurant is one of the best in the city."

Barry ordered for them an excellent traditional Lithuanian dinner. As the food was being prepared, Bruno explained the reason for their visit, to explain the murder of Simeon Calafifi on the Isle of Wight, and to obtain from Rabbi Barry an update on the situation regarding the return of the Talmud to Vilnius.

"Let me begin, Chief Inspector, by explaining our position. We are fortunate to have many supporters amongst the wealthy Jewish families in different parts of the world, who are intent on restoring the once thriving Jewish community to its former leading position in Lithuanian intellectual society. My wife and I came here from our wonderful community in Chicago, because we were asked by Rabbi Benjamin, an American whom I have known since college. He was familiar with my work in the deprived inner-city areas of Chicago. He knew that I could do the same work here. Since I came here, I have persuaded my friends to contribute several million dollars towards rebuilding the Jewish community. One of my ambitions was to return the Babylonian Talmud dating from 1800 AD, the Vilna Shas edition, to the Central Synagogue in Vilnius. I did not think I would ever achieve my ambition. Then, about two weeks ago, I received a phone call from a benefactor who regularly contributes to our communities in Vilnius, saying, that subject to a few legal issues, he was able to facilitate the return of the Babylonian Talmud to Vilnius."

Barry smiled with great satisfaction at this announcement and continued his narration.

"God has listened to my prayers and has found a way to answer me, I thought. However, the donor explained there were complications, namely the ownership had to be certified because the antiquarian bookseller in possession of the Talmud had been murdered, and the book stolen. But as if by a miracle, it had been saved from destruction by our benefactor and could be returned to its birthplace. I took that as an opportunity to inform the congregation that in time, hopefully soon, we could rejoice in its return. All our overseas benefactors were informed of this wonderful news and invited by us to visit us and celebrate."

"But you are not yet in possession of the Talmud?" This was the question that had justified the cost of their visit. Bruno looked the Rabbi in the eye as he answered.

"Not yet," said Rabbi Barry. "But it is coming," he said, his unwavering gaze declaring his veracity.

"Can you tell me the name of the benefactor?"

"His name is Wladimir Pivotkin, and he lives in London, England. We have not met, but he is I am told a wealthy industrialist and was born in Vilnius. I have his details, and I expect him to contact me when he is a position to return the book. It will be any day now. Then we shall celebrate in proper Jewish fashion."

"Can you tell us anything more about Mr Pivotkin?"

"I cannot, but I am sure from his manner that he will assist you in any way he can. He said to me that, at the same time as returning the Talmud to Vilnius, his associated aim was also to identify the murderer of the bookseller."

"But he gave you no details of who that person might be?"

"None. I think he might have thought that the gruesome details of a murder connected with the Talmud would dampen the joy of receiving this sacred testament."

"We would be obliged, Rabbi Barry, if you did not tell Mr Pivotkin that we have visited you before we are able to speak to him."

"I don't expect him to contact me until he is able to deliver the book."

They finished the meal in a very convivial manner, exchanging stories about their lives.

*

Rabbi Barry arranged for his driver to collect them at 9 a.m. on Thursday morning and take them on an extended tour of Vilnius and the surrounding countryside before their flight departure at 1:10 p.m.

It had literally been a flying visit for the detectives, but they had something to show for it, namely Rabbi Barry's revelation that Wladimir Pivotkin was in possession of the Talmud. They would validate this new information by visiting Pivotkin on their return. Bruno suspected that what Barry had told them would also be known by Hirshman and his contacts.

On the three-hour flight back to London they discussed the case and planned their next move. Ben Hirshman sat at the centre of their investigation. Bruno believed he possessed information that could help them find Calafifi's killer, but if he did have it, he could be bound by confidences as an agent which, if disclosed, would ruin his business reputation.

Had Mrs Calafifi innocently given information about her husband's business, and possibly the date that he intended to visit Tel Aviv to deliver the Talmud, thereby revealing that the Talmud was still in Shanklin two weeks after the Wheelers auction? Her planned departure from Ryde with her family signalled an urgency which was not helpful to the police, because it gave the impression that the immediacy of the departure was connected with somebody living on the Island who she suspected was involved in her husband's murder and the book thefts and whose existence she felt was a threat to her and whose identity she was afraid to disclose.

"Do you think she is moving away because she is afraid the killer might strike against her?" Andy asked Bruno.

"We can't rule that out. If someone is capable of killing her husband, that could make her want to get the hell off the Island with the two boys."

Bruno believed that Spens, the retired bookseller from Hampstead, had enough connections to know what was going on. He believed that most of the influential players in this antiquarian bookselling trade knew each other well, including Hirshman and Spens. As his agent, Spens would know that Pivotkin was the rich benefactor, promising to return the Talmud to Vilnius. Bruno did not think that Pivotkin would make a promise to the Vilnius Jews that he could not fulfil. So either he had the book, or was about to get hold of it, as a result of some kind of contact by himself, via Spens, with the killer.

Bruno was sure that Pivotkin had nothing to do with Calafifi's murder, but if he had the Talmud he must be seen immediately. This was the breakthrough they were looking for, namely that someone was in contact with Calafifi's killer and that he might fill in some of the gaps that could accelerate their investigation.

"We now know for sure the link between Pivotkin and the Talmud. And therefore between Spens and the Talmud. It helps our investigation to know that Pivotkin's intention is to return the Talmud to Vilnius. Whatever deal may have been entered into, those involved would surely want their participation to be useful in finding and apprehending the killer. Unless, of course, their participation in finding and obtaining the Talmud is part of the murder itself. This is the point, Andy, where we must look at everyone carefully and closely and then try and use that information to conclude this investigation. The final destination of this sacred book is not police business, but it could be very relevant to the murder of Simeon Calafifi. Let's put what we know to Hirshman, who may know where the Talmud is right now, before we get on to Pivotkin and Spens."

Bruno emailed Hirshman requesting an urgent meeting the next morning.

Chapter 18

B en Hirshman made himself available to the detectives late on Friday morning. He had promised, when they first met two weeks previously, that he would help any time they wanted to steer the right course around the antiquarian book trade. Bruno's first question, delicately put, required a direct answer.

"How well do you know Miriam Calafifi?" asked Bruno.

"I told you when we last met that I know the Calafifi family very well. The entire family. Even Simeon's grand-parents, from many years ago. David, Simeon's father, was a friend for many years, and I knew Miriam and her first husband as friends," he added.

"How long ago was that, sir?" enquired Andy, conscious that Hirshman had never mentioned the detail of knowing Miriam Calafifi that well at their first meeting and had certainly not alluded to a previous husband.

"Not recently," said Hirshman, "but I have been with Miriam at exhibitions and horse racing events. She has friends keen on the sport. She introduced me to Peter Rose, who owns racehorses. He collects racing books, old racing paintings and lithographs, which I come across from time to time. So I got hold of several interesting items for him. And of course, he came to me regarding the auction of the Talmud at Wheelers."

"You mentioned Mrs Calafifi's first husband. Is there

anything we should know about him that could be relevant to this case?"

Hirshman did not answer immediately but thought about the question for a minute or two.

"I don't think so. No, in fact, I would say nothing whatsoever, Chief Inspector. He lives in Paris and has done so for several years. His architectural practice is headquartered in Zurich. I see him occasionally when he visits London. He has an apartment in Knightsbridge and when in London is usually accompanied by his second wife, Catherine, and their three young girls. Both he and Miriam have moved on, you see."

Bruno returned to the subject of the Talmud: "We need to know who else at the sale of the Talmud was interested in buying it. Apart from Simeon Calafifi."

"Starting with myself," he said, "I was asked to bid for the Talmud by Peter Rose. He is a member of the Wood Green Synagogue, which has a fund for the purchase of special artefacts – not just old books, but other items you would see in a Jewish place of worship. They were aware of the history of the Talmud and wanted to buy it, probably eventually to return it to Lithuania, but not until time had passed, during which they would have studied it and probably had it copied by a language expert. And, of course, they would have had the kudos of owning it and so being part of its history."

Hirshman continued: "Your search for members of a consortium is a waste of your time, because for the Talmud there wasn't one. I can remember the other dealers who were present on that day and none of them wanted the Talmud. For Wood Green, £50,000 was their limit. And no-one else was bidding. Hence Simeon Calafifi was the successful and indeed only other bidder." He paused. "Have you spoken to Walter Spens?"

"Not recently," said Bruno.

"I suggest you speak to him before you leave here. He will be able to help you with something that has developed, of which I am aware, but I will let that information come from the source."

Whatever it was that could only come from Spens made the visit to Hirshman worthwhile. Immediately after they left, Bruno called Spens who invited them to come over right away. Bruno and Andy could not get there quickly enough.

*

It was a tube ride and short taxi journey from Hirshman's premises on Curzon Street to see Spens on Hampstead Heath. After making themselves comfortable, Spens asked them how they were getting on finding Calafifi's murderer.

"We are making some progress," said Bruno confidently. "We have just come from a meeting with Ben Hirshman, who suggested we contact you."

"I am glad you're here," he said. "What I am going to tell you does not identify the perpetrator but does lead on to something, which I hope will narrow your quest to find Simeon's killer. I tried calling you yesterday, but the receptionist at Newport Police Station could not contact you. Of course, I am aware that you know my client is Mr Pivotkin. I am also aware that you have made contact with him by telephone. For me to tell to you what my client reported would sound like fiction, something dreamed up by an old man. I think it would be best to introduce you to him, so that he can tell you himself what has happened. He lives opposite Regent's Park. Please excuse me while I call him and see if it's a convenient time to visit. If it is, I'll drive you straight over."

They were about to meet Wladimir Pivotkin.

*

The opportunity to meet Pivotkin was not to be delayed and avoided the need for an official police contact, or for appearing at Pivotkin's home with a warrant to question him officially as the law enabled them to do. Spens drove the detectives to a Regency house in an elegant crescent on the edge of Regent's Park. It was the kind of property that the two Isle of Wight police detectives rarely visited. Spens dropped them outside the house, explaining that his client had asked him to do so, and bid them farewell.

A smartly dressed woman opened the door. "Mr Pivotkin has just finished his luncheon and is expecting you in the library," she said, and led them through opulently furnished reception rooms to a spacious high-ceilinged library lined on three sides with floor-to-ceiling dark wooden bookshelves. Sliding glass doors opened onto a small, neat garden surrounded by bushes and shrubs. The uniformly green lawn owed more to the plastics industry than to skilled gardeners.

The library itself was furnished with a desk and a chair to one side and a set of leather armchairs arranged in the centre of the room around a central low table, on which lay newspapers. Before the visitors could sit down Mr Pivotkin appeared, smiling, and greeted them without any formal introduction, in a friendly manner, and said: "Gentlemen, I am Wladimir Pivotkin. Please sit down. I am pleased to meet you."

He was a handsome man in his mid to late fifties, fit, dressed in a jacket and tie. His demeanour concealed all the talents that a self-made billionaire would possess.

Bruno took the opportunity to introduce himself and Andy Bowen, and to explain the reason for their visit to Vilnius and their meeting with Rabbi Barry. Bruno then asked him if he would substantiate the rumour concerning the possible return of the Babylonian Talmud to the Synagogue in Vilnius.

"I hope you found my hometown enjoyable?" was his reply.

"Very much, sir," said Andy.

"First, and to answer your question, it is not a rumour. But, before I tell you how I managed to obtain the precious Talmud, I will explain my interest. I am Jewish, and for me to have such an interest in this Talmud is because I was born in Vilnius. I am a benefactor of the Central Synagogue and I support many Jewish charities in the city. Lithuania used to be part of the Russian Empire. Vilnius had a large Jewish population before World War II. The Nazis began their plan to exterminate all Jews, a project which the Russian armies continued. In a short time they nearly succeeded. Many Lithuanian Jews were lucky to escape, principally to Britain and America. Some became successful and wealthy. I am a descendant of that tradition. But we have never forgotten our homeland and have pledged to restore eventually every place to its former splendour. Vilnius currently has a small Jewish population

and still a few very elderly survivors of the horrors of their times. The sacred Babylonian Talmud was written by the Vilna Gaon, Rabbi Eliyahu Ben Shlomo Zalman, one of the greatest Talmudic minds. Returning it will have a great significance to the three thousand descendants of the Holocaust in Vilnius, and that is my intention."

He paused, then carried on. "Chief Inspector Peach, I have known Walter Spens for several years, and many of the volumes on these shelves have been acquired for me by him. The Talmud auctioned at Wheelers escaped our attention, because I was away sheltering from the English winter. As a collector, I am known by several dealers, and I receive emails from them often and my contact phone numbers are not a secret. But still, this most valuable book escaped my attention."

He continued: "I will cover the legalities associated with the ownership of the stolen book later, but first I will tell you how I got hold of it. So, prepare yourselves for an incredible story. I would appreciate it if you would not interrupt me, and if you would just let me speak. It is quite a long story so, please, make yourselves comfortable and relax."

Bruno and Andy both nodded in agreement. After all, Pivotkin had just admitted the momentous piece of information that the Talmud was in his possession. They were about to hear how and why. This was the most important piece of information since their investigation began.

"Two weeks ago yesterday, on Thursday 9th March, I received a phone call from a withheld number. The caller addressed me as, 'Mr Privotkin'; I did not correct him. He spoke with an English accent and came straight to

the point. He said: 'Do you want to buy the Babylonian Talmud?' I was surprised, and said: 'Is it for sale?' The caller replied, 'I have it for sale.' I asked if it was the same Talmud from a book dealer who bought it at an auction several weeks ago. 'It is the same book,' he said. I did not want him to think I was not interested and ring off, so I avoided asking questions about the murder of Calafifi and how the caller might have acquired it. He explained that it was available 'now' if I wanted to buy it, so I agreed that, subject to confirmation of the book's authenticity and our agreement on the price, I could be interested. My only task was to keep the caller connected. 'Let's start with the price,' I said. He asked for £50,000 and I explained that, for that money, I needed to be certain it was genuine, and my expert would have to examine it first."

Pivotkin then explained how he had obviously presented the caller with a problem by introducing another person and the reply had been that if he, Pivotkin, could not identify the Talmud himself, then they could not do business. This had prompted a description of the book, together with the provision of certain details which only someone in possession of the real Talmud could know.

Pivotkin explained: "I knew that with information I could obtain from Vilnius, I could further validate the Talmud's authenticity myself in person. I was relieved that I did not have to involve anyone else in a dangerous exercise of dealing with Calafifi's murderer, although I was not at that moment aware of the nature of the mission I was about to embark upon to secure the Talmud." He paused, stood up and stretched politely, and then sat back down, before continuing.

"I told the caller that I would authenticate it myself, which, after speaking to Professor Kazac in Tel Aviv and Rabbi Barry in Vilnius, I was confident of doing. They had told me of the key factors to look for, and I can read Hebrew and Yiddish. I listened to his proposition, ignoring the fear that lurked behind my brave front. Because if this person had killed a prominent bookseller and historian of religious books, I was determined to do my upmost to bring him to justice. You might say, Chief Inspector, that I should have reported the incident immediately to the police, but my concern was to lay my hands on the Talmud *and* somehow bring him to justice. In a police hunt it could have been destroyed by the murderer, as it was the hook that could catch him. I could not let him destroy the Talmud, so I promised to come alone."

Neither Bruno nor Andy commented.

"His proposal to me was as follows. He would deliver the Talmud to me on the Isle of Wight, which as the Talmud was stolen there and its custodian murdered there, I understood. His instructions were that I come alone to meet him at a secret venue which he later described. That I drive my own car to the meeting place. That I tell no one where I am going. That I bring £50,000 in used English notes, preferably £50 notes. I informed him that such a large amount of cash might take me a day or so to organise. 'How long will it take?' he asked, as if time was important. I confidently told him that I would need no more than 48 hours, including getting to the Island meeting point. He reminded me in no uncertain terms that if I came to meet him accompanied, he would destroy the Talmud and that I would come to some harm. I did not feel afraid for myself, but I really felt that I would do anything to protect the Talmud – and I think he knew that. So we agreed that I would go to the Isle of Wight."

As the story literally proceeded closer to home for the detectives, they inclined their heads and leaned forward to listen intently.

"He then instructed me to board the 4 p.m. Saturday car ferry from Portsmouth to Fishbourne. I was told that when I got to the Island, I should drive due south towards Niton. There I should continue west on the Blackgang Road to the viewpoint car park. He explained that this is the road that is called the Military Road running east to west on the south of the Island. Then I should 'head for the light'. That was all he said. I did not ask questions. I didn't want anything to derail my potential location of and acquisition of the Talmud. So, I got the money on the Friday and on Saturday I drove to Portsmouth, taking the ferry that we had agreed. On disembarking the ferry, I drove straight there to the car park, having looked at the map beforehand. I arrived at the car park at about 5:30 p.m. It was already quite dark. I got out of my car in the car park and looked around me. The place was deserted. Of course it was. I spun around 360 degrees, and I saw a light in the distance, north or northeast of where I was standing. Then I didn't see it. I soon realised that maybe 700 or 800 metres away someone was giving me a signal. I left the car park and crossed to the far side of the road and followed a public footpath leading to St. Catherine's Oratory – you would know the place, detectives. The ancient relic is high on the down. It was a straightforward walk, but I was alone, and it was dark, and I was beginning to have second thoughts.

But that was just fear talking and the driving force that I might be about to lay my hands on the Talmud kept me going. I was on a mission and determined not to fail."

As if on cue, the smartly dressed lady who had admitted them to the house arrived with a tray. Tea, bottles of fizzy water and some sweet treats that looked like baklava. The detectives tucked in. Neither said a word. They were genuinely spellbound.

"Although well walked in summer, the grass was cold and wet with shining evening droplets of dew already formed. It would have been a scenic walk on a clear day, but on that evening, the mist was descending to envelop the downs."

Bruno and Andy indeed knew the place well. It is a medieval lighthouse situated on the summit of St. Catherine's Down, one of the highest points on the Island. Constructed in 1328, the Oratory is a stone tower 35 feet high. It remains Britain's only surviving medieval lighthouse, a derelict octagonal building. Inside the octagonal stone building its many sides are covered in moss and it has a chalk encrusted dirt floor.

"As I reached the building, about 50 metres away at most, the light stopped going on and off. It was pretty dark now. I put on my own torch, the one on my iPhone. I knew it would mean that the person I was meeting would be at an advantage and would be able to see me. I figured that this was the point of me going so I continued regardless, albeit a little frightened by now. I found an entrance on the ground floor at the rear. The tower was not visible to me for the first half of the journey, but when it came into view, I understood why the thief had picked this place to rendezvous. He could watch my approach, even in the increasing darkness. If I were being followed or were accompanied, he could exit the tower and disappear into the mist. Inside the building it seemed larger, darker and more sinister than it looked from the outside. It took a while for my eyes to adjust to the absence of light. Within the bare walls of the ancient tower, which was riddled with mildew and damp for the lack of sunshine, I entered in the darkness, and for a minute or two I stood alone. Then from the far side of the tower a very bright torch was switched on and a person appeared carrying a parcel in his left hand and a handgun held tightly in his right hand. He was probably six feet tall, of an indeterminable age, probably between twenty and forty, to judge by what little I could see of him, and by how he walked".

Andy opened his mouth to ask a question, but Bruno stopped him with a look.

"He was dressed from top to bottom in black leather motorcycle gear, with black boots, black gloves, a black helmet and a visor – one of those ones through which you cannot see the wearer's eyes. In the dusk he stopped ten metres in front of me, creating an impossible-to-define shape in the glare created by his bright light. It felt very intimidating, and he shouted: 'Stand where you are! Do not come any closer. Do not be afraid of my gun. It will only be used for my protection should you try to rush me. In case you have such an idea, I will show you that I am not bluffing.' He fired one shot into the wall at waist height to my right."

Pivotkin explained how the bullet had loudly hit the wall and had created a deafening noise in such a confined space, which had left his ears ringing. It established the other man's command of the situation and Pivotkin had been terrified that he was about to be robbed and murdered. He was told to advance to the centre and to place the money on the ground, unwrapped, so that it could be seen. Pivotkin did as he was told and returned to his previous place just inside the entrance.

"Never taking his attention off me, he moved to the centre and laid the parcel, which contained the Talmud, next to the cash, which he picked up, and retreated to his previous place, continuously aiming his gun in my direction. When he was satisfied that I had met his requirement of £50,000 in used notes, he stuffed them into the zipped down front of his one-piece motorcycle suit. It was a squeeze and took him a minute or so. Having done so, he told me to 'Walk to the centre, retrieve the book and examine it.' I did that carefully and at first glance it was exactly what had been described to me by the two academics and what he had shown me in the photograph. I felt confident that it was the Talmud. Then he did something strange but which, on reflection, was very clever and bought him a lot of time. 'Throw your shoes to me,' he shouted, which I did. All the time he was fixated on me with his visored face, pointing the revolver towards me. He picked up my boots and threw one to the left and the other to the right, landing against the stone walls, some thirty or forty feet between them. 'Now drop your trousers and take off your coat and throw them both behind you.' Finally he told me to throw my mobile phone against the wall. I obeyed all his instructions."

Pivotkin explained that this was the point at which the mystery man grabbed his torch lamp and disappeared through the rear exit to the building leaving Pivotkin in darkness. It took Pivotkin at least ten minutes to find his clothes and his shoes and his mobile, and to re-dress himself. During that time, he had heard the noise of a motorcycle roar away in the now darkness, across St. Catherine's Down. Pivotkin had dressed, noted that his mobile was cracked but not broken, taken hold of the Talmud, and set off through the mist down the path back to his car as quickly as his legs would carry him.

"I did not venture to look out the back entrance, in case. Mindful of his loaded handgun and even though I thought I had heard him drive away, I just wanted to get away as soon as possible. I was worried that he might have an accomplice who could mug me for the Talmud. I was reliant on my torch beam to keep to the path and to ensure I did not fall into a ditch or tumble down a steep slope or even break an ankle in a rabbit hole. I eventually reached the unlit road. The car park was in complete darkness when I climbed back over the fence across the road to my car, which stood silently alone as I had left it. I did not linger, fearful of the motorcyclist's appearance, or of an accomplice, but I drove as fast as the road would allow back to Fishbourne and boarded the next ferry to Portsmouth. I was physically and mentally exhausted but uplifted by my possession of the Talmud."

Bruno knew that they would be able to verify this part of the story with the ferry company.

"In the warm and comfortable passenger lounge of the car ferry, I examined the Talmud, which had been very carefully wrapped. I found it in excellent condition, to my great relief. On my return journey I turned over in my mind the ethical issues involved, principally that in dangerous circumstances I had met and conducted business with the likely murderer of Simeon Calafifi, or at least with someone who had had dealings with the murderer. I decided that I would reveal the full circumstances to the police, but only once I had clarified the position on the ownership of the Talmud, which I have now done. It took a little longer than I had hoped, but now I am available to help you find this mysterious person, who I believe is from the Isle of Wight."

Whilst listening to Pivotkin's extraordinary story, which Bruno was convinced was wholly true, he had decided that he did not believe Pivotkin had broken any specific laws in deciding to act alone to save the Talmud from possible destruction. Obviously, it would have been helpful to know about this earlier, because two weeks had passed, but he sensed that Pivotkin was about to fill them in on this period.

"Next, I had to consider how I should accomplish my mission of returning the Talmud to its rightful owner. Not to have told Professor Kazac that I had redeemed the Talmud would have made me no better than the thief, and I had to persuade him to part with it, for which I would pay him handsomely. Before that I had to consider a number of ethical issues. First, I had confronted Calafifi's murderer, or murderer accomplice, alone and had allowed him to escape, thereby placing the importance of reclaiming the Talmud before the capture of a murderer. However, I consoled myself that I was retrieving stolen property belonging to Professor Kazac in Tel Aviv. The image of the threatening anonymous biker remains with me, and I am haunted with regret that I made no attempt to detain him. His demonstration of the loaded pistol convinced me not to mess with him."

This was the first time that Bruno had interrupted. He felt that this was not the time for whys and wherefores – that could come later – and he wanted Pivotkin to finish his story.

"Did you contact Professor Kazac?"

"Yes, I did, I called him. I explained how I had acquired the Talmud and why I had done so. He was impressed, I think. I offered to repay him the £55,550 he had paid Calafifi, out of my own funds. I reminded him that I would then have effectively paid over £105,000 for the Talmud, in an attempt to show my commitment to return it to Vilnius. He refused to begin with and explained that he had purchased the Talmud on behalf of the University of Tel Aviv, so that it was not for him to agree such a deal anyway. He added that he felt that they would want to receive the book that they had paid for, but that he would at least explain the situation to his fellow board members. We had a few telephone calls to and fro during that week. In the end, and with the full agreement of the other Tel Aviv university bigwigs, we agreed in principle to share the ownership of the Talmud. They would let me return it to Vilnius now as its spiritual home. But it would reside during all university terms in Tel Aviv as its academic home. And, of course, they took me up on the offer to repay them the £55,550. In some ways, it's a win-win for them."

It was hard not to be impressed with Pivotkin's ability to get a deal done. Then again, he was a very wealthy and astute man.

"I asked Kazac not to do anything or publicise anything until I had spoken to you, indeed, he agreed not to publicise the fact that I was in possession of the Talmud. This was mainly for safety reasons – someone had possibly murdered for it before, so they could easily seek to do that again. Professor Kazac had agreed, in principle, that the Central Synagogue in Vilnius should be the spiritual home of the Talmud. This was enough for me, and I am confident that I will achieve my goal in the end, after the paperwork and legals have been completed. But now back to today, Chief Inspector. The Talmud is evidence, and the police might wish to retain control of the stolen property, or rather the University of Tel Aviv's property, for the time being."

"It is an astonishing story, sir," said Bruno. "My colleague, Detective Sergeant Bowen here, and I need to digest everything you have said. Your description of the person you met is very helpful. His physique and demeanour indicate the type of person we could be looking for. In the absence of any other firm suspects, and to be on the safe side, we could for now assume he is the killer. Obviously, we cannot be sure if he is the person who called on Calafifi the night he was murdered. But the information you have given us is extremely valuable. We will need you to write and sign a statement for our files." Andy explained the protocol surrounding statement provision.

"I will certainly do that, Chief Inspector," he said. "And I would like to be of any other help that I can be."

"I do have a question, sir," said Andy. "Did you by any chance speak to George Deutsch?"

"I did," he said. "He comes from Bournemouth. He is an architect, and a nice man who intends to visit

Vilnius when the Talmud is – eventually – returned. His grandfather was from Lithuania."

"Will you also be sure to provide us with evidence of journey, tickets, booking details and the timing of the call you originally received?"

"Of course, in my statement. The call was from a withheld number as you would expect."

"We'll be on our way now, sir," said Bruno. "Thank you again for reporting your story to us."

Pivotkin added: "Chief Inspector, the Talmud is in perfect condition. If I had involved the police from the start, I'm certain I could not have retrieved it, and we'd have never seen it again. The man who delivered it to me I truly believe could have killed me if I had made any wrong move, and if there had been any visible police presence anywhere near the lighthouse, he would not have appeared. He would have ridden away on his motorbike, never to be seen again."

"You have heard him speak twice. Was the voice on the phone the same as the man who delivered the Talmud to you?" said Andy.

"That's an interesting question. They sounded different, yes. The man on the 'phone was southern, I would say working-class, English. The deliverer of the book sounded more middle-class, perhaps."

"Are we right to assume he is an Islander?" said Andy, as much to himself, but aloud, as to Pivotkin and Bruno.

"Yes," said Pivotkin straightaway, trying to be helpful, "it feels like a safe assumption, to me. He could not have delivered the Talmud to me on the mainland. He knows the Island geography very well, probably every inch, certainly on that remote patch above the Military Road. Chief Inspector, you might take a look at the Oratory for tyre marks or anything else suspicious."

"Mr Pivotkin, you have carefully observed the voice difference between the person on the phone and the person you met at the Oratory. That suggests maybe two men were involved. Would you agree?"

"It might seem that way, Chief Inspector, but not necessarily. You could put any variation down to the quality of the phone line. Both men were confident and authoritative. Yes, if they were different, they certainly presented the same kind of personality".

"From your description, he is not the type you would want to meet late at night in a dark alley. From his physical appearance, do you think you would recognise him if you saw him in a different setting not wearing the motorcycle gear, helmet and visor?"

"Possibly," said Pivotkin. "I remember the way he stood upright and perfectly still, and the careful manner that he placed the Talmud on the ground and picked up the cash. I said he was tall and physically fit. He seemed powerful and imposing. Yes, given a few minutes, I could possibly identify him. I would need to see him walk, crouch over – the movements he demonstrated at the monument."

"It is something for us to work on," said Bruno.

"Detectives, I wish I could have created circumstances whereby you could have made an immediate arrest, and if I can help further, I will do."

"Thank you," said Bruno, "We appreciate you telling us what happened. And congratulations on rescuing the Talmud. We travelled to your home city at the weekend and met Rabbi Barry, because we had heard that the Talmud was to be returned to its rightful home, and we wanted to make the connection. We may require your attendance if we have a confirmed suspect."

"Certainly, Chief Inspector."

The interview over, they departed. The two detectives walked to Regent's Park Station which was just minutes away. From there they took the Underground to Victoria station, and from there the train to Portsmouth. Most of the journey was spent in silence, as they both mulled over the momentous news that they had received from Wladimir Pivotkin.

*

It was 5:30 p.m. by the time they arrived back on the Island, but the clocks had gone forward the previous weekend and so the evening was light and there was time for them to retrace Pivotkin's rendezvous journey to the Oratory.

"There may be something to be learned and he, or the man he met, may have dropped something by mistake," said Bruno.

They took the quickest route to the Oratory to arrive at the car park where Pivotkin, under instruction, had left his car before trudging across the Down up to the medieval lighthouse. The detectives crossed the Military Road, as that section is called, and climbed the verge onto the Down. It was a walk that Bruno had done in daylight many years before, but it seemed quite new to him. Cattle grazing several hundred yards from them did not seem to be disturbed by the two men hiking by.

A cold easterly wind blew in from the sea, but no rain.

The grass was wet, as it was early evening. It was uphill all the way to the lighthouse, which came into view on the brow of the hill once they had passed halfway after about fifteen minutes. It was good exercise for a middle-aged detective.

Using the powerful torches they had brought with them, Bruno looked up inside the four-storey tower where four floors no longer existed. He looked right up to the stone roof.

The ground floor was how Pivotkin had described: a dirt floor with a rear exit through which the thief had come and gone. It was unpleasant and damp and they set about looking for anything that could become a clue. Nothing remained of the exchange that had taken place between the two men, but the firing of the handgun at the stone wall could have left an impression, which Andy set about searching for.

Both detectives diligently inspected the moss-covered walls of the Oratory using their torches, searching the surface with their fingers for the damage that must have been inflicted on the ancient masonry. It did not take more than ten minutes for Andy to discover an object embedded in the wall. Fortunately, the angle of the bullet caused a direct hit at more or less a right angle, meaning that it penetrated the crumbling surface of the wall, and there remained one-third of the bullet protruding above the surface. Had it ricocheted in such cramped quarters, it could have injured someone.

It was a significant discovery. Andy extracted the bullet using his Swiss Army knife, prizing it out of the wall. They could guess the calibre of the gun used, but the used bullet could enable police armaments to identify the weapon and, by reference to the police firearms licence database, potentially the owners of the handgun. The way it was used to frighten Pivotkin with such ease, suggested that its owner knew what he was doing and the ease with which it was fired suggested a properly serviced weapon.

The rear opening through which the killer departed, after leaving Pivotkin half-dressed, was covered in small plants, unlike on the south facing side. Studying the base of the Oratory, for several feet there was only weed covered scrub. There were no distinctive footprints or tyre marks from an escaping motorcycle. In the foreground 100 yards from the Oratory was a footpath leading down to the Military Road, along which one could ride a motorcycle at a fair speed.

"So, that was his escape route," said Andy. "Which suggests to me, more than anything else, that we are looking for an Islander who knows the terrain. Let's take a look at it."

Looking down the footpath, it was several feet wide. No one would have ridden more than ten miles per hour in fading light, but it was a solid surface that provided a firm escape route. Rather than return the way they had come, they continued down the gently sloping footpath. After what seemed about 400 yards they reached the Military Road, then walked a further 400 yards to their car.

The walk back to their car was downhill and gentle and their discovery had lifted their spirits. It had been a very long week, but at last they had found a link to the person who could well be the killer. By virtue of his use of a gun, so soon after the fatal stabbing of Calafifi, he was potentially proving to be an extremely dangerous and experienced criminal. A telephone call to the station confirmed that for proper analysis the bullet would have to be sent to Portsmouth's weapon establishment located inside Portsmouth dockyard. Given the importance of the discovery, Andy Bowen arranged to have the bullet taken over to Portsmouth the following morning, even though it was Saturday.

Before they went their separate ways, Bruno concluded their week with this thought: "Next week will be four weeks since Simeon Calafifi was murdered and next week we will make some kind of breakthrough. I really feel it, Andy. Get some rest this weekend – next week we are going to be even busier."

Chapter 19

At Newport Police Station on Monday morning, Bruno Peach tried to put into context the implications of what Pivotkin had discovered: that they were looking for Calafifi's killer within the Isle of Wight's community.

"Unless, of course," observed Andy Bowen, "the delivery of the Talmud on the Island had been staged to suggest that an Islander had murdered Calafifi?"

"I think that is too complicated for a non-Islander, and what would be the point? For a non-Islander to get on and off the Island affords too many opportunities to be caught out," said Bruno.

"There may be more to Pivotkin's story than he told us. We have no verification of how he came to possess the Talmud, just his word," said Andy.

"The ferry bookings, his descriptions of the incidents, and the bullet fired by the killer in the wall all provide some evidence. In fact, they all suggest that his story is genuine to me," said Bruno. "I also believe in his sincere commitment to get the Talmud back to Lithuania. He is also a very wealthy man so, under normal circumstances, he would have someone to undertake tasks for him. Certainly this kind of task where he could have sent a tough guy pretending to be him. The fact that he did this himself proves his commitment to getting the Talmud back. Having said that, would that overwhelming desire mean that he would kill to get the Talmud? Possibly."

"The date and ferry times of his return journey to the Island are already confirmed," Andy said. "It must be common knowledge among book dealers that if the Talmud re-surfaced Pivotkin was a potential, perhaps the only, buyer. But that would be on the illegal market, as it were, anyway, since the Talmud has already been sold to Kazac. Since the man in black at St. Catherine's Oratory is involved in the murder, or at least acting as an agent for the killer, through what channel or connection was he able to make contact with Pivotkin?"

Bruno admired his colleague Detective Andy's analytical mind which indicated that he could look forward to a very successful career as a detective.

"I certainly agree that just because he is a rich businessman doesn't absolve him," continued Andy. "On his journey from his poor Lithuanian beginnings to his immense wealth in England, there may have been some murky depths that he would be keen to conceal because they reveal his true character beneath the surface of his present respectability. Professor Kazac is somewhat out of the loop and probably simply relieved that the Talmud has been recovered. Provided it gets to him at the University of Tel Aviv, the university will not be out of pocket, and he will be in the same position as he intended to be in. Obviously, the Talmud is now somewhat tainted because of Calafifi's murder and so it may well be that Tel Aviv agree to sell it to Vilnius, brokered and paid for by Pivotkin, in due course. In which case, Pivotkin would have paid for it twice and we have an additional crime to solve. Namely, someone has £50,000 of Pivotkin's money for a stolen book."

"Yes, agreed. I think our position can be that we suspect the killer of Simeon Calafifi is at large somewhere on the Island with £50,000 cash," stated Bruno.

"So, do we put Hirshman back on to our persons of interest list?" asked Andy.

Bruno replied, "Yes, but not as a suspect. According to Pivotkin we are looking for a physically imposing man between twenty and forty years of age, six feet tall. We have no facial identification, but he knows St. Catherine's Down well enough to ride a motorcycle in the dark across it. That path did not look difficult for an experienced biker with powerful head lamps. He would know that trail off the downs very well."

"On the Ordnance Survey Explorers map it shows a footpath, which would be no wider than two yards running down west of St. Catherine's Oratory, which leads to the Military Road," Andy noted. "So, our thief could have watched Pivotkin park and begin his trek to the Oratory, then biked it up the footpath to meet him at the Oratory. He would have heard the engine, of course. The bike could have even been stolen, and he could have travelled on the same ferry as Pivotkin, ridden to a different ferry crossing and left the Island."

"Unlikely," said Bruno. "I am sticking with the belief that this is an Island person. We have effectively eliminated most of the persons of interest on our list, due to location, motive and now description. I feel we need to see Max Carter again and we still need to see Annabel Wilson's friend, Sam Trent. Remember Carter's warehouse? We have incidentally requested from the DVLA details of all motorbike licences on the Island."

When the file arrived by email it was a massive spreadsheet. Searching the list for the names of their suspects, only Max Carter's name was on the list, and his physique matched the man who had summoned Pivotkin to the dark tower.

"What about the motorcycle clubs on the Island?" suggested Andy.

"It's a long shot but you could check on what dates they meet," answered Bruno. "We have a description that fits many bikers, so we shall not spend too much time looking for him on that basis," said Bruno. "Let's make a call on Max Carter. He had two old bikes in his store. He might tell us about Island bikers. Remember also that it was Max Carter who told Pivotkin about the Talmud in the first place, not Hirshman, and I've always thought his connection with Pivotkin somewhat curious. I don't think Carter was involved in Calafifi's murder, but I do think that he likes to be involved in things. He likes to know what's going on. Hence, he has got loads of friends and acquaintants. He's a member of the Chamber of Commerce. No, I don't think he's shady, in fact I think he's a bit of a nosey know-it-all type. Let's try and use that to our advantage."

*

In Cowes, Max's welcome suggested that he was pleased to see them, and they were lucky to make their call on the off chance that he was there.

"Detective Chief Inspector, how nice to see you again! I take it you haven't found Simeon's killer yet, or you wouldn't be back. By now I must qualify as one of your suspects, or even your only suspect?"

"We might agree with you," said Andy. "But we haven't come over to arrest you for Calafifi's murder. We want your help."

"I have been racking my brain for something that could help you but come up with nothing. When you think of the complexity of this case, and the bareness of the book trade on the Island, who do you look for?" he said.

"We have followed up the leads you gave us, none showed any sign they'd be involved with owning or reading the Talmud," said Andy, who rather thought he had provided some of those leads for the sake of it, particularly the collectors. "However, there has been a significant development which we'd like to share with you."

Under a strict order of confidence, they told him Pivotkin's story, including the description of the murderer and the motorbike escape. He listened intently.

"Incredible," he said. "The type of person with knowledge of this coastal area is surely an Island person, who maybe even lives in that part of the Island. He may or may not be in the book business. He could just be an accomplice who is being paid, or someone who has a close connection with the killer. An ingenious plan, I have to say."

"He is six feet, possibly an inch or two taller, rides a motorcycle dressed all in black, suit, helmet, visor, has an athletic build, is an Islander. Any ideas?" said Andy, knowing his question was a long shot.

"That's helpful to a degree," said Max, with a rue smile. "Now I know the shape of your suspect, if I spot anyone,

I'll try to identify him, but I can't give you a name at the moment from my contacts."

"We actually believe that the murderer does understand the market in which Calafifi worked, knew what they were stealing, and that they could sell it for a large cash sum to one of a very small group of people. Looking at it from the other end, do you know a person who has just come into a load of cash, or has just had a debt repaid? From among your professional and social network of Island people. Someone who might also happen to fit the description Mr Pivotkin gave us?" enquired Bruno.

"I've already pointed you in all the directions I know," said Max. "But I will think again. I have thought about this killing a lot, because it's on my own doorstep. I feel I should be able to narrow the field down to one or two people, but it's difficult. It's a mistake to eliminate those who we believe must be innocent or incapable. Have you spoken to Nathan Philips yet?"

"Yes, we have contacted him and spoken to him briefly, but he has been away on holiday for three weeks. He actually returned last week but we were in Lithuania, so we have rescheduled our meeting with him for tomorrow."

"I keep telling you to talk to him. Now that he has had time to think about the loss of his principal competitor, he might have some ideas." He added, "And you could also speak to Bill Cockerton who owns the motorcycle shop in Ryde. Talk to him about off-road bikes, who he knows that rides them. Can't be too many people on the Island. But there is one aspect of this murder you may not yet have explored."

"What is that, Max?" said Andy.

"Imagine if the murderer did not kill Calafifi to get his hands on the Talmud but just wanted to get his hands on Simeon's successful business. Simeon's Bookshop has become a centre of the religious antiquarian book business in England. I shall be interested should his wife want to sell it, which I anticipate she will."

It seemed to the detectives that Max Carter did not know that Nathan Philips was to be the new owner of Simeon's Bookshop. Actually, when they first met, he didn't even know that Nathan Philips was on holiday. Bruno wondered what this said about their friendship and how Max Carter would feel when he found out. Bruno also pondered: if the killer had murdered Calafifi to get their hands on the business, who might that person be?

Before they departed Max's showroom, Andy wanted to take another look at the two vintage motorcycles he spotted in Max Carter's warehouse on their previous visit, so he asked Max if they could look around.

"Go ahead gentlemen, if there is anything of interest speak up and I will give you a special price," and left them to examine the contents of the showroom.

A diligent search did not reveal the bikes, so on their way out of the warehouse, Max said, "Nothing of interest, gentlemen?"

"I was interested in one of the motorbikes."

"Which one?"

"The BSA 500, 4 stroke."

"A classic bike in wonderful condition. I sold both the bikes last week to a mainland dealer in Pompey. I made a handsome profit and bought a new Triumph from him. I am still running it in. Are you a bike enthusiast, Sergeant? Tell me what you want, and I'll try and find it for you."

"Great. I'll let you know when I've firmed up what I'm looking for," said Andy.

"Another BSA 500 perhaps?"

"That would interest me, definitely," said Andy.

Back in their car, they agreed that Nathan Philips needed visiting as soon as possible now that he was back from his holiday. They did not believe that his absence so soon after Simeon's death was suspicious because they had checked out the truth about the bookshop's initially agreed exchange and completion dates. It made sense that he wanted to take a break while he could.

"Max Carter answered our questions, Andy," said Bruno, "and he seems to genuinely be trying to help us. On reflection, Pivotkin has exposed himself to great danger and invested a fortune to attempt to return a Jewish bible to its birthplace. It will give him great satisfaction in this symbolic act, to give peace and hope to the descendants of those who lost their lives in the events of 1942. That he may have risked his life would have added to his sense of fulfilment."

Bruno's mobile telephone rang displaying the number of George Deutsch. Deutsch had just returned from Vilnius and was able to give the police a first-hand report on his visit to the Vilnius Synagogue. He reported that the elaborate weekend was not the dedication of the return of Rabbi Eliyahu Ben Shlomo Zalman's Talmud to the Central Synagogue in Vilnius. However, he had heard the good – but fairly secret – news that Wladimir Pivotkin was now in possession of the stolen Talmud which he had secured for £50,000 cash and that it would be coming back to Vilnius before too long.

*

Carl Bullivent's business network was extensive and spread across the South of England. He called with another lead for the police to follow up which had come from a shipping agent named Jack Fisher, who lived in Southampton. Fisher's business was to sell space in containers to people wishing to send goods to overseas destinations, mostly private individuals moving permanently, or to holiday homes in Southern Europe, Malta or Cyprus.

Jack Fisher was a senior member of the Mormon church in Southampton, who had a close relationship with the church elders and with Caleb White, their leader. White had confided in him that the church had been offered a handwritten copy of the *Book of Mormon*, written by Joseph Smith in 1800, to purchase.

"Fisher approached me as someone in the antiquarian book business, and asked what I thought it was worth. That was two days ago, but I haven't replied. I didn't want to muddy the waters by talking about it or by saying anything about the murderous circumstances associated with it. No, I thought I'd leave you to investigate. I'll give you his details, and if you can leave my name out of it, I'd appreciate it. Furthermore, I know Jack Fisher to be a very honest man."

This was a red-hot lead from Bullivent and needed an immediate response, so a call was made to Fisher's business premises in Southampton and the detectives determined that Jack Fisher would be in, and able to see them if they dropped by.

*

Entering a modern ground-floor office, Bruno asked the receptionist to see Jack Fisher, presenting his business card for identification. From the immediate attention they received, it was clear that Jack Fisher was used to people calling in. The detectives were directed to a pleasant office overlooking a tidy garden square.

Fisher greeted them in a positive manner. "Detectives, how can I help you?"

By way of introduction, Bruno explained they had met the Mormon church leader Ronald Arnica at East Grinstead recently in connection with the stolen *Book of Mormon* and that they were searching for any information that may enable them to recover the book; this in turn might enable them to identify and potentially arrest the killer of Simeon Calafifi, who had acquired the book at auction.

"We believe you may be able to help us in our investigation. Some weeks ago, a rare book of historical Mormon significance was sold at auction for a substantial sum of money to a bookseller who specialises in religious books. Shortly after, this book and other possessions were stolen from the bookseller, and he was murdered. The *Book of Mormon* is being offered for sale to members of the Mormon church. If this book has surfaced in your church, we would like you to tell us about it."

"Detective Chief Inspector, I know little about this terrible situation, other than the fact that one of my church members spoke to me two days ago to explain that they had been offered a handwritten volume of the *Book of Mormon* by Joseph Smith. They asked if I knew what it was worth. I am still waiting for my contact, which I suspect you know is Carl Bullivent, to come back to me."

"Can we speak to this church member?"

"Let me call him now. I am sure he'll speak to you. His name is Caleb White." At which Fisher picked up his mobile 'phone and put it on speaker so they could all listen to the conversation. Caleb answered immediately.

"Caleb, it's Jack. Regarding the *Book of Mormon* you mentioned, I'm still waiting for my contact to come back to me with an estimate of its current value. In the meantime, I have with me Detective Chief Inspector Peach of the Isle of Wight police and his colleague. They are searching for a volume which was stolen from a bookseller on the Island. Can I pass him over to you?"

"Sure, Jack, put him on. Caleb White speaking," he said in an instantly recognisable American accent.

"Mr White," said Bruno. "We understand that you have been offered a copy of a rare edition of a Mormon bible to buy. Specifically, a handwritten edition by Joseph Smith."

"Correct, Detective Chief Inspector. Someone who claimed to be a book dealer in religious books phoned me. My question to him was simple: 'is it genuine or is it a copy?' He assured me that it was the original, handwritten work. I replied that I didn't have the authority to buy such a prized possession, but a higher authority could be interested. He said 'I'll let you find out if they are interested and I will call again'. When I asked the price, he said 'It's what the church can afford. I'll call you in seven days,' and then he rang off."

"How did he get your number?" said Bruno.

"I'm in the church directory, which is online. That's all I can tell you, Detective Chief Inspector."

"When did you receive this call?"

"Hmm, it was two days ago, so that would have been Saturday. Yes, Saturday 25th March."

"If you wished to buy the book, how much could the church offer?" asked Andy.

"I can see no reason why our church here in Southampton would want to acquire it with precious funds. But our central headquarters might consider it an essential record that should be acquired."

"Have you spoken to your leaders in East Grinstead about the book?" said Bruno.

"Yes, I have spoken to Ronald Arnica, who was positive, not exactly that we should buy it, but that we should not let the genuine article slip from our grasp. He told me that he would be contacting the police about this book. I assume that is you and your team." Bruno murmured some words of assent. He wondered why Ronald Arnica has not contacted him straightaway about this matter. In any event, Carl Bullivent had done so, and now Jack Fisher and Caleb White had explained the full story, so hopefully they had not lost too much time.

"The book is stolen property and belongs to the estate of a murdered man," said Bruno. "We want to apprehend this person who has approached you, who could also be the murderer of the owner of the book, or at the very least, who could lead us to the killer. The advantage we have is that this person has now made contact. We are desperate to find and arrest them, so cash for the book should be the bait. I can wait until this person makes contact, and together we should have a chance of catching them when they make contact. Today is Monday and they should contact you by or on Saturday, according to what they said to you. We would like you to express interest in buying the book and to agree to whatever proposition is put to you," said Bruno. "I imagine that it will involve a meeting where you exchange cash for the book. We will be present to protect you and make the arrest. We will not put you at risk. If you agree to call us the moment you are contacted, we can plan our moves."

"Detectives, I will do as you say and, with God's blessing, we will catch the killer," said Caleb White enthusiastically.

With that agreed, Bruno and Andy ended the call, explaining the need for discretion. They then left Jack Fisher and jumped into a taxi to return to the Southampton ferry terminal for the Isle of Wight. Their visit had been successful. They had a seller who, if it was the same person who had sold the Talmud to Wladimir Pivotkin, was a person willing to take risks for large chunks of cash.

"Greed is hopefully persuading the same person to try the same trick again, when he should have cut and run with the £50,000 for the Talmud. This time we will be present at the rendezvous," said Andy. "Carl Bullivent is wealthy and has provided us with two leads, completely unconnected, for the return of two stolen books. How could he have been so lucky in helping us find the murderer? To me, it makes Carl Bullivent a person of interest, sir."

Bruno could not openly disagree with his colleague, although he suspected that it was more an indicator of Carl Bullivent's good and clever connections than anything sinister or criminal.

"If Caleb White does a deal to buy the *Book of Mormon*, we will set a trap that will be impossible to escape from."

"So, we wait for Caleb to call us, sir? I can't think of what else we can do. Do you think this mystery caller could be Max Carter?" said Andy.

"No," said Bruno. "Even though, physically, in motorcycle gear, he is the right age and fits the bill."

"Carter's alibi for the evening of 28th February is sound, but isn't watertight, so he could – at a push – have killed Simeon, but I can't see him doing that, nor can I see him trying to sell books for a murderer. And for a successful businessperson like Carter £50,000 is not a life changing sum of money. He would be risking too much for too little."

"Our killer has £50,000 cash which could have a material effect on his immediate activities, either in business or socially. However I doubt that the cash will have been used yet, and I am certain that it won't have been banked. It is looking increasingly like this murder is to do with money. Possibly someone who understands the antiquarian book business and has a definite plan for the cash," concluded Bruno.

"Let's hope he calls Caleb White again, as he said he would, and we can make some progress," said Andy.

"Yes, let's hope so, indeed. I told you this week was going to be busy."

Chapter 20

"What reason do we have for visiting Philips?" said Andy, as they prepared to visit his Bembridge bookshop. He was talking to himself evidently because he carried straight on: "Well, Nathan Philips and Simeon Calafifi were competitors. However, Calafifi had sold the bookshop business in Shanklin to Philips. So, effectively, Calafifi was no longer a competitor to Philips, even before he was murdered. I think if Philips was going to murder Calafifi, he would have done it prior to a purchase, thereby eliminating Calafifi and allowing himself to take over as the leading Island antiquarian bookseller without shelling out a penny. Murdering him after the deal was done? Surely not – for starters he wouldn't want the bad press around a bookshop business that he had just bought."

"Agreed," nodded Bruno. "The only reason we haven't seen him before now is that he has been away. I don't think his absence is suspicious in any way. I think he rushed to exchange on the bookshop before going on holiday, which was also convenient personally because it gave him and his family the opportunity to have a break between exchange and completion. Presumably after completion it would be a terribly busy time for him. Let's pay him a visit now this morning. He is expecting us. Sometime very soon he will acquire Simeon's Bookshop in Shanklin and break the news to Annabel that she is working for him, and any hopes she had of acquiring the bookshop will vanish."

*

When the detectives arrived, Nathan Philips was in the midst of a physically arduous task. He and his assistant were busy unpacking new stock that had arrived that morning. They adjourned to his back office, away from his assistant's ears. He was in his late thirties, married to Natalie, with two very young children. He lived in Bembridge, in a sought-after property near to the harbour, which was rife for re-development. He was well built, not overweight, six foot two and fit, capable of lifting heavy boxes of books. He was handsome, had graduated from university, where he had majored in American literature. He had an intellectual interest in books. It had taken him fifteen years to establish his bookshop in an affluent part of the Island, and to gain a reputation that Simeon had recognised and encouraged. Simeon Calafifi, Max Carter and Nathan Philips were all involved in trying to establish the annual Island Literary Festival in Cowes as the major literary festival in Southern England.

"I've heard about your investigation. How is it going?" were his first words to them.

"Slowly," said Bruno. "We've had to spend a lot of time on the mainland, where Mr Calafifi did most of his business."

"Was that helpful?"

"Yes," said Bruno. "While you have been away, we have been investigating three crimes, which we believe to be linked – two thefts and a murder. We understand from

Miriam Calafifi that you had been in negotiations with Simeon Calafifi to acquire his business here on the Isle of Wight, and that the deal was signed right before Simeon's murder, the day before, I believe. Since then you have been away. Now you are back, we would like to talk to you about your relationship with Simeon Calafifi, in the hope that you might have some information that will help us in our investigation. Perhaps you could tell us about yourself and your business and your dealings with Mr Calafifi."

Nathan Philips paused. He looked calm and not at all stressed.

"First, I'll give you some background about my business. When Simeon moved to the Island, he was really keen on getting involved in the literary festival. Max Carter and I are both on the committee. He thought it would stimulate his business and show the Island as a place that could be developed as a literary mecca for writers, but that did not really happen. The development of the Island Literary Festival, which happens in early October, has been impressive but it didn't really have the effect that he wanted. I don't think he and Miriam were really suited to Island life. They'd lived in London; she has a pretty dynamic job. So we discussed his future here and he had decided to relocate to Bournemouth."

"Tell us more about Mrs Calafifi. How well do you know her?" asked Andy.

"Well, I do know that Miriam has found it hard to pursue her career living on the Island. They had lived in Ryde for three years and they decided that relocating to Bournemouth would suit them both better. In the autumn, Simeon approached me to see if I was interested in buying the Shanklin shop and I jumped at the chance, although it meant mortgaging myself up to the hilt. It's the business breakthrough I've been looking for and helps me to soak up not just all of the business in the east of the Island but also opens me up to new kinds of sales. Obviously, Simeon's death is a shock and a tragedy and part of me wonders whether it is a bad omen, but I can't back out – I don't want to anyway – and I know I take it on with his blessing. In many ways, it is a blessing – certainly for Miriam and the boys – that it was sold just before he died."

"Could we ask you about Annabel Wilson? I presume you know her. How will the sale affect Annabel's position?" said Bruno.

"She's likely to take it very badly and will probably leave straight away," said Nathan.

"How do you feel about that?" said Bruno.

"In the past year, she has spoken to me about taking over the business herself, so to find out there is no chance of that will affect her negatively. It's going to be awkward if she stays and it will be cheaper for me if she does leave. Under the circumstances, I will be glad to see the back of her. I've known her for many years, Chief Inspector, and I don't want a fight with her," said Nathan.

"What will she do?" asked Bruno.

"No idea. Leave the Island, maybe?"

"She doesn't have much in the way of information about Simeon's contacts or business methods that have helped our investigation," said Andy. "Max Carter has been very helpful, as have other contacts that he has directed us to." Andy explained in brief about the Talmud and the *Book of Mormon*, but he did not give all the details of Pivotkin's involvement nor Caleb White's recent information.

"I don't have anything else to add either," said Nathan. "I will keep thinking about it and if I think of anyone who might be involved or anything else helpful or important, of course, I'll let you know."

"When do you intend to take over the Shanklin business?" said Bruno.

"Funny you should ask that. It should have been yesterday, which was a month to the day since we exchanged. But I've told Miriam Calafifi that I can be flexible, and we should wait another month to see what happens with your investigation. She actually said that she would have preferred to stick to yesterday's date, but I wanted to wait until I had at least seen you. I'll probably call Miriam at the end of this week and come up with a plan."

"Please keep us updated," said Bruno.

"I'll do that, Chief Inspector."

With that they departed the bookshop, which was now busy out the front.

Back in their car, Andy said, "Did you notice the motorcycle helmet on the table behind his desk?"

"Yes," said Bruno, "I did."

*

Back at the office Bruno picked up an email from Caleb White at the Mormon Church in Southampton informing him that Ronald Arnica had instructed White to use central church funds to buy the *Book of Mormon* if it was offered to him and that he must keep the Isle of Wight police informed of any developments. White had further explained that he was fortunate that the congregation in Southampton consisted of many friends and fraternities throughout South Hampshire and was one of the wealthiest Mormon fraternities in England. A handful of wealthy members had in fact agreed to contribute up to £10,000 between them to buy the *Book of Mormon*. This had been communicated to Ronald Arnica who had agreed with White that this should be the approach: to use these special funds, of £10,000, to purchase the item and to only offer that amount.

Bruno and Andy had only just read White's email and were talking about it when a call came in from White himself.

Caleb White had important news for them. He had just been telephoned by the holder of the *Book of Mormon*. It sounded like the same person who had called White on Saturday. Bruno was pleased. A second call fairly soon after the first meant that the person holding the *Book of Mormon* was starting to get a bit jumpy. A more confident thief would have waited the full week like his initial call stated.

White's offer of £10,000 was at first rejected by the seller, until Caleb explained that that was the limit of funds that could be raised, so it was take it or leave it. He had then accepted. This was also regarded by Bruno as positive.

White confirmed to Bruno that he was prepared to risk attending the designated venue to exchange the cash for the book on the understanding that there would be a police presence to protect him. White had learned that the book had been recently sold at auction for £42,000 so he was confident the financial risk to the church would be minimal and would reward his church handsomely for the personal risk he was taking dealing with a murderer.

White had received instructions for retrieving the book. It would be delivered to him on Thursday evening, at 7:30 p.m., at the entrance to Bembridge Fort. He must arrive alone and wait at the gate to the Fort, which would be locked, and where the book would be delivered in exchange for £10,000 in cash, in a mixture of used £20 and £50 notes.

Bembridge Fort is a disused Fort on Culver Cliff, halfway between where you turn off the main road signposted to the Haven Inn. It is exceedingly popular with walkers and the road is suitable for cars and motorbikes. Between the point at which you leave the main road and the Haven Inn there are no buildings except the Fort. Caleb White would need to drive to get to it. A motorcycle might be the transport that the thief would use and the previous experience with Wladimir Pivotkin at St. Catherine's Oratory suggested a bike could be used again. This time the police would need to be prepared and, if the escape was to be made on a bike, the entire motor division of the Island police motorcyclists would need to be on hand to assist with the apprehension of the thief.

White reported to Bruno the caller's words: "You will arrive at 7:30 p.m. Alone. As long as you have not informed the police, I will deliver the book to you. I shall be watching the whole road and, if I am not happy, then I will not meet you, and I will burn the *Book of Mormon*." This must have been an idle threat, as it was out of character from the profile of the thief the police had compiled, but it was surely designed to affect a deeply religious man like Caleb White and frighten him into complying.

Bruno thanked Caleb White for his call and then made arrangements for an unmarked police car to collect White from his home in Southampton at midday on Thursday to bring him over to the Isle of Wight. He would receive a briefing and some training prior to the early evening meeting at the Fort. Bruno had reassured White that he would not be alone. After the call ended, Bruno and Andy also started to make the necessary arrangements for the police presence at the Fort.

"The Fort is the highest point on the cliff. We can seal off both ends, so that when the thief appears we shall see him, albeit from a distance," said Bruno. "If he is on foot, he will be caught and if he rides off on a motorbike, he will be intercepted by our police presence. Inspector Downing, head of the Island Motor Division, will need to ensure there are enough of the police bike squad to stop him by whichever road he tries to escape on."

"Let's visit Bembridge Fort to survey the land properly and check for entrances and exits, to see what trap we need to set. It's our last chance to catch him. We must ensure that Caleb White is properly protected with body armour."

The two detectives were, to say the least, excited at the prospect of catching the murderer.

Chapter 21

The following morning, Wednesday, Bruno Peach and Andy Bowen accompanied by Inspector Downing, head of the Island Motor Division also based at Newport Police Station, drove from Newport towards Sandown, turning off along the B3395 towards Bembridge. They took the first right after a 90-degree bend, which rose sharply to Culver Down towards the Haven Inn, a little more than a mile from the turn-off. They passed Bembridge Fort on the cliffs, halfway between the turn-off and the Haven Inn car park.

Bembridge Fort is a formidable structure. Owned by the National Trust, it is the highest point on Bembridge Down. A notice states that it was built between 1862 and 1867, a defence against an anticipated invasion by the French that never happened. Today it is generally unused, although a commercial sign was affixed over the main entrance, establishing that events took place in the Fort on summer festival days. A heavily policed 'Fright Night' on Halloween was a well-attended, unique Island event in October.

Standing at the entrance of the Fort facing the sea it was obvious why the site had been chosen to build a defence against the threat of a French invasion in the mid-nineteenth century. It provided a 360-degree panoramic view and, from the high brick walls, a perfect angle to fire cannonballs at French invaders. It was now to serve as a meeting place for Caleb White to meet the suspect in the case of the murder of Simeon Calafifi, and Bruno could see why he had chosen this place.

The Haven Inn serves the small community who live in the Coastguard cottages, and farmers whose sheep and cattle roam Culver Down, together with the walkers and tourists who come to admire Sandown Bay and visit the monument. The Inn looks down on a row of Victorian brick-built terraced cottages on the cliff edge a hundred metres across from the Inn, two hundred metres above Sandown Bay and, to the east, towards Culver cliffs.

Culver Down is a white chalk ridge which faces south, with the beach several hundred feet below, stretching back to Yaverland, to Sandown sailing club, and to the holiday attractions of Sandown and the Esplanade.

Bruno knew that a large visible police presence spread across Culver Down would frighten away his suspect and their best chance of cracking this case would be lost, so he and Inspector Downing examined the proposed meeting place at Bembridge Fort. It was an unusual place to meet and one from which the murderer must have been completely convinced he could successfully extricate himself. That worried Bruno, because it bore the same stamp of cunning as securing the payment for the Talmud. What did this person have in store? Meeting in a remote location had the potential of enabling the suspect to deliver the *Book of Mormon* safely and then to make a clean escape. Hence Inspector Downing's determination to block every possible escape route, and back across fields from the Fort.

Access by motorcycle was what Bruno anticipated, because that was how the thief had made off from St. Catherine's Oratory. From Bembridge Fort the only route off the Down was back along the road to the junction with the B3395, or to the north across farmland, a distance of half a mile to meet another road. That would have to be on foot and would be a most unlikely exit route. Heading towards the Haven Inn would lead to a dead end. So how might he leave unhindered from the rear of the Fort? Having studied the Ordnance Survey Explorer map, the B3395 lay just 500 metres from the rear of Bembridge Fort. Using the same method of escape as he used at the lighthouse on St. Catherine's Down, it would be feasible for him to reach the road in a couple of minutes. He'd clearly be familiar with his route and, as long as no police presence was noticed prior to his meeting, he could make off with his £10,000 on his bike, as with the Talmud.

Inspector Downing committed to having his motor-cycle team all over the area, at the beginning of the Cliff Road and, at the cattle grid, with more police at the Haven Inn. On the B3395 at the nearest point to the Fort, he would have officers in cars and on motorbikes, so there would be no chance of his escape on a motorbike, and if he chose to abscond on foot they would close in on the Fort within minutes. Downing studied the terrain for some time planning their approach, knowing that Caleb White would phone the police the moment the transaction was done and the thief was out of sight. Then the police could home in on him from every concealed place on the Down. Bruno and Andy agreed to leave the policing to Downing.

They would wait at the cattle grid to be summoned to make the arrest. The main problem was that the officers would need to be concealed – which would mean arriving much earlier, and risking being seen. Or they would need to arrive bang on time, right when the suspect was meeting Caleb White, which would risk them being heard. Either way, it was a risky and difficult operation. White's safety was paramount. Bruno was anxious that there were many opportunities for this operation to go wrong.

*

Bruno and Andy updated Chief Superintendent Barlow with the latest developments in the Calafifi case. He was interested in their plan to arrest the person they believed to be the thief and possibly the murderer, on Culver Down. True to form, he was keen to make the point that they would need to have enough evidence to charge the individual.

"We won't fail this time, sir, as long as he shows up with the book," said Bruno. "If we get him, I think the whole case will unravel pretty quickly."

"I wish you luck, Detectives. Let me know how you get on as soon as you can. I have confidence in you both."

Chief Superintendent Barlow made them feel optimistic that the suspect was about to make a mistake that would result in his arrest. If he had been satisfied with the £50,000 he had received for the Talmud and had walked away, perhaps he could have escaped justice, but greed and the relative ease of luring Pivotkin to the Talmud had likely tempted him to try to clean up and sell the *Book of Mormon* too.

After they had completed the paperwork obligations regarding their use of the resources of the Island Motor Division, they spoke to Caleb White to prepare him a little more for his Thursday evening meeting. They confirmed timings and plans with him. He told them a little about himself and Bruno conjured up an image of a man in his thirties, clean-cut and neat, in the tradition of the young missionaries from the Church of the Latter-day Saints that you see knocking on doors with a well-rehearsed pitch to try to recruit you into their church. He came across as a thoroughly nice and reliable person and Bruno felt that they had an excellent candidate in White for the task ahead. He claimed to be fully prepared mentally, and Bruno assured him that his safety was the most important aspect of this operation. He also explained that, in case the suspect knew or had seen Caleb White, it was not possible for them to use a stand in. As such, a lot rested on Caleb White tomorrow.

*

Having enjoyed the luxury of a visit to Vilnius the previous Wednesday, this Wednesday was closer to home. As it was a beautiful spring day, Bruno phoned Janet and invited her to drive over to meet him after school finished. He suggested they drive to the Haven Inn at Culver where they could explore the surrounding area on foot, visit the pub, enjoy an early dinner and then take a stroll in the early evening sunshine the half a mile back to the Fort.

There was a serious reason for inviting Janet along. Bruno planned to wear a cap and sunglasses and carry a backpack and the walking pole he kept in the back of the car. He asked Janet to change into walking clothes too. This would make them look like any other couple hiking around the east of the Island, rather than a Chief Inspector casing the joint for the meeting the next day. It was quite possible that the suspect would be visiting there himself just to check all was well on his side prior to the Thursday rendezvous.

Bruno wanted to reassure himself about the safety aspects of Caleb White's involvement at Bembridge Fort on the next day at 7:30 p.m., at the time chosen by the murderer. Presumably that time was chosen to make identification in the dusk more difficult, and the ability to vanish into thin air more possible. However, Bruno was uneasy about the location and believed that the British Army of 1849, fearing a French invasion, would not have risked being trapped in the Fort by invaders. Perhaps a tunnel existed, surfacing some distance from the Fort, to provide a means of escape?

It was serene and windless as Janet and Bruno sat on the grass verge in front of the entrance to the Fort, staring towards Sandown Bay. Staring over the cliff in front of the entrance to the Fort, one looked down on a steep, vertical drop, before reaching a grass covered cliff 200 metres below itself, from there descending steeply to the beach a drop of at least 300 metres from where they sat.

It was conceivable, thought Bruno, that the murderer could escape by abseiling down the steep cliff to the beach below. Janet agreed that it was a potential escape route, if a sound anchor for the abseil equipment could be found where they were sitting, but in the minutes and seconds the murderer would have to escape it would be impossible for him to set it up. It would have to have been done before hand and was fraught with possible shortcomings. It was a far-fetched idea they decided could not be implemented in the time frame, and their reconnaissance of the meeting point confirmed to Bruno that the police had all bases covered. Nevertheless, he still felt nervous and anticipated a sleepless night ahead.

Chapter 22

Thursday morning was full of anticipation. If an arrest was made that afternoon, the case could be concluded very quickly. Revealing the identity of the culprit would be a welcome event, as could discovering the motive for the unexplained murder of Simeon Calafifi.

The arrival of Caleb White at lunchtime was expected with a high level of anxiety. In police work, even the best-laid plans did not always work out as intended. In this case Caleb White's safety was all-important, so both detectives were nervous.

At Bruno's insistence, Caleb put on a police issue bullet-proof vest beneath his jacket. He could have been Moses going to receive The Ten Commandments on Mount Horeb in the desert of Sinai; instead, it was the *Book of Mormon* at Culver Cliff on the Isle of Wight.

"Once the transaction is complete, you will phone us on the number we have given you, and which you have stored in your mobile 'phone. We shall be all over the place within minutes," said Andy.

Caleb told them that he believed he had been selected by God to retrieve the *Book of Mormon* from the thief, and that this act would guarantee him a preferential place in the life thereafter. At his church in Southampton his mission would be celebrated. Those who had contributed towards the £10,000 that he carried with him were gathered together in their church this afternoon in solemn prayer that his mission would succeed.

It was a cold windy evening, with the wind blowing from the south. Caleb's appointment with the killer was at 7:30 p.m. at Bembridge Fort. At 6:15 p.m. they set off slowly from Newport. Caleb was to follow the detectives to Sandown where they would lead him to within half a mile of the rendezvous location. They must not be seen to have any contact with him, in case the killer was watching the approach to the Fort from a distance. Caleb remained at the agreed distance behind their car, until the turn-off at the signpost to the Haven Inn. It was just after 7 p.m. when Bruno pulled over, stopped and parked in a secluded parking spot. Caleb carried on, passing them, following the clear directions to the Fort which he had memorised earlier and where he would arrive at around 7:15 p.m.

It was not without a feeling of concern that Bruno watched Caleb White proceed past them towards the Fort and Culver, admiring the faith of the young man, who was confident that he would bring back the original teachings of the founder of his beliefs, despite being fully aware of the potential risk. Surely within the Fort, a large and spooky place, somewhere could have been set up unseen to trap the killer before the meeting with Caleb White, if they had had more time to plan. If this endeavour went wrong and Caleb suffered an injury, Bruno would never forgive himself. They remained silent and hidden beneath overhanging trees until 7:25 p.m. and then drove very slowly to the cattle grid at the entrance to the Cliff Road. In their unmarked car, Bruno and Andy could have been visitors watching the last of the day's sunshine vanish as a gloomy dusk fell over an incoming tide on a cold, windy Sandown Bay.

A police motorbike sat out of sight, its rider wearing dark motorcycle clothing. He did not move from a concealed position beneath evergreen shrubs, waiting for instructions from his controller.

Barely concealing high levels of anxiety, at 7:30 p.m. Bruno and Andy were sat still, in complete silence, concerned only for the safety of Caleb White, who was alone with a person who was likely to be armed and capable of killing. As the minutes passed their concern increased. They went over what they thought was happening and how long the meeting should take, but the call from Caleb did not come, not even a text message, so their concerns increased.

Then at 7:45 p.m., as darkness was closing in, Caleb White's car became visible on the Culver cliff road approaching at speed until, slowing dramatically, he crossed through the cattle grid and shuddered to a halt beside them.

Caleb jumped out of his car shouting, "He's gone! There was nothing I could do! He flew away."

The detectives could not believe what Caleb had just said. They were speechless.

"I sat outside the locked gate to the Fort. He was on time, he slowly walked towards me from *inside* the Fort *behind* the locked gate, carrying a handgun pointing towards me. He wore a rucksack and told me to pass my 'phone to him through the wire gate at the entrance to the Fort, which was locked with a large padlock. He then threw my 'phone into the deep trench that surrounds the Fort. He then asked for the cash. I gave him the cash. 'Don't move,' he said, and he checked the money."

Caleb spoke quickly, breathlessly. "He was wearing a helmet and visor. His clothes were dark, but lightweight, not heavy motorcycle gear. He wore gloves and after he checked the cash, he handed to me over the gate a plastic bag containing the book. He did not wait while I checked the contents of the bag, which could have contained anything. 'You must wait here for five minutes before you leave, or I'll shoot you. And I will be watching you,' he said. He then backed into the Fort, about twenty metres away from the locked wire entrance gate and disappeared. I stood motionless, as instructed. After no more than two minutes, from the grass verge, high up above entrance to the Fort, the man who had just presented me with the *Book of Mormon* launched himself towards the cliff edge flying a blue and white paraglider, and once clear of the trench, the wind lifted him into the air and I watched him fly higher and higher out over the sea, until I could only see him in the distance, the wind taking him swiftly that way. I could not 'phone you because my 'phone lay twenty feet down in the trench, completely out of reach," Caleb pointed in the vague direction of Sandown Beach.

Distraught, Caleb explained further. "With the precious book, I drove here as fast as I could. If you look towards the sea or that way, he has disappeared."

Having listened to an emotionally exhausted Caleb, Bruno's instruction to the police motorcyclist was to drive to Sandown and see if he could spot a man, any man, on a motorcycle or a man descending on a paraglider; he was then to follow and detain him. He called Inspector Downing and updated him with the turn of events, informing him that the suspect had got away on a paraglider. Downing sent his entire team to Sandown to search for a man who might have alighted from the glider and be hiding in the beach area.

The killer's escape was an embarrassing moment for the police. However, his skill as a paraglider had given them more information about him and narrowed the field through which to identify him. They had not explored the Island's motorcycle clubs because they did not believe their man was the type to join a club, but as a paraglider he had changed their perception of him. There were fewer paraglider clubs than motorcycle clubs on the Island. Those might be worth a try. From Caleb White's report, this man was experienced and relied on his skill as a glider to escape.

"He is also a gambler," pointed out Andy Bowen. "Because if there had been no wind, he'd have been on foot and certainly apprehended by police. Those paragliders check the wind all the time, he would have known this evening's wind conditions, but they can change without much warning."

"Now is the windiest time of the year," said Bruno. "But you're right, it was an incredible gamble. He would also have to know the area very, very well to be confident in the semi-dark. A really very daring and very dangerous escape."

"We should have thought about this possibility, given the location of the rendezvous, and had a different plan, given our experience with this man. These paragliders find wind once they are ten feet in the air," said Andy. "Shall we join the search on Sandown beach, or drive along to the Haven Inn for a pint?"

"Take me back along Sandown Beach," said Bruno, frowning slightly at Andy's suggestion.

There was no doubt that the killer was extremely clever and had anticipated police presence within range. He was ingenious enough to engage in a unique method of flight. Bruno now knew they were searching for an exceptional individual, in every respect, but for them there could be no excuses. From now on their plan had to succeed to bring the killer to justice. Fortunately, the press could not report on the day's events – one could only imagine the sensational headlines.

Downing phoned Bruno to report they had found no one obvious in Sandown who could be the paraglider. He had informed the coastguard in case the paraglider had gone off course and ended up in the sea, in which case they would be looking for a body. Bruno hoped that was not the case, as it would potentially be a very unsatisfactory end to the case.

Downing added: "I believe, sir, that paragliding is a specialist activity and that on the Island there will be someone who knows this man. You need equipment, and the right conditions. It is not the kind of sport you can do on your own, so it attracts attention. Let's talk to some of the people who do it."

"He must've been driven to the Fort by someone?" said Bruno.

"Maybe he was, sir, but all of the equipment you'd need to fly can be carried in a large backpack. So, he could have walked from where he parked his car or motorbike and flown his paraglider back to his bike and been away before anyone got down to Sandown beach. Or it could have been further away, say on the concrete seaside pedestrian walkway beside the stretch of beach between Sandown Pier and Hope Beach in Shanklin."

"We'll research paragliding tomorrow after reporting to the Chief," said Bruno. "We must keep Barlow close to us on this case, because he will have questions to answer to the Chief Constable, so everything we are doing must seem right to him."

*

It was a late supper that night with Janet, to whom Bruno revealed the whole day's activity. To escape by paraglider was straight out of James Bond, she thought, and proved that they were dealing with someone with a physical prowess, high intelligence, resourcefulness and a huge amount of daring. Assuming the same man had met both Wladimir Pivotkin and Caleb White, surely there were not many people who possessed motorbikes and paragliders – and had the facilities to store, maintain and use them. Janet's conclusion was that he lived remotely on the Island, where he was not overlooked by curious neighbours and had space to store his equipment so he could go about these activities, including the murder, undetected.

Chapter 23

On Friday morning, Bruno reported the latest developments to Chief Superintendent Barlow; surprisingly he commented favourably on their effort and organisation.

Bruno then phoned Carl Bullivent and thanked him for his assistance with his introductions to both George Deutsch and Jack Fisher, and to gauge his reaction to Caleb White's successful recovery of the stolen *Book of Mormon*, with which he was delighted. His information had opened up both the south coast Jewish and Latter-day Saint communities to them, and had effectively resulted in the return of the sacred volume to the Southampton Mormon Church, albeit at a substantial gain to the murder suspect of £10,000, and sadly leaving the police no wiser as to the person's identity.

"Paragliding is a specialist sport," claimed Bullivent.

Bruno agreed. "From Caleb's description, the killer's launch from the ramparts of Bembridge Fort could only have been made by an experienced glider with expert knowledge of the launch platform. He must have had previous access to the Fort, which is normally securely padlocked. Although wind conditions on the night were perfect, paragliding at dusk would have required great skill to guarantee a safe landing, notwithstanding the well-lit esplanade. We'll be investigating how many paragliders there are on the Island. It will be a very small circle."

Bullivent offered, "I can speak to the South of England paragliding schools to find out who the most renowned gliders are," he said.

It was another offer to help the police find the killer, who, the longer he remained at large, the less likelihood there existed of finding him. They were looking for a thief who threatened others, possibly in the same or similar business to Calafifi. They had no time to lose to prevent another attack, or even a murder.

Having exhausted their enquiries amongst the persons of interest on their list, they felt as if they were going back to the start of their investigation. Nothing they had discovered so far led them to think they were about to make an arrest, for example. This led them to question their police methods. Could they have acted differently? Was something about this murder staring them in the face? It was possible that they had taken completely the wrong turn from day one.

*

Andy arranged with Bembridge Council Public Works Department to have access to Bembridge Fort in the early afternoon. They had avoided this before the Thursday evening meeting, for fear of an informal leak, which could have derailed the plans and put off the suspect from coming to the rendezvous. Bruno and Andy had to examine the position above the entrance to the Fort from which the paraglider had launched himself in search of a clue.

They were met at the gate by Ralph Stone, driving a Bembridge Council van. When Ralph Stone attempted to open the padlock on the wire gate, the key that he had brought would not fit the padlock.

His response was immediate. "This padlock has been changed! This isn't even a Council-issue lock. I've got some cutters in the van. I'll have to cut it off and replace it," he said.

Whilst he was searching for his cutters, Bruno took a small plastic bag from his car and placed it over the padlock, so that Ralph did not touch it while he snapped through the padlock bar.

"Good thinking, sir," said Andy, realising the padlock could prove important evidence as it must have been replaced on the gate by the suspect.

It took one pinch from Ralph's wire-cutters to open the lock covered by the small plastic bag, which Bruno pocketed carefully for forensic examination. An eerie, damp, steep tunnel rose up to the open area, which was 100 metres square in the centre, indicated by a sign as the Parade Ground. The Fort was a formidable structure surrounded by a high grassy bank, which had proved the launch platform for the paraglider. The view down to the beach in the distance was not only beautiful but showed a safe landing place for a glider. Bruno imagined that, depending on wind conditions, in five minutes he could be on the beach and in five more onto his motorbike or into his car, which he might have carefully parked out of sight late in the afternoon, before any police arrived on Sandown Esplanade. If he had had an accomplice waiting for him, it could have been even quicker.

Having examined the paraglider launch area they climbed down several flights of steps to the trench, which was dry, having never been a moat filled with water around a medieval castle. There they retrieved Caleb White's mobile telephone, undamaged, and, after a short search, the original Council padlock that the killer had clearly discarded from the Fort gate.

"We're not looking for any ordinary paraglider, but a very experienced one, and one who probably also rides a motorbike," said Andy.

"That narrows the field significantly," said Bruno. "What a sense of exhilaration our killer must have had as he took off, leaving Caleb White standing in front of the locked Fort gates, watching him escape with £10,000. It's an exciting sport, not for the fainthearted," he said to Andy.

Investigating the origin of the replacement padlock, and the prints on it and the cut off original council issue lock were Bruno's next actions.

Hughes Ironmongers in Newport was a short walk from the police station. When he presented the non-council padlock to the shop assistant, she conducted him to their padlock selection. It took Bruno seconds to find an identical padlock for £6.50, which he purchased.

At the till he asked the salesperson if she remembered selling one of these recently. She couldn't. However, she keyed into her computerised till system the stock item number from the plastic wallet and confirmed that an identical padlock had been sold from the Newport shop three days previously. It could well have been the one used at the Fort.

That suggested that the killer had arrived at the Fort early, cut off the old padlock to gain entry, thrown the old lock into the trench, entered the Fort and put on the new padlock. He had then prepared his glider out of sight on the ramparts, in readiness to meet Caleb White, complete the transaction and fly away.

Back at the station, Bruno called Inspector Tommy Dodd and asked him to examine the padlocks he had taken from the Fort for fingerprints. He also gave him Caleb White's mobile telephone to be checked for prints before returning it to White by personal messenger. While Andy chased a reply from the Firearms team in Portsmouth and researched the Island paraglider and motorcycle clubs, Bruno paid a visit to Simeon's Bookshop.

*

Annabel was busy, but Chloe, her new assistant, afforded her the luxury, as she put it, to sit with a cup of tea and plan the development of the business. She said she was reluctant to let the reputation of the business as a specialist in religious books lapse with the demise of Simeon. She was confident that her own experience in the Jewish Library in Israel, together with what she had learned from Simeon, would enable her to continue the business very successfully. She was determined to sustain and maintain the valuable goodwill created during Simeon's stewardship. To that end she was studying a mountain of literature on the subject.

"Has Mrs Calafifi advanced her plans to move back to North London?" said Bruno.

"Yes, term ended on Wednesday for her two sons.

They will move during their Easter holidays which last for almost three weeks," she said.

"And the business?"

"I have offered to run the business for her until probate has been granted, on the condition she sells it to me at market value as soon as possible after that. Otherwise, I will leave now and open my own shop in new premises just along the High Street. She has agreed to my suggestion, so I shall stay and develop Simeon's Bookshop here."

Miriam Calafifi was clearly taking advantage of her deal with Nathan Philips in Bembridge, in which he'd agreed to delay completion until her situation had normalised, and thereby stringing Annabel along. Annabel's arrangement falsely appeared to guarantee her the purchase of the business once probate had been granted, meaning that Simeon's murder actually conferred a significant benefit to her, provided the deal with Miriam Calafifi was true. There was a degree of ruthlessness in her dealing with Miriam Calafifi, who she assumed was in a weak position as a seller. Little did she know.

"On the day of Simeon's murder you said that you went straight home to prepare a meal for a guest?"

"Correct, Chief Inspector, and on my way home I stopped at the Co-op to buy food. Sam Trent visits me on Tuesdays. He brings the latest draft chapter of a book we are writing, which we then edit together, amend and rewrite."

"What is the book about?"

"The mother of Alexander the Great, which I research for him. But you know all this. He writes the narrative from a son's perspective – as in Alexander the Great's perspective – and then we edit his work."

"How is it going?"

"Very well. I'm pretty involved in it. By editing you could say re-writing."

"Remind me, what is Sam Trent's role at Ryde School?"

"He teaches Latin and Greek, and he takes sport for the senior boys."

"So, he must be quite fit?"

"I would say so. He is a young man, Chief Inspector."

"The person we are looking for in connection with the book thefts is young and fit. Perhaps you would go through your records and see if a name stands out, particularly if they live on the Island? I think most of your customers are of an older demographic, so I hope any younger men might stand out?"

"Do you think the murderer is an Island resident, Chief Inspector?"

"The evidence we have gathered so far suggests that the person we are looking for in connection with the thefts and the murder is a man, an Islander who has learned enough about the book trade to find a buyer," he said. "You might help us find Simeon's killer if you can try and identify the evening visitor to Simeon on 28th February."

Bruno left the bookshop feeling he had achieved something, but he wasn't sure what. Her unwillingness or inability to contribute anything helpful toward his investigation was beginning to annoy him but was possibly somewhat enlightening.

*

Back at the station Andy read out the report he'd received from the Portsmouth Police Firearms team on the bullet he had sent for analysis.

"It had been fired from a semi-automatic handgun, a Beretta M9. The cartridge is a 9mm or 9 × 19 Parabellum. It is a weapon used by the US Military and considered to be accurate and high performance. It does, however, require a gun licence and would only be held by an experienced gun user."

The Portsmouth Police Firearms team had checked the British firearms licence holder database and discovered that this weapon had been licensed to the Portsmouth Rifle Club, which closed ten years ago. Then all the weapons and ammunition were sold at auction through a licenced auction house, which had unfortunately since closed down and so could not provide details of the sale. The Beretta M9 was a weapon sought after by collectors and private buyers.

Andy's research into paragliding had produced a pile of information on how and where on the Island the sport could be enjoyed. A map of the locations that were suitable for the experienced pilots and a couple of telephone numbers for individuals who were prepared and accredited to teach people how to paraglide on a one-on-one basis. The Island Paragliding Club produced an excellent daily weather bulletin on the wind status, available online for anyone going gliding daily. However, there were no club details with membership names, as the pilots came from all over the South of England to the Island, because of the favourable weather conditions.

Andy summarised to Bruno what they knew about the thief and murder suspect so far. "He appears to be aged between twenty and forty, to have an athletic build – a narrow waist, broad shoulders, a flat stomach, tall in stature. This description as reported by Wladimir Pivotkin, an intelligent observer, can be relied upon. It is consistent with Caleb White's description too. He can ride a motorcycle off-road across different terrain and he knows the Island roads well. He carries a gun and has demonstrated that he was prepared to use it. He is an experienced paraglider pilot. He is confident in his behaviour and does not appear to have an accomplice, although we don't know that for sure. And now he has vanished, making our chance of finding him difficult. He has potentially risked his liberty for a mere £50,000 for the Talmud and £10,000 for the *Book of Mormon*. So why did he do it, and what connection does this person have with the book trade?"

Bruno was thinking.

"Even though we seem to have gone forward in our investigation, we are at that point where I think there are so many unanswered questions," Andy added.

"Yes, but that is always the case so don't worry," Bruno reassured him. "Was the theft planned? Was the murder intended? Was the motive just to make £60,000 – or indeed as much as possible? The proceeds from the sale of the Talmud couldn't have been enough, so he needed more from selling the *Book of Mormon*. At this particular moment, I wonder what the suspect will be thinking. Has this crime been undertaken by a murderer with a big ego, who will be basking in the satisfaction of having succeeded? Or will he think he has failed? A murder for £60,000? What other motive could there be?"

"Where does that all leave us, sir?" said Andy.

Bruno didn't answer. He was thinking again.

"Who amongst the persons of interest we have seen recently has a motorcycle?" he said.

"Max Carter has a new powerful bike which he is learning to ride, and Nathan Philips has a motorcycle helmet. We've already basically discounted Max for reasons not connected with motorcycles," noted Andy. It was time to revisit Philips.

*

On the thirty-minute drive to Nathan Philips's bookshop they carried on discussing the mentality and intellectual capability of the suspect.

"Every move the suspect has made so far seems to have paid off, but his luck cannot hold out forever," said Andy, staring out of the window.

"We have missed two opportunities to catch him. The first we didn't even know about; the second – well, we were very unlucky with that," said Bruno.

"The newspapers have little interest at the moment," said Andy.

"That's because the details of yesterday's dramatic escape have not been released by the police press office to the *County Press*," remarked Bruno.

As soon as they arrived at the Bembridge Bookshop, Nathan showed a keen interest in how they were progressing. Bruno described the two missed opportunities at St. Catherine's Oratory and Bembridge Fort. Andy was charged with watching Philips very carefully while he, Bruno, spoke, even though they believed that Nathan

Philips had no motive to kill Simeon Calafifi, mainly because of the bad publicity that would then surround the bookshop he had bought and because of the complications it would add to the purchase.

Bruno amplified his theme. "The common thread in these two escapes is that they are intended by the perpetrator to be noticed. You could say that he wants to demonstrate his ingenuity, his masculinity and his skills. He carries a gun without the intention of using it for harm, as far as we know. He wants to show that he is a seriously clever operator, with an intellectual flourish."

Bruno alluded to the fact that both Caleb White and Wladimir Pivotkin had braved the meetings with the suspect and had been terrified. Both were on a mission to preserve a sacred volume, which both succeeded in doing perfectly. They were responding on behalf of their respective religions and, if they had not survived their ordeals, they would have been canonised as martyrs.

"You're right, Chief Inspector. When their respective religious congregations learn about Pivotkin's exploits in returning the Talmud to Lithuania, and White's rescue of the original *Book of Mormon*, these two individuals will become heroes," Nathan replied.

"Nathan, when we last visited, my ever-observant colleague Detective Sergeant Bowen here spotted a motorcycle helmet on your table. Are you a member of a motorcycle club?"

"I'm not that kind of enthusiast. I have a 1000-cc Honda, which is a powerful bike, but I regard the power of the bike as a safety feature. It enables me to accelerate through gaps in traffic, and to escape situations which

246

might otherwise result in a crash. I never exceed the speed limits, and I never carry a pillion passenger. I travel all over the South of England visiting booksellers, buying and selling by motorcycle. I can normally park on a pavement or outside a premises, do my business and get back in good time. And in answer to your next question, I don't know anyone else who owns a bike on the Island. I bought my bike from that main dealership for new motorbikes in Ryde. They might be able to help if you have an accurate description of the man you are looking for."

"Thank you," said Andy, "but the little information we have does not include a sighting of any specific motorbike, so I doubt he could be of any help."

"Any ideas on the paraglider?" asked Bruno.

"I know quite a bit about this because I have a friend involved in paragliding," Nathan's words got the attention of both Bruno and Andy who weren't necessarily expecting a direct hit. "A lot of that goes on over the cliffs that stretch from Whitecliff Bay, Culver, Sandown, Shanklin and Luccombe. It's usually windy there, and it's safe. If you fly beyond Luccombe, the prevailing winds will always bring you back. There are something like fourteen or fifteen different take-off areas all across the South Downs on the Island. Some are attached to B&B hotels for visitors who come and remain while the winds last. Most of the paragliders you see are visitors whose home surroundings cannot offer or allow paragliding. The most important thing in this dangerous sport is safety, and the Island is a very safe flying area. There are a couple of recognised flying schools. The biggest is High Adventure Flying, based on a farm at Wellow in the north-west of the Island."

Nathan went on, "This friend of mine works for the National Trust. He lives in Luccombe Village and his house has views over various take-off sites that are on Trust land. He might be of some help. Shall I call him and arrange a meeting? I won't explain your mission. He will tell you more than I can."

"An introduction is always an icebreaker. Yes, please, we can meet him tomorrow."

"I know him because he is a local author and writes about the Island coast. His name is Bradfield Gittley. He lives in a cottage high on the cliffs at Luccombe, next to Haddon's Pits, which stretches down to the cliff edge. It is a National Trust paragliders' take-off station."

Nathan tried phoning him, but Gittley was out. He promised to try again later that day and introduce them.

"I'll phone you, Chief Inspector, and give you a time."

*

On their journey back to the Police Station, Nathan called. He had succeeded in contacting Bradfield Gittley who had invited them to call on him at home at any time the following morning. Nathan gave them Gittley's contact details. Andy was confident that they could get an insight into the escape from the Fort by visiting paragliding schools.

"Let's see what Bradfield Gittley has to tell us about paragliding on the Luccombe Downs tomorrow," said Andy.

"Tomorrow is Saturday, so there should be some activity," Bruno noted. He reflected on the fact that the next day was the first day of April. He felt the passing of time and would have liked to have made, in his opinion, more progress by now than he felt they had done.

Forensics' response to their examination of the padlocks confirmed thumb and forefinger prints clearly taken, but none matched prints discovered on the safe door in Simeon's offices, from which the books had been stolen, or any other prints from the shop.

"That is kind of a win," said Andy. "Fingerprint evidence could prove to be crucial."

"Before tomorrow," said Bruno, "I want to visit Simeon's Bookshop this evening as Mrs Catchpole arrives, because I want to watch her arrive from a distance and speak to her as she opens the shop. The time between the killer's departure, and her arrival at 6:45 p.m. was very short. If the killer knew the expected time of Mrs Catchpole's arrival, they would have had to leave in haste. Anyway, with the passing of time, she might have remembered something that she hasn't told us before."

Andy remarked, "The profile of the suspect thief we have is based solely on the descriptions given by Pivotkin and White. They are similar enough to conclude they are the same person. But is this the person Simeon was meeting at 6 p.m. on 28th February? We don't yet have anything concrete to say that the person selling the stolen books is the murderer."

Bruno replied, "Agreed. Just going back to the shop, for a minute. The time of the killer's arrival and departure is so far based upon guesswork and based upon the times given us by Annabel Wilson and Sheila Catchpole. Annabel Wilson says that the shop closed at 5:30 p.m. and she left at 5:45 p.m. Sheila arrived one hour later.

Annabel told us Simeon said he was expecting someone at 6 p.m. We're assuming that Calafifi knew his caller and therefore knew his killer, but we have no evidence of that. Likewise we have no evidence that the person described by Pivotkin and White is the killer. He is undoubtedly a clever person, but is he someone Simeon would meet in his office after hours? If not, then the person delivering the books and collecting the money is not the killer. He may be working for the killer. That does not lessen our search for both, because both people have acted against the law. Furthermore, if we catch the person who sold the books to Pivotkin and White, I think we catch the killer."

*

Bruno and Andy arrived in Shanklin at 6:30 p.m. They parked opposite Simeon's bookshop. It was closed. They waited fifteen minutes for Mrs Catchpole to turn up, which she did, on time. Whilst she was searching for her key, they stepped out of the car and reminded her, in the nicest way, who they were.

"Oh, Chief Inspector! And you, Sergeant Andy. You gave me such a fright! I don't know what I'd have done if it wasn't you."

"Can we come in?" asked Bruno.

"Of course. What can I do for you?"

"We just want to look around and replay certain parts of the crime. It would help us if you could walk us through what you did on the night of the murder."

"After unlocking the door, I put the keys on the inside of the mortice lock. The Yale lock clicked shut automatically and I turned the mortice as I always do. For safety." She seemed unaware of the irony in her words.

"I switched the shop lights on and walked through the shop, past the two unlit offices on the left of the building. Poor Mr Simeon was in one of them. Then I moved on through the glass-panelled door to the back of the offices. There was the kitchen, with a double sink with cups and saucers, mugs and several glasses for me to wash up…"

Bruno interrupted her as she led them into the kitchen, "Mrs Catchpole, I'm just wondering, how many sets of office keys are there?"

"There's my set, Annabel's set, and Simeon has a set. That's all I know of," she said.

"Could you take us outside to look at the car park?"

"I'll show you," she said, and took them to the back door and opened it with her key.

"Mrs Catchpole, I see spaces to park four cars."

"Mr Simeon and Annabel used two of them."

"Mrs Catchpole, please now show us what you did when you found the body."

"I saw Mr Simeon right there, slumped over his desk. I thought he must be asleep as the lights were off and it was dead quiet. When I couldn't wake him up, I ran to the front door, turned my key in the mortice, opened the Yale and so the door, and then left the shop quick as I could."

"Are you certain that the back door was unlocked, and the alarm had not been set?"

"Yes, Chief Inspector. I told you that when I rang you. I think the killer must have left by the back door. The alarm was usually set by Mr Simeon when he left for home," she said.

"But not by Annabel when she left at 5:45 p.m.?"

"No, she wouldn't set the alarm if Mr Simeon was still here, would she?" she said. "I am not sure what time she leaves exactly. I might expect her to lock the door but not necessarily. If someone was still in the building, she probably just shut the door, Chief Inspector. But I told you that the back door wasn't just unlocked and clicked shut, it was actually open. The Yale lock button had been moved across. So anyone could have just walked in. I clicked it across after I did the bins."

"Thank you, Mrs Catchpole, I think we will leave you to carry on. Thank you for being so helpful and have a good weekend."

As they left the shop by the rear door and walked down the cobbled street, Bruno said, "If Annabel locked the back door, Simeon must have unlocked it to admit his visitor."

"Unless she did not lock it?" said Andy.

"I think she said that she shut it but did not lock it," said Bruno. "We will re-confirm that with her. Although it doesn't really matter because it seems that the murderer entered and left through the back door. There are then three options: if the door was locked by Annabel, Simeon would have to unlock it to let the caller in. If the door was just clicked shut by Annabel, Simeon would still have had to open it. If the door was left open, with the Yale pushed across, the killer could just have walked in. Did Simeon do this? Did Annabel do this? Or did the killer do it – maybe as he entered to ensure that his escape was as easy as possible?"

Andy liked and agreed with Bruno's summary of the options for the back door.

"What did our meeting with Sheila Catchpole tell us that we didn't already know, sir?" said Andy rhetorically. "Not much at all. The killer must have known she arrives at 6:45 p.m. That's weird for a stranger to know the cleaner's movements. I think our biggest problem is that we have no record of who the person was who had an after-work appointment with Simeon? What happened to his diary, probably stored on his missing mobile 'phone, which could tell us? Where is the murder weapon? Why did they kill him? And could this killer strike again?"

"Actually, we have no record that there actually was a person who had an after-work appointment with Simeon," said Bruno. "Just Annabel Wilson's word for it, really. Which reminds me – we must see Sam Trent in person."

"Okay, sir, let's consider that the real motive for this killing was the elimination of the bookseller. Yes, let's say that this murder was about Simeon Calafifi. It was personal. Taking the books after the murder might have been intended to throw us off the track. Was to make it look like a thief murdered Simeon for the books?" suggested Andy.

"And let's be clear about the facts that we know about the evening of 28th February. The only person who knew Simeon was waiting for a visitor after 6 p.m. was Annabel. We know from the CCTV footage that the only person to enter the shop after it had closed was Mrs Catchpole via the front entrance at 6:45 p.m. The killer, for want of a better word, came and went through the rear door, and would have been admitted by Simeon. The killer had, say, thirty minutes to engage with Simeon, stab him to death, and leave the premises in darkness carrying the Talmud, the *Book of Mormon*, and the cash takings. To undertake this robbery and the murder in this manner, in this time, in this window, required a knowledge of the shop and the whereabouts of the books, and the safe key," Bruno pointed out. "Apart from Simeon, the only person with that knowledge was Annabel."

"But we don't suspect her of killing Simeon, do we, sir?" asked Andy.

"Not of the murder, but she could have provided the killer with information accidently or with a slip of the tongue to a customer in the shop. If she is in any way involved with Simeon's murder, then we are still searching for her male accomplice. That's why we should see Sam Trent. Nothing has come up on any records so far that he is a paraglider or a motorcyclist, but we need to confirm that for sure."

Andy was ready to go home. It was Friday night, and he was looking forward to fish and chips. "I'll pick you up tomorrow morning, sir, at 9 a.m. Then we'll go and visit Bradfield Gittley in Luccombe, to see if we can catch a paraglider."

Chapter 24

Bradfield Gittley lived in a modernised house at the highest point of Knock Cliff, with a view of Shanklin and Sandown to the north and Luccombe Bay to the south. Either side of his house was grass and National Trust shrub farmland, called Haddon's Pits because of its downward slope towards the edge of Knock Cliff. It was a popular take-off point for paragliders. Bradfield Gittley had clearly been briefed by Nathan Philips as to what this was about.

"Good morning, detectives. Bradfield Gittley," he announced, holding out his hand, to which both detectives responded. "I understand you're looking for a particular paraglider?"

Andy said, "It is clear that the person who paraglided off the Bembridge Fort ramparts at dusk two days ago was an experienced pilot, very sure of making a successful flight. He was also very sure of his intended destination. Once he'd cleared the road, he rose above it and took off towards Sandown beach. In doing so, he escaped the police cordon we had set up around Bembridge Fort. We think if he had landed on Yaverland beach, we'd have caught him, the same with Sandown – certainly on the beach, before you get to the town," said Andy.

"In your opinion, Mr Gittley, could he have flown further than Sandown that evening?" asked Bruno.

"Certainly," replied Gittley, who then explained what he knew and had observed about paragliding.

"Let me describe him to you," said Andy. "He is 6 feet tall with an athletic physique, aged from twenty to forty. We have no facial description. We believe that he rides a motorcycle and knows the Island very well. The only identification we have for the paraglider is that his equipment is blue on top and white underneath."

Gittley replied, "You know that before anyone paraglides, they must call Sandown Airport and take a weather forecast. Last week the weather was perfect for paragliding, and an experienced paraglider would have known this. Do you think he might sometimes fly from this take-off point at Haddon's Pits?"

"We don't know. But what I'm asking is this: could he have landed, for example, this far away from Culver to guarantee his escape?" said Bruno.

"Yes, I think so, if he was familiar with the landing zone in the dark. Difficult, yes. Dangerous, yes. Impossible, no. So, yes, if the wind was in the right direction, he could have done," said Gittley. "I can confirm online the weather for last Thursday evening. You say he rides a motorcycle?"

"Yes, sir."

"I will look out for that too. I have your details, gentlemen. I am going to keep my eyes and ears open, and I will call you if I've anything to report."

*

Bruno knew Shanklin very well. As it was Saturday, on their way back towards Newport they took the opportunity of calling on his eighty-year-old mother who lived in a flat in Hope Road, which is the road that leads to Shanklin Beach. She was reading the newspaper, trying to work out if any of the stories was an April Fool's Day joke, and was pleased to see her son and his colleague. She never tired of hearing about the Island Murder Squad. Bruno introduced his mother, Emma-May, to Detective Sergeant Andy Bowen, whose usual ebullience was a gift for older ladies. She took to him immediately.

"Are you working on an interesting case, Andy?"

"We are trying to find the person who killed the bookshop owner in Shanklin."

"How interesting," she said. "I've been into that shop. It's near the bus station and if I have to wait for a bus I go across and usually buy a book. They sometimes have a box of second-hand novels out the front. Who would kill the owner of a bookshop?"

"That's exactly what we are trying to find out."

After discussing the case in more detail Emma-May concluded, "It must have been a person he knew, who wanted something he had," she said. "It's not about books. Bruno, it's about jealousy. A woman, maybe?"

"I shall certainly consider what you've said, Mum," said Bruno.

They stayed for half an hour while Bruno read the meters, heard the update on her wide network of friends, and left with her fondest love to Janet.

Chapter 25

As Bradfield Gittley was looking out of his kitchen window in Luccombe Village, watching two paragliders preparing to take off, another paraglider appeared from Luccombe Down, the high point behind Luccombe Village. The paraglider had arrived from behind Gittley's house, and descended in a wide arc over the sea, Horse Lodge and Knock Cliff, before landing gently beside a rucksack. As the paraglider touched down, Gittley noticed the sail colours matched the description given to him by the detectives: white and blue. He couldn't believe what he was seeing. He immediately grabbed his phone and called Detective Chief Inspector Peach. So it was on Sunday morning at 9 a.m. that a call was received on Bruno's mobile phone from Bradfield Gittley. At that time, Bruno's phone was turned off as it always was when Janet and he attended the 9 a.m. communion service at their local church, hence the phone was unanswered.

Meanwhile the pilot was folding and packing his glider into a rucksack.

Gittley decided that he had to do something to discover the identity of this paraglider, who would vanish within a few minutes. He grabbed his keys and climbed into his car. He set off and turned down Luccombe Road towards Haddon's Pits just in time to see the paraglider, his equipment neatly packed into his backpack, set off on a motorcycle 100 yards in front of his car. He was now at a loss at what to do apart from follow the motorcyclist until he had reached his destination. In his excited rush to leave the house he had left his 'phone on the table next to a half-eaten boiled egg.

Keeping a safe distance, Gittley followed the motorcyclist along the road towards Sandown. He noted the registration number of the motorbike which he would be able to give to the police.

Of course, the man on the bike might be an innocent paraglider catching the wind while it was still blowing, as surfers do any time during the day when the winds are right. At the first traffic light, at the top of Shanklin town, outside Daish's Hotel, Gittley, four cars back, was stopped as the lights changed while the motorcyclist continued. The motorcyclist had turned left and proceeded along Victoria Avenue, but Gittley lost him. He searched Victoria Avenue, along with the adjoining roads, but saw nothing of the bike or the rider.

Gittley drove around for nearly an hour, to no avail. Back home, he finally succeeded in getting through to Bruno and explained exactly what had happened and gave him the number on the bike registration plate.

Bruno thanked him profusely for his effort and promised to identify the owner of the bike from DVLA records first thing on Monday. What a co-incidence and what luck, thought Bruno. Maybe the tide was turning on the perpetrator of the crime at Simeon's Bookshop?

Chapter 26

On Monday morning, Bruno and Andy were at their desks very early, by 7 a.m. Bruno had texted Andy the afternoon before to share the news from Bradfield Gittley. Both detectives displayed a mix of nerves and excitement. Bruno called the DVLA to give the motorcycle registration. The silence at the other end of the phone seemed to last an eternity while he waited to hear the name and address of the owner.

"Mr Jonathan Cladmore, The Meadows, Ferry Road, Fishbourne, Isle of Wight," came the reply.

*

A lady, who Bruno guessed was in her mid-fifties, opened the front door to a substantial detached house a few hundred yards from the entrance to the car ferry terminal.

"Good morning. Can I help you?" she asked, surprised to see two policemen standing on her doorstep on a Monday morning.

"Good morning, madam. Is Mr Jonathan Cladmore in? We're from Newport Police Station," said Andy. "Detective Chief Inspector Peach and Detective Sergeant Bowen," he added, each holding up the accepted identity to her.

"Perhaps you'd better come in," she said. "Is Jonathan in trouble? Is he okay?"

"Yes, we haven't come with any bad news, we'd just like to ask him some questions," ventured Bruno.

"Jonathan is my son, but he doesn't live here anymore. He moved to a new job in London two months ago."

"Was he on the Island yesterday morning?"

"No, but I called him at his home in London mid-morning. He was definitely in London yesterday. He said he was meeting his friends in Battersea for a pub lunch."

"We want to speak to him about his motorcycle."

"Oh, if that's what this is about, I can help you. He sold his motorbike two months ago, literally a couple of days before he went to live in London."

"Have you any idea who he sold it to?"

"It was to a man who answered his advert in the local paper. I don't know his name. I would call my son, but he is at work just now, so I will give you his number and, if you like, you can ask him yourself."

"Okay," said Andy. "We'll do that. I presume you are Mrs Cladmore?"

"Correct, Chief Inspector. Sarah Cladmore."

"Did you by any chance see the man who bought the motorbike?"

"Yes, I was here when he called."

"Can you describe him to us?"

"Let me think. I would need to remember. Perhaps thirty-five, older than Jonathan I would say, tall, fairly well-dressed. One thing, he had the same size head as my son, because he didn't come with a helmet, so Jonathan gave him his, which fitted perfectly."

"Was he alone?"

"No, a woman drove him here, but she stayed in her car."

"Can you describe her?"

"I am not sure about her age, Chief Inspector, but she was attractive, blonde, I think."

"Did you notice what car was she driving?"

"I can't help you there. You will have to ask Jonathan. I don't really know much about cars. The sale took about an hour, during which time the buyer went for a short test-ride. I know he paid cash, and that was it. He spoke to the woman before they left, but she never got out of her car, even while the man was test driving the bike."

"Thank you, Mrs Cladmore. You've been extremely helpful. We will call Jonathan."

"Is everything all right?" she said.

"Absolutely nothing for you or your son to worry about. We'd just like the name and address of the man he sold his bike to."

*

Jonathan Cladmore answered Andy's lunchtime call and gave him a name of the man who bought his bike: Alan Bristow of 18 Campbell Road, Ryde. The police checked the house. It was a large property, split into bedsits. One of the people living there was able to provide the details of the owner. He was a helpful old man, who lived nearby, and who was able to confirm that none of the tenants was now or ever had been called Alan Bristow.

"That name and address shows that the buyer of the bike found it necessary to use a false name. In turn that suggests, as much as two months ago, the purchaser might have had it in mind to use the bike as part of some kind of criminal activity," suggested Andy.

"Although you would be surprised how many people give a false name and address for the sake of it. Sometimes, when asked for an address – whether they have a valid reason for not giving it or they don't – they just blurt out the first road that comes to mind. That might have been this person's reaction. Who knows? I think we should drive to where Bradfield Gittley lost him on Sunday morning. I don't believe the motorcyclist knew that Gittley was following him and therefore I don't think he was trying to give him the slip. More likely he knows this area well and was going to a property in this area. We can drive around Victoria Avenue, which consists of flats and substantial private houses, it's a really nice part of Shanklin to live in."

Bruno and Andy spent thirty minutes combing the streets in the immediate vicinity in search of a parked motorbike but saw nothing. Andy parked the car and asked, "What is our next move, sir?"

"The only person on the fringe of this investigation we have not eliminated is Sam Trent. He should be back from his Italian trip now. The events of the last week or so have rather shifted the focus away from him but, on reflection, I think we now need to see him as soon as possible," replied Bruno.

Andy reminded Bruno, "When I was looking through our to-do list last week, I called the school secretary to re-confirm the Classics trip dates and those of the Easter holiday break. She is obviously aware now that we really want to speak to him. In fact, she offered to give me his CV and I accepted."

Andy opened his smartphone and read out from the email attachment he'd received from the school. "Sam Trent is twenty-eight. He's from Abingdon in Oxfordshire. He graduated from Loughborough University with a degree in Sports Science and English. After a PGCE, he moved to Croydon to take up a position as an English and Sports teacher at a preparatory school. Because he had studied Latin for A level, he started teaching Latin too. After a few years there, he had proven his capability to teach English, Sport and Latin. When he applied to Ryde School, his application was accepted. He has been living at the school in staff accommodation since he moved to the Isle of Wight. This is his second year at the school."

"Seems like a decent CV," Bruno agreed. "Let's get over there now."

*

It didn't take them long to find Sam Trent. He was in the staff accommodation eating tea and toast in the staff kitchen.

"We would like to ask you a few questions, Mr Trent. We have been making routine visits, to everyone who is remotely connected to Simeon Calafifi. We know that you have a professional and personal relationship with Annabel Wilson, who was Simeon Calafifi's colleague. We also know, confirmed by yourself, that you were with Annabel on the evening of Tuesday 28th February. I appreciate that it was almost five weeks ago now, but could you run through what happened that evening? The more detail, the better."

"Sure. On Tuesdays I go to the school gym and work out straight after school finishes. Then I tend not to even shower but cycle – fast – on my road bike to Shanklin. I'll shower at Annabel's, and we'll have dinner and work on the book we are collaborating on."

"Can you talk us through your evening after you left the gym?"

"That's what I normally do, but on that Tuesday, it was different, Chief Inspector."

"Different? What do you mean by different?" Andy almost spat out the words.

"Well, on Tuesday morning before school started, she called me and asked if I could meet her in the car park at the back of the shop at 5:45 p.m. She said not to cycle but to come on the bus. I agreed, because of what had happened on the Saturday before, although it meant missing my gym session and having to get the bus rather than cycling. "

"What had happened on the Saturday?" asked Andy, but Bruno interrupted and told Trent to continue with the events of the Tuesday.

"So, I finished lessons, got changed, got my stuff together and then I caught the 5:05 p.m. bus to Shanklin. It's due at Shanklin Rail Station just before twenty to six, and then it's just a couple of minutes to walk from the station to the shop. Unfortunately, just outside Ryde there was an accident that blocked the road, and I didn't arrive in Shanklin until 6:15 p.m. She was waiting for me outside the shop at the back in the car park. She hadn't texted or called to see where I was. She was just waiting there. She told me to drive her car home, via the Co-op, and to wait for her there. She was irritated and said she was going to meet someone in the Conservative Club for really a short discussion. She gave me the key to her house and said, 'I'll meet you there in forty minutes maximum.' I wasn't too bothered. It meant I could choose what we ate in Co-op, and she'd given me her card to pay for the food anyway, which was a win-win. And if she was back home at 7 p.m. or around 7 p.m., which she was actually, that was usually the time we got together on a Tuesday anyway. All it meant was that I didn't do my gym work or get my cycling in. Oh, and I'd need to get a taxi back to Ryde late, when we'd finished working."

Bruno noticed Sam Trent's commitment to physical activity and his very athletic build. He was young and strong.

"You didn't think to tell us any of this earlier?" asked Andy.

"I haven't met you before. I thought Annabel would have told you this anyway. It's not like I haven't told you this or I've avoided you deliberately."

"You referred to something that happened on the Saturday before that. It would have been Saturday 25th February. Could you elaborate?"

"Usually, if I have no school sports commitment on Saturdays, I will cycle over to the shop in Shanklin and have a sandwich with her. As far as I know, Simeon tended not work at the shop on Saturdays so I could kind of hang out in there. On that Saturday when I arrived, she had discovered some news that really upset her. It's fair to say she was really pissed off. Fortunately, the shop was not overly busy, so I spent the afternoon trying to calm her down – unsuccessfully, I might add."

"What was the news?" asked Bruno.

"It seems she had found some paperwork in a file, which showed that Simeon had made arrangements to try to sell the bookshop through some agents in London, dated last November. Annabel claimed that Simeon had promised, if he ever sold, to give her first refusal. She thought this was going against that."

Bruno and Andy were extremely interested.

"But the correspondence that made her the angriest, which was in the same file, was an offer from Nathan Philips, the bloke over in Bembridge, to buy the bookshop from Simeon and it appeared that Simeon had accepted this offer in writing. It's fair to say that she was seething."

"Did she say that she was going to speak to Simeon about this?" Andy asked.

"She spoke as if she was even more pissed off about Nathan Philips, as if he should have spoken to her before he'd agreed to buy Simeon's business. She seems to know Philips."

"How?" said Andy.

Trent didn't answer Andy's question but just shrugged before continuing. "I eventually spent Saturday evening with her. She calmed down and so we went to the Village Inn. I had quite a few beers and she had loads of wine, and we ate there. Afterwards we walked back to her house in Victoria Avenue. I'd left my bike there before we went for a meal, and so I stayed the night with her. She has plenty of room. We'd drunk too much for her to drive me to Ryde, same with me cycling."

"Did she tell you what she was going to do? Was she planning to confront Simeon? And what about Nathan Philips?"

"On Sunday morning, she seemed normal. I cycled back to Ryde and hoped that by Tuesday evening she'd have accepted it. I mean, she had a job, she's really well qualified. Even if she wasn't going to be able to buy the bookshop, she could easily start another one."

"Can we go back to Tuesday 28th February now? When she arrived home from the Conservative Club, how did Annabel seem to you?"

"Tired, preoccupied, not that eager to start work on the book. We discussed some aspects but finished earlier than usual."

"Did she talk about who she met at the Conservative Club?"

"Nope."

"Did she mention anything further about what she had had found out on Saturday 25th?"

"Nope."

"Did you ask anything?"

"No, she just came back from whatever she was doing at the Conservative Club and – well, I was hungry, so I just wanted to get on with dinner, to be honest."

"You are aware that Annabel's employer, Simeon Calafifi, was murdered early on the evening of 28th February, at about the time you were meeting her at the bookshop. We believe that he was killed soon after 6 p.m. We were told that Annabel left the shop at 5:45 p.m. and that the cleaner arrived at 6:45 p.m. In that hour, Mr Calafifi was murdered, and valuable property was stolen, together with approximately £600 in cash. Your connection with Annabel has prompted us to speak to you. We were not aware that you did not go straight to her home that evening. As you met her in the vicinity of the shop, you might have spotted something unusual. It also makes you a person of some considerable interest to us."

"I was flustered at being late because of the bus thing, so I wasn't looking for anything unusual."

"Has Annabel discussed Mr Calafifi's murder with you?" said Andy.

"Only to say that she didn't think you were making much progress."

"Has she ever mentioned the mysterious visitor that Mr Calafifi was expecting on the evening of his murder?"

"No, I haven't seen her much since the murder. Anyway, I've been away."

"Are you sure that she arrived home at 7 p.m. on 28th February?"

"Yes, Chief Inspector, it was about 7. Maybe 7:15, but no later."

"Did you ever meet Mr Calafifi?"

"I met him once, a couple of months ago; I dropped into the shop briefly just as Annabel was leaving. Just an introduction. We didn't have a conversation. I called to pick up a Latin text that I had ordered from the shop. That's when I met him. I like that bookshop. Annabel loves it."

"What do you do in your leisure time?"

"This is a boarding school so there is always some sports activity going on, and I am Head of Sport for the whole school. I like playing games. I love the job, but during term there isn't much leisure time."

"How is your book going?"

"Really well, thanks. We have finished the first draft,

and we have a publisher who is interested in publishing it. That is good news," he said.

With that Bruno decided the interview was over – for now. They left the school, giving Sam Trent strict instructions not to leave the Isle of Wight and to ensure that he was available the next day in case they wanted to speak to him again.

In the school grounds Andy said, "Why didn't you ask him if he had a motorcycle?"

"The same reason I didn't ask him if he was a paraglider. It was our first meeting, let him relax. If he is guilty, he might give himself away."

"What do you make of him, sir?" said Andy.

"He behaved exactly as I would have expected for someone who is guilty, as if butter wouldn't melt in his mouth. Having said that, he is relatively young and open."

"Do you believe he is connected with the murder, sir?"

"My gut feeling is no. I don't think he would have told us she was late home on the 28th, if he'd any connection with the murder. I am puzzled about their relationship though. He is twenty-eight, she is forty-one, writing a book about Alexander the Great's mother. Is there something else? Sex, intimacy, other common interests? What do they talk about when they are alone together?"

"I bet writing the book was her idea," said Andy. "Killing Calafifi would have taken some planning and if it was them, or just him, or just her, they are both serenely calm about it. If we assume they are guilty, what do we need to find out?"

"We need to find the weapon, a motorbike, some kind of paragliding equipment, clothing you would wear to do both of these activities. And of course, what has happened to the money," Bruno replied. "A bank or building society account, newly opened, would require identity, passport or driving licence and a current utility bill. So, a look at their existing financial accounts will tell us something."

"How do we do that, sir?" said Andy.

Bruno answered, "There are official routes but I've got an idea, which could actually kill two birds with one stone, but we need to speak to Mrs Calafifi first."

"Then maybe we let Sam and Annabel carry on as they are for the moment," said Andy.

As they walked back to their car, a further thought occurred to Bruno. "Although Simeon was a distinguished antiquarian book dealer, I would like someone to take a close look at the shop's records during the past twelve months. I am interested in the other books bought by Calafifi at auction or from dealers: what did he buy, what was he sold and by whom, the margin achieved. I want an independent audit of the business for the past year to prove that everything was properly run. We have information and lists given to us by Annabel, but they lack detail, and she is never going to show us discrepancies. I want the whole business re-examined. I'd like someone to look at bank statements, and all the business expenses. Start with the basic questions. If he bought twenty-three books at auction, what were the titles, how much did he pay for each title? If sold, at what price, and if not sold, is it still in stock? We must do this before we interview Annabel and Sam Trent again. If this murder is about money, then it is possible there have been other thefts and sales, and an audit will reveal any discrepancies," Bruno observed.

"I think that's the right approach," said Andy. "We could ask Jim Duncan, our local Chartered Accountant, to do an inspection."

"Good idea," said Bruno, "I'll tell Mrs Calafifi what we are doing. He will take a day or so, and our two suspects will think it is just a routine probate or company valuation related audit conducted by Mrs Calafifi's lawyers. If it throws up discrepancies we can tackle Annabel straight away, confident that Duncan's professional report can be relied on. In the meantime, we shouldn't indicate to either Annabel or Sam Trent that we have any suspicions or concerns about their actions or behaviour."

Chapter 27

Very helpfully, Jim Duncan was available to undertake the audit immediately. Without giving notice to Annabel, he turned up at Simeon's the following morning at shop opening time with supposed instructions from Miriam Calafifi. At first, Annabel claimed to be too busy to co-operate, needing time to prepare, but on the insistence of Jim Duncan, she reluctantly complied with his polite, but firm, requests.

By 4 p.m. Jim Duncan had completed enough of his assignment to covertly give Bruno and Andy a preliminary report, despite Annabel's continued responses that 'all this used to be Mr Calafifi's responsibility'. She claimed to not know much about what happened to the valuable books that he acquired. Some were not recorded in the sales or purchase ledgers and nor were they in stock. There were just sales invoices from dealers and payments through the bank. A significant number of purchases indicated on the bank statements as payments to auctioneers and booksellers amounted to £63,000 for a total of thirty volumes. These ranged in cost from £150 to several thousands and were properly recorded as book purchases. A total of eleven out of thirty were still in stock and nineteen presumably had sold; however, there was no record of onward sale for the nineteen volumes which had cost over £50,000.

Bruno had accepted Annabel's explanation that this part of the business was Calafifi's private domain. However, as she had stated previously, she was responsible for the business accounts and the stock records. These discrepancies, in Bruno's opinion, were down to her, and blaming Calafifi for stock shortages of rare and valuable books that he had carefully selected was not acceptable. The audit confirmed his suspicion that such a level of bookkeeping irregularities and monies missing was her responsibility. In essence she was running the business badly or, worse, stealing from the business.

*

By 5 p.m., Bruno had emailed a list of the nineteen missing and unsold books to Nathan Philips in Bembridge, with a short note asking if he had been offered any of them to buy in the past six months. His immediate response by telephone was a huge surprise.

Of the nineteen books on Jim Duncan's missing list, all had been offered to him during the past six months. He had bought some of the books offered, from a man in his thirties, carrying no more than a handful of books on each visit. They were in excellent condition, but expensive, rare first editions.

"I spent £7,000 with him in all, but not all in one go, on five of the nineteen books on your list. I had Hemingway's *The Old Man and The Sea*, a signed first edition. I gave him £1,200 and sold it to a mainland collector the following day for £6,000. I presumed the vendor was in the business and had struck lucky finding such desirable books. He might have been a collector needing cash or have been left the books in a will by a collector who had passed away. That happens often. I did not enquire. When a book collector dies, his or her beneficiary might give a private collection to anyone who will take it, not aware of its true value. That's when, as I did, you can get some really good deals."

"Can you describe this man?"

"Tall, strong build, fit and I think he actually did know about books by what he brought in, and how he spoke. Oh, and he came on a motorbike."

"Any name?"

"Said his name was Brian, just Brian. I didn't ask for a surname or for any ID. Perhaps I should be more careful, but when I'm offered a rare book, I always pay cash. Does that help, Chief Inspector?"

"It might have been more helpful if you had asked Brian for some kind of ID, given the size of the transactions. It means that you can be easily absolved of any wrongdoing if the goods later turn out to be stolen," Bruno pointed out somewhat sharply. "I will come back to you if I need more on this man, whoever he is. If he returns, please be sure to call us, or Shanklin Police Station, get a photo on your phone, and keep him talking him until we can get here?"

"Yes, Chief Inspector, I will do my best on that one."

Bruno rang off. Andy had been listening.

"Either Brian is a regular book thief from Simeon's, or Annabel is providing books to him," Andy remarked. "So, books bought by Simeon are sold by Brian, and no records of these transactions appear in the business books of account. I'm sure that Annabel will plead ignorance of the loss of the nineteen valuable books, suggesting that it was Simeon's area of responsibility. My guess is that she will indeed claim either that the books must have been stolen by this Brian, who she doesn't know, or that Simeon and Brian were in it together, as a way for him to extract money from the business tax free, for example. Should we speak to her straightaway, or first thing tomorrow?"

"Not yet," said Bruno. "How long has she been on the Island? Some verification on her past history might fill in some of our gaps in this investigation. We need to confirm she is the academically qualified professional she seems."

Andy added, "What about her out-of-hours activities: what does she do outside the office, and who are her friends?"

Bruno replied, "Annabel has no criminal record, we know that. And she has told us quite a lot about her career. Show me the file that has been building up on her, please."

Andy read from his screen: "She's forty-one. She studied at Somerville College in Oxford. It says here that there is no graduation record for her. That's not what it says on Simeon's website, is it? At the same time as she should have been completing her degree, she seems to have been in the USA with an American student, who was a few years ahead of her at Oxford, and who had graduated with a first-class degree in English after a three-year course at St. John's College. They lived in an apartment in Brooklyn, New York, for several years, where they both worked for the New York Public Library; she in the cataloguing department, while he was a research scholar. She left ten years ago and travelled to Jerusalem, where she worked in the Hebrew Library as an assistant curator, eventually returning to the UK three years ago, and to the

Isle of Wight at the time that Simeon was opening his new bookshop in Shanklin."

"It seems that she has possibly misstated or exaggerated her qualifications. She wouldn't be the first person to have done that. And presumably she was actually capable of doing the work in New York and Jerusalem, notwithstanding the underlying exaggerations which got her those jobs. That doesn't necessarily make her a murderer," added Bruno.

Andy continued, no longer reading from his screen: "She and Sam Trent are writing a book, or say they are. Do you think we should ask to see it? There might not even be a book."

"Again," said Bruno, "That doesn't make them criminals. He's a teacher at a prestigious school and she is a lady over ten years his senior. This might be the cover they need to conduct their relationship. I kind of get that."

"I think we should see them both first thing tomorrow, separately."

"Not until we find the motorcyclist," said Bruno. "We need for it to be Sam Trent. Then we can certainly link him, and potentially Annabel, to the thefts of the Talmud and the *Book of Mormon*. And perhaps to these other nineteen missing books. That establishes them as thieves running an expensive book trade under the counter, as it were. If Simeon had found out about this, maybe he challenged Annabel, and even Sam, and that confrontation led to the murder. I'm not sure about that yet, but it certainly brings us right back to Simeon's Bookshop."

"Given Sam Trent's trip to Italy, could he actually be involved? Does that absence eliminate him from our enquiries? I mean we know he was away, there are tons of witnesses to confirm that he was with a big bunch of teenagers in Italy for ten days."

"The dates work, Andy," Bruno got out his notebook and read from some calculation notes he had made. "Sam Trent went to Italy on the term time school trip on Monday 13th March. Wladimir Pivotkin obtained the Talmud from motorbike man on Saturday 11th March, which was two days before Trent went away and – interestingly – was a Saturday, so not a school day. Sam Trent returned on Wednesday 22nd March, late in the evening. Caleb White picked up the *Book of Mormon* from paraglider man on Thursday 30th March. That Thursday, usually a school day, was one day after term ended on Wednesday 29th March. The dates work but I don't want you to do anything other than find evidence of the book they are writing. That you can ask her about."

Andy called Annabel Wilson on her mobile. She said that she had just got home and didn't have time to talk. Andy asked her if Sam Trent was coming over, it being a Tuesday evening.

"Not tonight," she said, "It's the school holidays and he's busy." Andy asked if he could meet her the next day for her to show him the book on Alexander the Great's mother. She sounded surprised. She explained that she'd have to ask Sam, because he was responsible for the written copy of his book and, as she had said, she thought he was busy this week. Andy insisted that this activity was important to the police investigation, to which her response was again negative.

"Sergeant Bowen, I cannot see any reason why our regular Tuesday collaboration should be of any interest to you. It is completely unconnected with anything to do with Simeon's murder. It's an academic exercise."

"Miss Wilson, I'm afraid that is for us to decide. Your cooperation would be much appreciated."

"I have told you. It's not ready for anyone to look at. It's in the very early stages," she countered. She sounded very irritated.

"Your partner in this work, Mr Trent, has indicated the opposite. He told us yesterday that the book is at a completed first draft stage that can be submitted to a publisher."

"He is wrong, so let's leave it there."

Frustrated by her reason for not allowing the police to look at their work, but mindful of the need to make progress, Andy changed tack. "It doesn't matter what stage your book has reached, Miss Wilson. We simply need evidence of your activity on the night of the murder," he said. "We will come over to see you tomorrow. You can ask Sam too, if you like."

He left it at that and finished the call.

Chapter 28

On Wednesday morning, Bruno drove to Ryde to see Miriam Calafifi. She was in.

She looked tired and like she had lost weight. Nevertheless, she sounded confident and asked Bruno the first questions.

"How are you, Chief Inspector? Can I ask you a few questions about this investigation? How are you getting on? Do you have any suspects? Are you close to making an arrest?"

"We are progressing. Yes, there have been developments. Importantly, we have recovered the two books which were stolen from Simeon's safe on the night of the murder. I am confident that we will get there," he said.

"Things have developed at my end since we last spoke. Annabel has agreed to stay on and run the bookshop for me. Of course, this suits me because I need to keep it going until Nathan Philips takes over. A few days after we had agreed that she would stay on, she called me and said she had been made another job offer – she didn't say what – and that she was considering her options, but that she would stay if I agreed to sell her the business to her at a fair price. I didn't tell her that a contract has already been signed to sell the business to Nathan Philips."

This was consistent with what Annabel had told Bruno herself.

"And now what?" asked Bruno, curious about Miriam Calafifi's way of thinking.

"In fact, she made me an offer for the business."

"When was this, Mrs Calafifi?" Bruno wondered why she hadn't rung and told him before, although he had learned over many years that his thoughts on what might be helpful additional information were not necessarily shared by the general public.

"About a week ago, maybe ten days. I can look back and tell you for certain."

"Did you agree a price?" asked Bruno.

"Yes, she offered £50,000 for the business, and £10,000 for the stock, which is the kind of figure my lawyer said was a fair price, given the circumstances."

Bruno was silent. It had to be too much of a coincidence, surely, that these were the exact amounts received by the suspected thief of the Talmud and the *Book of Mormon* respectively.

"So I told her I would accept her offer. Obviously, I can't really sell the business to her because I no longer own it, but what I have told her keeps her on side for a bit longer. She will think the sale to her is going through until I can announce that I've already sold it to Nathan."

Bruno was interested in the cool, calm way Miriam Calafifi was stringing Annabel Wilson along. Given that she was coming to terms with the recent and unsolved murder of her husband, Bruno had some sympathy with her.

This was the moment when Bruno saw his opportunity.

"Will you now do something for me, Mrs Calafifi? I will explain clearly exactly what I need you to do.

This is important and I will need you to act in complete confidence."

Miriam Calafifi nodded.

*

Over in Shanklin, Annabel Wilson was sitting in the office which had previously been occupied by Simeon Calafifi, when she received a call from Miriam Calafifi.

"Hello Annabel, this call will need to be quick. I have had another offer for the bookshop. I would, of course, prefer to honour our agreement but I feel that I need you to commit now, today. I know it's somewhat short notice but there are others who are keen to buy the business, and I don't want to risk you backing out and leaving me high and dry without a buyer. To that end, you are shortly going to receive an email from my solicitor. I hope that's okay. Anyway, I've got to go now. Goodbye."

As instructed by Bruno, Miriam Calafifi gave Annabel Wilson no time to reply.

True to her word, Mrs Calafifi instructed her solicitor, Arnold Robinson, to request by email an immediate same day deposit from Annabel Wilson or she would consider another offer. Annabel's response was to transfer £25,000 from a bank account, with the reference "50% Purchase of Simeon's Bookshop – Annabel Wilson".

Determined not to lose the purchase, Annabel made the transfer within minutes of receiving the request.

Bruno was now becoming more confident that she was in possession of the proceeds from the sale of the two valuable books, something which he would be able to confirm by an information request to her bank. The problem was that, in addition to the theft of the two books, and even more important, was the murder of Simeon Calafifi. He didn't want to jeopardise the murder investigation by only solving the two thefts. A 'softly, softly' approach was required.

*

"What do you think of the amount of cash offered by Annabel for the business?" said Andy.

"It was no coincidence," said Bruno.

"We must assume that cash for the Talmud and the *Book of Mormon* was received by Annabel, and that she had a male accomplice. It feels almost too stupid that she would offer the exact amounts received for the books. Do you think she could be playing with us?"

"Anything is possible. Coincidence, not a coincidence; a game, not a game. Experience has taught me never to be surprised at anything. Regarding the amounts, all we have proved is that she does have money – and plenty of it – and that she is desperate to acquire Simeon's bookshop. Furthermore, I imagine that a bank request will show significant, accountable, balances from some time ago. If she is the ultimate recipient of the £60,000, it will either still be in cash or it will be washed through in chunks to arrive in her account at a later date. As of now, we do not know for certain the identity of her accomplice. We are assuming it's Sam Trent, and we know he was in the UK at the handover of both items, but we need to know two things urgently: is he a paraglider, and does he ride a motorcycle?"

"Okay, sir," said a thoughtful Andy. "Whoever we are looking for – whether it is Sam Trent or someone else –

is in some kind of relationship with Annabel and she is running the show."

"Not necessarily. She could be just taking care of the cash for the killer on his instructions. If we charge her with Simeon's murder, the actual murderer could vanish, whether she reveals his identity or not, leaving the cash behind. She could deny murder and all knowledge, stating simply that she is acting for a third party whose identity she will not reveal to us."

Andy suggested, "We need to determine whether the motorcyclist and paraglider are the same person and whether or not that person is Sam Trent or the mysterious Brian."

"We have the registration number of the bike, which has been circulated throughout the Island, and we have the colour of the paraglider used at Bembridge. We also have the description from Pivotkin, White and now from Nathan Philips."

"Okay, sir, I think we need to talk to Annabel Wilson, to Sam Trent and to see if we find out about this Brian. I'll make the calls to confirm the appointments with Annabel and Sam now."

*

At 5 p.m. on Wednesday afternoon, Bruno and Andy arrived at Simeon's Bookshop to interview Annabel Wilson. They had asked Sam Trent to come along too. They sat Annabel in her office and Sam in the shop. Bruno talked to Annabel; Andy talked to Sam. This was intentional. Suspects were often unnerved at the clear sight of their contacts being interviewed.

In the interview on Monday, Trent had detailed his movements precisely. He had said that he waited until approximately 7:15 p.m. for Annabel to arrive home on Tuesday 28th February.

Bruno's first request to Annabel was to ask her to explain her movements between the time she left Simeon's at 5:45 p.m. and her arrival home at 7:15 p.m. That request came as an unpleasant surprise for her, and he received a fairly unconvincing answer.

"I met a friend, Chief Inspector, who was feeling depressed, so I took him into the Conservative Club, and bought him a drink to cheer him up and listen to him. What he needed was some human contact."

"Could anyone confirm your presence at the Club on that evening?"

"Yes, the staff could. I can't remember who served us, but I would have paid for the drink on my card. I'm sure I can dig out the credit card receipt, Chief Inspector, if you need it."

"We are just trying to fill in the gaps," said Bruno "So, you arrived home at..?" He waited for her to answer.

"Sam can tell you exactly, because I was a little late and he was waiting. It didn't affect our Tuesday evening session on Alexander," she said.

"What was the name of your friend?"

"You wouldn't know them. It was an old friend. He's married so I would rather not say. The staff though will confirm that I was with a man."

Bruno decided to move on and tackle the identity of the friend a bit later. He wanted to switch tack and turn to the audit carried out by Jim Duncan the day before. "Can you tell me about the audit Mrs Calafifi had Mr Duncan carry out yesterday?"

She was prepared. "Yes, the accountant was very helpful, and we identified a number of discrepancies, all things Simeon was dealing with, sales made by him that were missing from the accounts. As a result of his findings I can now start with a clean slate. I am grateful, Chief Inspector, to Mrs Calafifi for arranging that," she said in a more positive tone than when Jim Duncan started his audit.

She had replied in exactly the way Bruno had anticipated.

*

In the shop, Andy was talking to a very relaxed Sam Trent.

"I do have a question for you, Mr Trent. You are a fit young man. You are Head of Sport at Ryde School. Do you paraglide?" asked Bruno.

"Interesting that you should ask that. I do. Annabel introduced me to a friend of hers who has a paragliding school and he is giving me lessons."

"Can you tell me where you are learning to paraglide?" asked Andy.

"It's a school based at the Luccombe Village Hotel. It's up on the hill, south of Shanklin. It's run by this guy called Brian Lindsey, who also owns the hotel. I've not been doing it long and I get the feeling that paragliding might be comparable to golf. What I mean is that to become highly skilled requires constant practice over a number of years."

"You've not lived on the Island long enough to have

that kind of command of the sport, unless you'd been at it before you came to the Island?" enquired Andy.

"No, Sergeant, no one knew about the sport where I lived before. Nobody is paragliding in Croydon. Conditions here are perfect for it, though. That's why I've taken it up. It's pretty exciting and I think could be good at it."

It had not escaped Andy's attention that Sam Trent's introduction to paragliding had been made by someone called Brian: Brian Lindsey, a friend of Annabel's. However, Andy tried not to look pleased at the discovery.

"Can I take a look at your book on Alexander the Great?"

Sam took a ring binder out of his rucksack. It was the latest draft printout. Andy had a flick through it and acknowledged, "Goodness, that's a substantial work of research, running to hundreds of pages. I can appreciate why a publisher would be interested."

"Thank you," said Sam. "We are currently checking the extensive footnotes we've compiled on each page. Referencing properly is really important. I hope this shows you how purposeful Annabel and I are in our Tuesday evening get-togethers."

*

On their journey back from the Shanklin bookshop interviews, Bruno and Andy traded information.

Andy pointed out the two, linked, significant pieces of information to Bruno that had been mentioned by Sam. First, Sam he said that he had been introduced to paragliding by a friend of Annabel's. Second, he had named that friend and the owner of the paragliding school as Brian Lindsey.

Bruno shared the expected reaction of Annabel to the anomalies uncovered during the audit. He also noted that they would need to press her for the name of the friend she had supposedly met at the Conservative Club. He had deliberately chosen not to press for that during this discussion.

"As a friend of Annabel's, surely this Brian Lindsey must be the same Brian who sells books for her?" mused Andy. Bruno agreed that he should be visited urgently.

Chapter 29

For paragliders Thursday was a gift from God, a very windy day. At 7:45 a.m. Detective Chief Inspector Bruno Peach and Detective Sergeant Andy Bowen sat in their unmarked police vehicle watching the main exit from Ryde School. Their assumption that Sam Trent would take off for some kind of exercise early in the morning was correct. At 8 a.m. he emerged from the school exit dressed to go running. He took off quickly towards the High Street, downhill to the Ryde Esplanade. He kept to the shop side while they followed inconspicuously at a distance in their car, keeping him in sight until he took a sudden right turn, which required them to drive further to a roundabout and return, by which time he had disappeared into the maze of little back streets behind the main Ryde Esplanade.

"As we heard yesterday, sir," said Andy, "Sam said that he was recommended to go to the Luccombe Village paragliders by Annabel, whose friend Brian runs it."

"You're right, Andy. That has got to be her connection with a paraglider. I am convinced that whoever our man is will not allow these perfect paragliding conditions to pass without enjoying a flight, so let's call the Luccombe Village Hotel Paragliding School to see if the owner can give us any information. We can pop in to see Bradfield Gittley while we are up there."

When Andy phoned to make an appointment, Brian Lindsey hesitated. He sounded as if he had something to hide, which naturally made Bruno even keener to pay him an official visit. Andy said that they would come down this morning, which put his back up even more.

"Not the right day for it, to be honest. Perfect weather means we are really busy," said Lindsey. "Can't you come another day?"

Bruno had observed a similar evasiveness from men who had served time and who were still involved in something criminal. Bruno wanted to ask Lindsey about his connection with Annabel Wilson.

*

It was a thirty-minute drive to Luccombe from Ryde. During the journey, Bruno started to doubt his belief that the lure of perfect gliding conditions would entice Sam, or whoever they were looking for, to paraglide today or, under the circumstances, in the near future. Whoever the paraglider was who took off with Caleb White's cash, the suspect had demonstrated a fairly unique skill in escaping from Bembridge Fort. He was probably too clever to risk putting himself on show again. He was potentially a hunted man for a most serious crime and a life in prison was something he would do everything to avoid.

They had lost Sam early in the morning running, but, on reflection, that was to be expected, because joggers make split-second decisions based on the conditions. Turning off the Esplanade to escape a cold blast in his face, he had found the shelter of the closely packed houses in the narrow roads behind. If he was the accomplice in

Simeon's murder, then his relationship with Annabel must consist of more than a once-a-week meeting to discuss a writing collaboration. It had been revealed earlier that their original connection was based on the fact that Simeon's Bookshop supplied the school with textbooks, and he was the contact. Could that be the only reason for their friendship?

*

Bradfield Gittley was pleased to see the detectives and unnecessarily apologised at losing sight of the paraglider suspect at the last moment at the Shanklin traffic lights last Sunday.

"You did very well to spot him at all, Mr Gittley. We're going to call into the Luccombe Village Hotel Paragliding School to see if the owner can give us any information."

"He should be able to," said Gittley. "He is a big paraglider himself and will know of anyone who is really skilful on the Island. I don't know him, he's a bit of a strange man, uncommunicative, but he has good staff, so I assume he must treat them well."

Bruno asked, "Have you witnessed any spectacular gliding in the past few days? The weather has been good for it, from what little I know. I can't help thinking that paragliding must be very high on the list of dangerous sports."

"Most paragliders are very careful not to risk their life, Chief Inspector. I haven't seen anything noteworthy since Sunday. If I do, I will take photos to present you with something useful next time."

They left him to carry on with his day and went on their way to the Luccombe Village Hotel. Gittley had painted a picture of Brian Lindsey in his mind. Bruno's sixth sense had induced him to arrange for one uniformed police constable to accompany them to the Luccombe Village Hotel in a marked police vehicle.

*

Sitting on the veranda when the police arrived were two teenage boys waiting for an instructor to arrive to provide paragliding instruction. The arrival of the police aroused their interest. Ernest and Tom were regular visitors to Shanklin during the school holidays, and delighted in the freedom to do things they were never able to do at their homes in London.

"They're cops," Ernest said to Tom. "What are they doing up here?"

"Something's going on. I wonder who's committed a crime?" Tom was curious.

The small hotel was situated on the clifftop, where the National Trust grazing land sloped down towards the cliff edge 300 metres away from where they sat. This cliff made the hotel's paragliding school an ideal location for teaching courses in the sport.

Given what was at stake, a uniformed officer driving a marked police car was the correct method in which to approach and interview Brian Lindsey. Being visited by a police car would make anyone anxious but Lindsey was waiting for the detectives at the bar in the reception area appearing self-confident; he looked about forty, maybe a bit younger, fit, and with an apparently open manner.

Bruno thought that he answered the description of the person provided by Wladimir Pivotkin and Caleb White, and by Nathan Philips. His manner seemed more amiable than during their phone conversation earlier. He was certainly a bit younger than the name 'Brian' had led Bruno and Andy to assume. That was an important rule of policing which they had overlooked – assume nothing.

After making the usual introductions, Andy said, "Mr Lindsey, we are trying to find an experienced paraglider, who flies in this area and therefore knows it well, and who is sufficiently skilled to fly from Culver Cliff to anywhere beyond Sandown Beach. With your knowledge of your sport, where would you fly to from Culver if you were headed towards your hotel? What would be the maximum distance you might fly if it was getting dark?"

"Depends on lots of things," he said. "You always have to bear in mind the wind speed and direction, so if you are flying over water you keep to the coastline. You don't fly in the dark, as soon as the sun sets you head for home. Accidents can take place on landing and take-off in paragliding. Culver is quite a long flying distance, but doable. It'd take twenty minutes in good conditions."

"Would any paraglider do that flight just before sunset?"

"Yes, if he had to, but he'd have to know the terrain very well."

"Where would he choose to land?"

"There could be several places, depending on where he lived or where he was going. I don't think he would take off at dusk, fly until it was dark, land, pack up his kit, unless he was aiming for a particular spot."

"Like in front of this hotel?"

"He could do that from Culver," said Lindsey. "But I wouldn't let any of my pupils try it. What would be the point?"

"Can you tell us about your friendship with Annabel Wilson at Simeon's Bookshop?"

Lindsey was surprised at Bruno's sudden change of direction and direct, personal question, and did not answer straight away. His face seemed to darken, and his brow furrowed until he spoke. Bruno's question had touched a nerve.

"What do you want to know?" he said.

"Do you know her well?"

"I do work for her occasionally. When she has a problem in the house, plumbing or electrics, she calls me, and I fix it. Nothing more than that, Chief Inspector."

Coming from the veranda outside of the hotel, the two boys who had been waiting for their lesson now appeared in the hotel lobby and approached them.

"Sorry to interrupt you, Mr Lindsey, but we've been waiting for the instructor for ages now. Can you tell us whether we're going to get our lesson today?"

"Just wait outside a few more minutes, lads, and I'll come and talk to you."

The boys sauntered off slowly, clearly trying to listen in and work out what was happening. Sitting in the police car on the hotel drive was PC Peter Tinkler, ready and waiting for the two detectives to finish their meeting with Mr Lindsey.

As they reached the police car, one of the boys, Ernest, said to his friend, "That's PC Peter Tinkler! Do you remember him from last year?"

Level with the police car driver's open window, Tom leaned forward and spoke to the PC in the driver's seat.

"PC Tinkler?"

"Yes? Can I help you?" said Tinkler.

"It's Tom Coombs. You remember us from last year?"

"Refresh my memory, young man," he said, climbing out of the car.

"The crash, sir, in the centre of Shanklin Old Village. We were your key witnesses."

"Of course I remember you. Tom Coombs and Ernest Wright?"

"Correct," said Ernest. "Good to see you again, sir," He held out his hand to shake the PC's hand, as did Tom.

"How are you both doing?"

"It's the Easter holidays, so we are back for a few days. We've got our GCSEs in a few weeks so we are supposed to be revising," Tom explained.

"We didn't hear from you after the crash, sir," said Ernest.

"Well, your statements were registered along with the others, but we didn't need to call you. It turned out to be an easier trial than we had expected."

"How long did they get, sir?" said Tom.

"Life for murder for the lady, and her accomplice got a long sentence for manslaughter."

"So, it was murder?" said Ernest.

"Afraid so," said PC Peter Tinkler.

"Are you here to make an arrest, sir?" said Tom. "Can you tell us what's going on?"

"To tell you the truth, I don't know why I am here today. I am just a uniformed presence backing up the Chief Inspector and his Detective Sergeant."

"Is Mr Lindsey under suspicion?" asked Ernest.

"I really can't say anything."

"We are very interested in police work," said Tom.

"There is a place in the police for bright, young men like you. How old are you?" said Tinkler.

"We're both sixteen, sir."

"Come and see us when you have finished your A levels, and I am sure we can give you some advice. A university degree will start you off on the right foot."

"How about a summer job in the control centre?" asked Ernest.

"That would be a start," said Tinkler. "You could write to the Chief Super in Newport. His name is Barlow. You never know, you might be lucky. Where are you off to now?"

"We've been waiting an hour. Our instructor shows no signs of appearing and we've got to meet my grandmother soon in Shanklin. We can't wait any longer," said Ernest.

"Can't you call him?"

"We've tried texting him, sir, but no answer," said Tom. "And Mr Lindsey is busy with your Chief Inspector, so he can't sort it out."

At that moment the two detectives, Peach and Bowen, emerged from the hotel, deep in conversation.

"Excuse me, sirs," said PC Tinkler. "Can I introduce these two young gentlemen? They completed witness statements last year because they saw the Shanklin Carnival Queen's float crash into the Crab Inn in the Old Village."

"Nice to meet you, boys," said Bruno, and gave each one a welcoming handshake. PC Tinkler formerly introduced

Detective Chief Inspector Bruno Peach and Detective Sergeant Andy Bowen as the detectives who had been in charge of the Old Village murder investigation.

"I told these young men, who offered to appear as witnesses last year, that they were not needed to testify in the end."

"Thank you for your offer anyway, we always need all the voluntary help that is offered to us," said Bruno. "Are you still waiting for your instructor? Mr Lindsey may be able to help you now we have finished our meeting."

"He didn't look like he was going to be doing instruction today and the usual guy hasn't arrived, so we've run out of time. We have to go back to Shanklin now anyway. He's probably been frightened away by your car, sir," said Ernest. "The mystery at the Luccombe Village Hotel," he added with a grin.

"Many a true word is spoken in jest," said Andy.

"Are you investigating a crime here, Detective Chief Inspector?" asked Ernest. "We are willing to help in any way we can. We could come back later, stick around, make searches, anything."

"How far does your instructor have to come?" asked Andy.

"He lives in Ryde, sir," said Tom.

"Is he a good teacher?"

"Truth is, we don't really know. So far, we've only had one theory lesson from him," said Tom.

"What's his name?"

"We don't know his surname, sir," said Tom. "We just call him Sam. You will have to ask Mr Lindsey if he is any good."

"We'd prefer Mr Lindsey to teach us. And I think he will when we get past the theory and the land practices. He's the best glider on the Island," said Ernest. "He is not going to let us fly over the sea, although he does it all the time, of course. We haven't actually done any flying yet at all."

"Do many people come here?" asked Andy.

"Loads," said Ernest. "It's quite a popular and growing pastime. Mr Lindsey says we are only on the margin to control a paraglider anyway as we are only sixteen and we need to be a little heavier and a little stronger and a bit older."

"Yes, next year we will be better," agreed Tom.

"Where did you say you were going, boys?" said PC Tinkler.

"We've got to meet my gran," said Ernest. "She's very old and we promised to carry her shopping home for her."

"Where are you meeting her?"

"Shanklin Co-op, sir."

"When?"

Ernest looked at his watch. "Now, sir! We'll have to run."

"Tinkler, take the boys to the Co-op and come back for us," said Bruno. "I want to go back inside and talk more to Mr Lindsey," he said to Andy.

Both detectives had simultaneously picked up the name Sam, and Bruno's reaction to the coincidence clicked immediately, which had the effect of connecting a series of facts that were otherwise unconnected.

Inside the hotel reception Bruno said to Lindsey, "Our driver has left for a short duty call. He'll be half an hour. Could we have some coffee, please, while we wait for him?"

"Of course, you chaps sit down and I'll go through to the kitchen and make it myself. Give me five," he said and vanished.

"The boys' reference to Sam is a connection which we can investigate," said Bruno.

"Should we speak to Lindsey about it?" said Andy.

"No," said Bruno. "Let him calm down. Despite his demeanour, he must be rattled by our knowing about his connection with Annabel. We should go back to Ryde and speak to Sam first," said Bruno. "Lindsey is not going anywhere, so we can come back and speak to him at any time.

"OK, let's go to the school now," said Andy. "We are assuming that Sam the paraglider instructor is Sam Trent. If he is qualified to teach paragliding, then he is much better at paragliding than he led us to believe."

"Although, to be fair, he is only teaching those boys theory. Sam Trent is a teacher and a Sports teacher at that, together with Latin and English. Even if he had only been learning paragliding himself for a short while, he has all the raw material skills to teach a couple of teenage boys the theory. Anyway, it's the holidays, and it might be a way for Sam to get a bit of extra cash."

After twenty minutes Tinkler arrived back and drank a coffee with them before returning with the detectives to Newport.

Lindsey was more relaxed when he served the coffee, confident that he'd dealt with the police questions.

"I took them to the Co-op, sir," reported PC Tinkler. "And the grandmother was waiting outside with several food bags, too much for them to carry really. It was quite an event for the old lady seeing the two boys get out of a police car. They are full of it, those two boys. They climbed out of the car saying, 'We are under arrest!' holding their wrists together, as if they had cuffs on. They are staying a half mile down the hill on Luccombe Road, at a block of flats called The Reach. So, as I was coming back that way anyway, right past the door, I loaded the three of them and the bags into the car and dropped them home on the way back. It only added a couple of minutes to the journey and gave me time to get their numbers, just in case, with the grandmother present, seeing as they are only sixteen."

*

On their return journey back to Newport, Bruno and Andy passed two large white buildings. "That's The Reach, where the boys are staying, sir."

"On top of the cliff, they must have a great view out to sea," said Andy.

"And of paragliders passing by," added Bruno.

"Sir, if Sam is a decent paraglider, then everything comes together. We could be in a position to make an arrest," said Andy, exhilarated by their chance discovery.

Bruno pointed out, "Apart from the name drop by the two boys we have nothing on Sam Trent based on actual evidence. We are not yet sure it's the same Sam until we talk to him. I think we did the right thing not asking Brian Lindsey too much. When we get to paragliding, is Sam a beginner, just helping Lindsey out, teaching the basics to youngsters? Is he connected to Lindsey in another way? My guess is that he will be open about everything we ask him. He seems to have been so far," said Bruno.

Andy had a dental appointment at 3 p.m. and they had started work very early, so Bruno decided to go home, have some tea and have a think. Before leaving for the day, Andy called Sam Trent and invited him to visit Newport Police Station at 8:30 a.m. the next morning, Friday 7th April, to tie up a few loose ends, and to sign a statement confirming his movements and activities on the day of the murder. "A routine requirement," he said to him. Sam happily agreed to attend.

*

Janet's view was that if Annabel had the slightest whiff of where the police investigation had reached with the money, she could be off, disappearing into thin air.

"The bookshop is open until 5:30 p.m. I know you've only just come back from that way, but why don't we drive over to Shanklin? This Annabel doesn't know me. I can go in and buy something and get a feel for her mood while I choose a book and have a chat. I might find out something," Janet suggested.

It was a helpful idea, and Bruno was of a mind to take all the help he could towards achieving his objective. To him it seemed that the villains were suddenly all on the doorstep, and he could pick them up, one by one, or all together and the case could be solved. But he knew that detective work was not as straightforward as that. If one piece of the jigsaw was in the wrong place his case would fall apart, and the information he'd gathered from Luccombe Village Hotel did not prove anything beyond doubt.

The bookshop was busy when they arrived in Shanklin. Bruno parked in the main Co-op car park and Janet walked up to the shop on her own. Janet was able to slide in and mingle with the customers and take in the atmosphere. There was no hint that five weeks previously the owner had been murdered on the premises. Today everything appeared to be in order and the shop was running normally and smoothly. Annabel ended up serving Janet and there was nothing at all untoward about her manner or her attitude. Janet had tried to ask Annabel a couple of leading questions, without seeming like she was too obviously asking probing questions, but Annabel had replied with general answers and platitudes.

Bruno was encouraged with Janet's assessment of the business. Furthermore, she had bought him a present: a copy of a novel called *Trust* by an American writer about a crooked Wall Street banker. It was a small blessing that would transport him to a different world for an evening.

Chapter 30

Sam Trent arrived at the police station a little before 8:30 a.m. on Friday morning.

"Good morning, Chief Inspector. And you, Sergeant Bowen. I am glad you invited me over. All people like me ever see of a police station is what we see on television. If you show me around, it's something I can tell the boys about – what it's really like!"

Andy was surprised at how relaxed Sam appeared, showing no concern that he might have been invited for a serious discussion. He did not come across as a person with something to hide nor was he anxious at being in a police station.

"Where did you park, Mr Trent?" Andy asked, intrigued to know whether he had arrived by motorcycle.

"I came on the Newport bus that stops outside Ryde School. I know some of your colleagues in the Ryde Police Station, as we are often asked about school matters by the police. We ask them to visit the school to talk to the boys about safety matters," he said.

"Mr Trent, we have asked you to come to the station because we want you to fill in some gaps for us about the day of the murder of Simeon Calafifi."

"I'm very happy to do that," he said.

"On that evening of 28th February you met Annabel at the rear of the shop at 6:15 p.m. Is that correct?"

"Yes."

"Did you enter the shop?"

"No. Why would I have done? I told you. She was outside waiting for me."

"Why wouldn't she have waited inside the shop? It was cold. You could have gone in there and got her," suggested Bruno.

"How would I know why she was waiting outside? She was waiting by her car. She wasn't in it. The only thing that was strange was that it was cold, and she didn't have a decent coat on. But maybe she hadn't planned to go to the Conservative Club. Maybe she was just planning to drive home. Who knows?"

"So, how long were you in the car park? Did you see anyone else?"

"No. And I must have been there less than two or three minutes. I got in her car, and I drove it to the Co-op. I went in there and bought the dinner. You'll be able to check all this."

Andy and Bruno said nothing to this. They had in fact already confirmed the delay to the bus and the Co-op purchases. Unless Sam Trent had run into the shop and stabbed Simeon Calafifi and then run out again and driven to the Co-op in less than six minutes, it would have been impossible for him to have murdered Simeon Calafifi. The lack of time and of forensic evidence rendered this proposition virtually, but not completely, impossible.

"So, you had dinner with Annabel Wilson, as you have already told us. Can you tell us about any other activities you engage in with her when you are not working at school?"

"With her? None at all," he said. "We meet once a

week and may also talk on the phone at other times about Alexander matters," he said. "Occasionally I will drop in to the shop on a Saturday. On that particular evening, 28th February, I mean, she didn't arrive until maybe an hour after I got there. In other words at, say, 7:15 p.m. I had put the television on, and I know that the program on BBC1, with the Welsh lady presenting it, had started. But I wasn't watching the clock or noting the time. Why would I have been? I had kind of started getting the pasta ready and by the time she got in and we had had a drink and finished cooking it, it must have been about 8 or 8:15 when we ate. So we ate later than we usually do. She was quiet when she arrived, but only at first. Once we got onto the work, she was her usual self."

"What do you do outside of school?"

"I play tennis at the Ryde Tennis Club. I am also a member of Ryde Golf Club with Jack Welsh from the school – off peak only, as it's cheaper. I run with Ryde Harriers Athletic Club, and I go to the Ryde Chess Club. That's about it. We are a boarding school, so there is plenty going on in the evenings and at weekends, which as a junior master, I have to attend and usually be responsible for. I don't have that much free time, and I like to be busy. I've got no family down here, so my time is my own."

"What about the paragliding club?"

"I've only just taken that up. It's not a club I actually belong to."

"Have you been there often?" asked Andy.

"Not often. I try to show up on Saturday mornings, the golf club is busy on Saturdays, and Ryde is only a nine-hole course. Annabel has a friend, Brian Lindsey, who owns the Luccombe Village Hotel, where the Paragliding School is based. I have been up there a few times. I make short flights testing the techniques that I've learned from him. I hope that next time I go, if the conditions are right, we will fly out over the sea."

"How well do you know Mr Lindsey?"

"I've met him at his hotel, but he knows Annabel very well."

"'Very well'? Would you say they are in a relationship?" asked Andy.

Sam looked taken aback and thought for a few seconds before he gave his answer.

"God knows, Chief Inspector," he said with a smile. "I haven't tracked that one. Could be, he spends a lot of time at her house –"

"– where you go on Tuesdays?" Bruno interjected.

"Correct, Chief Inspector."

"What can you tell us about him?"

"I've never actually seen him when he's at her home. He's not my friend, I don't think he is really Annabel's friend either."

"Does he have a wife or girlfriend?"

"Not that I've seen, but he does have a live-in manager. Her name is Pat Lee, she does all the work. She's nice."

"Do you have a motorbike, Sam?"

"No, I have a bicycle. It's very good racing bike. No motorbike, no car. But it is a good bus service on the Island, which suits me, because I don't need transport to get to work. I can walk to the tennis club and the golf club from school."

"But you can drive a car?"

"Yes, I have a licence, and I can drive. But I don't have a car."

"We spoke to two young men, Tom and Ernest, who you taught to paraglide at the hotel."

"I have only taught them once. Lindsey had overbooked. Yes, nice boys. Ernest's parents have an apartment in The Reach near the Luccombe Village Hotel."

"Would you say that Mr Lindsey was a good paraglider?"

"Definitely. He has all the certificates, and he is a former British champion. May still be."

"Interesting," said Andy.

"Do you think you'll go back to the Luccombe Village Paragliding School?" asked Bruno as he was about to leave.

"Hmm," said Sam. "Probably. I don't think there is anywhere better necessarily. Brian might be a champion paraglider, but he is not a teacher. There is always somebody waiting to speak to him and that makes for a disjointed lesson. I only went there because Annabel suggested it, and he gave me a few free lessons because she sent me there."

Bruno and Andy were in unspoken agreement that Sam Trent had not murdered Simeon Calafifi. Although Sam had been in the country on the dates of both the meeting with Wladimir Pivotkin and with Caleb White, some background checks suggested that he could not easily have been at either St. Catherine's Oratory or at Bembridge Fort at the early evening meetings. Furthermore, the lack of skill had made it apparent that Sam was not the paragliding phantom they were looking for.

At this stage, they agreed that Sam Trent could be of no further interest, but he had opened the case spectacularly, enabling them to put enough pieces into their jigsaw, so they could now begin to see the faces of the people involved; Brian Lindsey was a man who they needed to know more about.

"Sam, that's been very interesting. One of our team is going to help you prepare a statement covering what you have told us today and on Monday morning at school and on Wednesday in the shop. You will need to read the statement carefully and if you consider it to be an accurate report of our conversations, please sign it," said Andy.

"After the statement bit, will that be everything done?" he said.

"Yes, for now. Thank you for coming over," said Andy as Sam left with a junior officer to give his statement formally.

"Do we have the missing link?" Andy asked Bruno, knowing the answer.

"Not with Sam Trent, but let's see if Brian Lindsey has form before we pursue him. We know our killer is dangerous, and if we corner him, we can't guess his reaction."

"We've not seen him paraglide, have we?" said Andy.

"We don't need to," said Bruno.

"From what Sam has told us, Lindsey is a champion paraglider. He is totally familiar with this coastal area, and he has a strong connection with Annabel Wilson."

Brian Lindsey did not show up on the police database as a person with a record. Setting that aside, the key question to put to him was his whereabouts on the early evening of 28th February.

Andy went on: "By his own admission, he is a friend of Annabel's, though Sam Trent has just said 'I don't think he is really Annabel's friend'. He is able to arrange local support when necessary to fix plumbing, electrics and minor household jobs. He is a single man, and he has a decent business. He doesn't have a wife or girlfriend that we know of. He is in good shape, and he looks like he regularly works out, possibly to enable him to have the physical prowess for paragliding. The fact that he is at Annabel's beck and call suggests that he has designs on her, even if they are not reciprocated. It also suggests that they could be linked by the activities we are investigating."

"I think that we can set Sam Trent to one side for now. Brian Lindsey should be our focus," said Bruno. "We need to question Lindsey, and discover what he was doing on Tuesday 28th February, on Saturday 11th March and on Thursday 30th March. We also need to find out who Annabel was meeting on Tuesday 28th February at the Conservative Club. Finally, I want a search warrant for both the Luccombe Village Hotel and for Annabel's home."

"I'll get straight on it, sir. In fact, I will go and get Brian Lindsey myself right now."

Chapter 31

Brian Lindsey had been waiting in an adjoining interview room. He had been swiftly, and surprisingly for him, brought in for questioning at 10 a.m., based upon his involvement with Annabel Wilson, the theft and onward sale of books from the bookshop she worked in, and his skill as a paraglider. Otherwise, they had no evidence to connect him with Simeon Calafifi's murder. He had been brought in quietly, without notice, by Andy himself, so that word would not reach Annabel Wilson that he had been taken in for questioning.

It was still before 11 a.m., after another busy week, and Andy Bowen felt that he was a strange mix of exhausted and energised. He opened the questioning by asking Brian Lindsey to repeat his whereabouts on the evening of Tuesday 28th February.

"I was in my hotel serving dinner to my guests."

"What time was that?"

"Well, dinner is at 6:30 p.m. There is only one sitting at this time of year. I serve drinks from the bar, then I help serve and oversee the meal."

"How many guests did you have for dinner that evening?"

"Not many. As far as I can remember, it was half a dozen," Lindsey replied.

"And what time does dinner end?"

"By about 8 p.m. at the latest. In the winter it's not a long drawn-out affair. Then I clear up and lay the tables for breakfast. It is only at this time of year; we have very few guests in February, you see. It gets busier now, around Easter, and then in the summer I have staff to do all these jobs."

"Can you prove you were in the hotel between 5:30 p.m. and 7 p.m. on that evening?"

"Of course I can. My manager, Pat Lee, and the guests could confirm that. They would have noticed if there was no-one to serve drinks and dinner, I can tell you."

Brian Lindsey's prompt confirmation to their question about his whereabouts was expected. They had discounted that he might have been Calafifi's mysterious guest on that fateful Tuesday evening: they had already confirmed his alibi with the hotel manager, Pat Lee, and with the part time chef, and with one of the dinner guests, who was a regular and to whom Pat Lee had easily directed them. This eliminated him as a suspect in the murder of Simeon Calafifi.

However, the detectives had inferred that with his skill at paragliding, he was the person responsible for the Bembridge Fort escape, and physically that he closely resembled Pivotkin's description of the man in the tower. They would come on to that.

"When we last met, we told you that we wanted to meet an experienced Island paraglider. Someone who could fly at dusk from Culver Down to the beach in Sandown to Shanklin. Or even further, as far as Luccombe, or where he might touch down and quietly vanish." Bruno wasn't sure that they had actually used these words but that wasn't the point of the question. He wanted to see Lindsey's reaction to a question where the answer was very close to home.

"You did, Chief Inspector. And I said I couldn't put a name to anyone."

"Do you know Sam Trent?"

"Yes, he comes to my school."

"Could he have flown a paraglider that distance in those conditions?"

"Possibly," he said. Then Lindsey thought about it, and said, "Actually no, Chief Inspector. He came to the school because Annabel sent him. I used to be the UK national paragliding champion twelve years ago, and he wanted to learn the difficult turns and manoeuvres, the things the experts do. So I gave him the benefit of my knowledge. And if he told me that he was planning to fly from Culver Down as far as Luccombe, I would have put him off. He's not even completed a sea flight yet."

Lindsey was proving to be an ample source of information. He had supported what Sam Trent had told them and helped to confirm that Sam Trent could not be the paraglider they were looking for. This was surprising on the one hand but also to be expected. Lindsey's prowess at paragliding was public, celebrated and beyond doubt; there would be no point in him pretending otherwise.

"Are you aware of the seriousness of this meeting, and why you are a person of interest to us?" Bruno asked.

"Yes," Lindsey replied. "You think I had something to do with the murder of Annabel's boss?"

"We do not believe that you murdered Simeon Calafifi. However, we believe you are associated with the theft of books from Simeon's Bookshop and therefore that you are potentially connected with the murder. What is your relationship with Annabel Wilson, who manages Simeon's Bookshop?"

"When you say 'relationship', I can tell you that I'm not 'in a relationship' with her. It's more than likely you should talk to Sam Trent about a relationship. He's in and out of her house all the time. I just go to the bookshop when I'm in Shanklin."

"Have you ever sold books for Annabel?"

"Where did you get that from?" he said in an aggressive tone.

"Please, just answer the question, Mr Lindsey."

"Yes, I have sold books for her. Ones that she said they didn't like to stock."

"To whom?" said Andy, continuing his line of questioning.

"To people and to other bookshops on the Island."

"Have you ever sold books to Nathan Philips in Bembridge?"

"Yes. Why? That's hardly a crime, is it?"

"Was it profitable?"

"Yes, it was. Otherwise I wouldn't have done it. We split the money. I got twenty-five per cent of whatever I could get for them."

The detectives now understood the connection between Brian Lindsey and Annabel. He was her runner. Nathan Philips in the Bembridge shop had said he bought expensive books from a man called Brian and Brian Lindsey had confirmed that he had sold books to Nathan Philips. It would be difficult to prove that Brian Lindsey had had any knowledge that the sales of these books was fraudulent in any way. For all he knew, they were indeed stock that the shop had found it difficult to shift, and he could reasonably have assumed that his activities were in the full knowledge of not only Annabel but Simeon also.

"Did you often go bookselling for Annabel?" asked Andy.

"Quite often. I've made a few hundred pounds over several months. These books are not rubbish. They're special editions that collectors look for. On a couple of occasions, I've made telephone calls to offer books to clients."

"Have you ever called someone called Michael Turner in Petersfield?"

"Can't remember."

Bruno was certain that Lindsey was their pistol-toting gunman at St. Catherine's Oratory, and the ace paraglider who escaped from the Bembridge Fort. It seemed an easy step for Annabel to persuade Brian to negotiate the sale of the two religious books.

"Mr Lindsey, do you know what a Talmud is?"

"A what?"

"A Talmud", repeated Andy.

"No. Don't think so."

"Have you heard of the *Book of Mormon*?"

"You mean like the musical? Yes, sure."

"Have you ever been asked by Annabel Wilson to sell either of these books?"

"I've no idea. I don't notice the title of everything I sell for her."

"What is the highest value book you have ever sold for her?"

"I've no idea. Why are you asking me this?"

"Okay," said Bruno, "Let's ask you two different and direct questions. What were you doing on Saturday 11th March this year? And on Thursday 30th March?"

"I have absolutely no idea, Chief Inspector. I can't remember."

"So, you can't remember what you were doing last Thursday, eight days ago, but you can remember what you were doing exactly on Tuesday 28th February?"

"If you say so," replied Brian, who was starting to get a little agitated.

"Let's work backwards. Thursday 30th March. Not yesterday but the Thursday before that. Eight days ago. A windy day. Did you go paragliding in the late afternoon, early evening? You would have had to miss the 6:30 p.m. dinner service at the hotel, something we will be able to check very easily. Did you go paragliding on Thursday 30th March from Bembridge Fort back to, say, Shanklin or even Luccombe?"

Brian Lindsey did not reply. He then asked a question of his own:

"Am I not supposed to be offered a solicitor during an interrogation?"

This told Bruno and Andy everything they needed to know for now.

*

Brian Lindsey's request for legal representation gave the two detectives the opportunity to adjourn the interview for a couple of hours while this was arranged for him. Fortuitously the search warrant for the Luccombe Village

Hotel and for Annabel Wilson's house had been approved while they had been interviewing Brian Lindsey. The detectives agreed that Bruno and Andy would go straight to the Luccombe Village Hotel as quickly as they could and without delay.

On the way there they would stop at Simeon's Bookshop. They would make an appointment to see Annabel Wilson at the shop the very next morning, Saturday 8th April. They planned to be friendly and make out that it was a routine follow up to the audit, the findings of which Mrs Calafifi had shared with them, and that their concerns were mainly financial and, even, tax related. They would not mention the murder of Simeon Calafifi. Nor would they mention that they had Brian Lindsey in custody back at Newport police station awaiting a second round of questioning by Bruno and Andy, following the imminent search of the hotel, which he did not know was about to happen. This was a benefit for the policemen.

"It won't do any harm for him to have to sweat and to wait for us for a bit. And, depending on what we find, it will determine how we speak to him."

*

Pat Lee was busy with a small group of what turned out to be locals at the Luccombe Village Hotel bar. They were eating ham sandwiches and drinking half pints of shandy. She looked like she had her hands full with the Friday lunchtime crowd.

Discreetly, Bruno informed her that they had come to search the office and private accommodation used by Brian Lindsey. She showed them the office. Having found a set of keys to his living area, which was a private apartment on the eastern side of the building, she left them to return to the guests in the hotel bar.

Pat's offer to help their search had been politely declined. Bruno and Andy had a number of objectives. Assisted by some junior officers, and observing the strict police searching protocols, they set about diligently opening every cupboard, every drawer, a desk with unlocked drawers, and a bedside cabinet.

Transferring his attention to the kitchen, after opening cupboards, biscuit tins and drawers, in a large turquoise Fortnum & Mason tin of wrapped teabags, Bruno found what he had come for: a Beretta 84 handgun, and a cartridge of bullets. Obviously this would need to be looked at by Forensics and by the Firearms team in Portsmouth, but this was enough to confirm to Bruno that it was Brian Lindsey who had collected the ransoms from Wladimir Pivotkin and Caleb White in exchange for the Talmud and the *Book of Mormon*. It was Brian Lindsey who had threatened both men with a handgun and who had fired a warning shot into the ancient wall of the lighthouse at St. Catherine's Oratory.

The paragliding equipment building was full of stuff, including two or three distinctive blue and white sails. Andy had found nothing conclusive in there. Bruno and he decided that it was Brian Lindsey's skill, rather than the equipment itself, which was the most persuasive evidence that Lindsey was the paraglider from Bembridge Fort. Very few people could have made that flight successfully.

There was no sign of any large sums of cash. 25% of the £60,000 total received for the two books would have been £15,000. In a hotel, with a cash bar and a paragliding school offering lessons, it would be relatively easy to spread the cash around over a period of time to avoid its detection. Bank a bit here, pay for a few things in cash there – that kind of thing.

Before leaving, the two detectives interviewed Pat Lee briefly as she washed glasses behind the bar. It wasn't long before they had heard what a difficult evening she had had on Thursday 30th March, when Brian had not shown up for the dinner service.

"Me and chef had to manage all on our own. I was running around like a blue arsed fly. I mean, I didn't mind and all that, but I was supposed to be going to bingo on Thursday evening in the Baptist church in town at 8 p.m., so I had to leave at 7:45 p.m. at the latest. And then Brian waltzed in at 8 p.m. and asked if he could help. As I say, I didn't mind as he's a pretty good boss. I'm going to my niece's wedding in Cyprus in a couple of months and, when I told him how I'd missed the bingo, he gave me £500, cash. Out of the blue. Straightaway. Said it would make up for any winnings I'd lost, and I could use it to buy my ticket to Cyprus."

Chapter 32

Emboldened by their findings at the Luccombe Village Hotel, Bruno and Andy decided to accelerate the search of Annabel Wilson's home. They were waiting outside when she arrived at 3 p.m., accompanied by the two uniformed officers who had collected her from the shop without notice. She was more than a bit annoyed.

"What the hell is going on?" she demanded as soon as she emerged from the back seat of the squad car. "I was busy in the shop, and you've dragged me over here. We agreed to meet at the shop tomorrow morning. What the hell has happened in the last hour and a half to change things?"

"We are not going to speak to you, here, Miss Wilson. We would just like you to give us your house keys to enable us to enter and to search your home without the need to force entry. We have a warrant to conduct a full search. These two officers will be taking you to Newport Police Station where we will come and speak to you when we have concluded the search of your home."

She threw the keys at Andy and got back angrily into the police car.

"Let's see what we can find here then," said Bruno as they let themselves in.

*

Annabel Wilson's home was that of a successful, professional woman. There were towers of stacked books in the lounge, bedroom and the bathroom. Everywhere there was a space or shelf, it contained books. It was an extension of Simeon's shop. It was chilly inside Annabel's house.

"We need a clearer picture of her, and to discover a motive. Look for personal letters, information about her, her family, her friends. We need to understand the kind of person she really is."

The detectives started upstairs. The house was furnished as you might expect of a woman in her forties: modern, stylish, clean, with colourful bedlinen and a duvet laid over a five-foot king sized bed, leading to a modern bathroom with sweet-smelling essences adorning the shelves and surfaces. Two other bedrooms were similarly laid out and spotless, and a shared bathroom existed between the second and third bedroom. The upstairs suggested that she had visitors to stay sometimes. Her clothes were properly arranged in floor-to-ceiling wardrobes. Nothing upstairs provided a clue that helped them in their search.

Bruno knew that Annabel was obsessed with the book business, and the contents of the downstairs of the house confirmed that conclusion. One particular book interested Bruno. He'd hoped to find a clue for this brutal murder that might show her in a better light, but what he now discovered had the opposite effect.

Inconspicuously, on a bookshelf, was a slim fifty-page pamphlet in the *Teach Me Anatomy* series. The copyright page was dated that year. It had not been lying about on a bookshelf for years. It had been bought very recently.

It showed graphic illustrations of every part of the body, male and female. The pages revealed skeletal representations detailing bone structure and the position of the organs in the upper body in relation to the vertebrae and ribcage. The location of the heart was shown a little below the shoulder blades. The drawings were all to scale indicating the distance from the body surface to the heart and liver. Bruno indicated to a junior officer to bag and label the book as evidence.

Bruno reflected how these days most forms of communication are electronic, because there were few personal letters or cards to look at. On the bottom shelf of a bookcase, with outsized books, were a few slim photo albums of young people at a holiday camp, a music festival, and some university groups.

"Were they taken on the Island?" asked Andy.

"Hard to say," said Bruno. "Take a closer look."

Many of the photographs included Annabel and gave the impression that they were of her and friends whose pictures she wanted to cherish.

The detectives continued looking through the photo albums. There were holiday photos, and also more groups of friends who attended activities on the Island together, all some time ago. One particular photograph caught Bruno's attention. It was a group of nine adults, including Annabel, in front of a poster for the Isle of Wight Music Festival. Bruno estimated that Annabel would have been about 25, maybe a year or two older. So the photograph was about fifteen years ago.

Standing next to Annabel, Bruno recognised Nathan Philips. He had his arm draped around Annabel's shoulder.

He was younger, naturally, but instantly recognisable. So, at the very least, he was an old friend, closer than the impression he had given when they had visited him at his shop. As an old friend, her present predicament must be of concern to him. Nothing else in her house indicated any present-day connection between them.

Bruno had wondered why, after Annabel's travels in America and Israel, she had returned to the Island. Was it to seek out Nathan Philips, who had already married? She must have regarded it as home, where she lived when the pictures in the albums were taken. Bruno decided to revisit him at his Bembridge bookshop to see if he might fill in some of the gaps about Annabel's background.

Andy had discovered a ring binder with some important and revelatory documents. The label on the front of the binder said: "Simeon's Bookshop." Inside the binder were the original purchase memoranda for the lease of Simeon's Bookshop. The terms and conditions were fully documented. Simeon Calafifi and a Derwent Property Company representative had signed the lease soon after his move to the Isle of Wight three or four years ago. The lease ran to the usual thirty pages containing the conditions and obligations of both parties.

That was not the most interesting item in the binder. It also contained printed copies of emails from some business sales agents in London called Clifford Thompson, whose first letter on the file was dated just the previous November. That letter confirmed instructions from Simeon to sell his bookshop. It stated the price of £100,000 for the lease, plus selected stock at valuation.

Behind the lease for the shop and the sale instructions

was the single most important document as far as the detectives' investigation was confirmed. It detailed the offer from Nathan Philips to purchase the bookshop, which Simeon had accepted on 1st February. This proved that Annabel had discovered that Simeon Calafifi was selling the shop behind her back to Nathan Philips. The same Nathan Philips who she had some kind of history with. Given Annabel's desire to own Simeon's Bookshop, it would have come as a bombshell to her and certainly gave her a motive to murder Simeon Calafifi.

On Bruno's instruction, Andy called Nathan Philips at the Bembridge Bookshop. He asked Philips to drive over to Newport Police Station straightaway in connection with the murder of Simeon Calafifi. Philips agreed to leave then and there. Bruno was keen to have a quick word with Philips before the interviews with Annabel Wilson and Brian Lindsey. He asked Andy to stay behind and complete the search of Annabel's house. The garage needed properly going over and the Forensics team had just arrived.

Chapter 33

Nathan Philips was oddly pleased to see Bruno. Bruno couldn't put his finger on Philips' mood and attitude. If pressed, he would have said that Philips seemed relieved. It was almost as if he was about to get something off his chest.

Bruno quickly got down to business by producing the Isle of Wight festival photograph he had found in Annabel Wilson's house.

"Do you recognise this picture?"

"I recognise some of the people, but I've never seen the picture."

"I have brought it with me to show you because I was told by Annabel that she came to the Island three years ago, when Simeon opened his shop, and we believed that she was new to the Island."

"No, that's not true. She has been on and off the Island most of her life," Philips said. "She went away to University, she also went to the States with an American guy, she worked in New York, and then she went to Israel for several years. But in between she was here, on the Island and, yes, I knew her."

"Was she born here on the Island?"

"No. Her mother came here in the 1980s, when Annabel was about five, I think."

"Where from?"

"I don't know."

"No husband?"

"You mean did Annabel have a Dad? Obviously, she must have done but not that I know of, and not on the Island."

Nathan Philips explained that Annabel had attended a local school on the Island where she did exceptionally well, and then went on to Oxford University, where she took a degree in Latin and Ancient Greek. Nathan didn't know whether she had finished her degree or not. He knew that she had also worked at a London Museum for a bit.

"I had known about her for a year before that Isle of Wight Music Festival photo was taken. It was after Oxford and the US, but before Israel, I think. Anyway, right after that photo must have been taken, I mean like a few weeks after, her mother died in peculiar circumstances in The Eagle pub in Shanklin."

"Tell me about that", prompted Bruno.

"Well, as I recall, the barman had reported that this respectable couple came into the pub early evening and sat in a quiet corner. The man ordered the drinks at the bar, a pint for himself and a gin and tonic for the lady he was with. This may seem like minute detail, but that's how Annabel recalled the events to me. And I remember her telling me the story very clearly, because it was so strange."

Nathan continued, "After about half an hour, the barman apparently saw the man get up and leave the pub, having finished his beer. The woman was still sitting in the corner. Nothing strange. He thought, at first, that the man could have stepped outside for any number of reasons. However, after another half an hour, the lady had not moved and the man had not returned, so the barman approached her to collect the empty glasses. She didn't move, sitting bolt upright, staring ahead. It transpired that she was dead."

"Dead?"

"Yes, dead. Nothing suspicious was discovered at the post-mortem. She had died from a heart attack and the man she came in with was never traced. Of course, every attempt was made to find him according to the barman's description. Her strange death was widely reported, and the police were involved, but he never came forward, and there was nothing in her belongings that had a name that could be traced. Annabel didn't know who her mother had been with. It had a profound effect on her, from which, I don't think, she has ever recovered. She may appear perfectly normal. She is attractive and kind in her own way, but her mother dying in that way without saying goodbye, in the company of a stranger who has never been traced, or come forward, has had a lasting effect on her."

"This is a devastating story," said Bruno, "but it must have been, what, fifteen years ago and I don't recall reading anything about it. Were you her boyfriend at that time?"

"I was. We were close, and I did love her. Then she left, a month or two later, by which time I was pleased that she had moved. I believed that the memory of her mother affected her more than she could bear, and it is undoubtedly still there."

"So why did she come back?" said Bruno.

Nathan didn't answer that question. His admission that he had once been in love with Annabel had changed Bruno's view of him.

"Has she been charged with the murder of Simeon Calafifi?" asked Nathan.

Bruno decided that by telling him some details of the case and the current position, he might reveal more about Calafifi's murder.

"No, but we know that she was involved in the theft of the Talmud and the *Book of Mormon*. I anticipate that she will end up being charged with involvement in his murder too. However, our investigation is continuing as we have a suspicion that another person could be involved, someone whose identity she is concealing. Perhaps the actual murderer."

Bruno looked Philips in the eye as he added, "And we hope the realisation by her of her position will persuade her to confess to us."

"You will find that difficult, almost impossible," said Nathan. "I was in love with her, but didn't know her at all, and when we parted it was as if we had never known each other. She remains a stranger to me, and since her return to live on the Island, I have seen no change. She is a person who wants to be in control but she's also very fragile, Chief Inspector."

"Is there anything else you would like to tell us about her?" asked Bruno.

"When that photograph at the Isle of Wight Music Festival was taken, we had known each other for a year or so and we had planned to save enough to open a bookshop together. That dream was shattered when her mother died as I've described. Her death happened a few weeks after the festival. The effect on her was devastating. She treated me as if I was the man who had abandoned her dying mother in The Eagle. She believed that if that man had alerted the barman, a paramedic team might have saved her mother. So we parted one day. I didn't think I could help her. I did not call her again, and she did not contact me."

Bruno sensed this was difficult for Philips and waited for him to continue.

"When eventually I did try to see her, she had left the Island. She returned three years ago, after an absence of twelve years. I bumped into her and I saw her here and there. At first, she appeared to be changed and to have come to terms with what had happened. It was a welcome surprise to me that she had gone to work for Simeon. Then she sent Brian Lindsey to see me with a good selection of titles that helped my business survive a rough patch, and we remained friendly, on a professional level. From time to time, whenever I was in Shanklin, I would call into Simeon's. We'd have a coffee and discuss business. I admired Simeon. He was a proper antiquarian bookseller with an unblemished reputation nationally, even internationally. I could see he would do well. With the establishment of the Isle of Wight Literary Festival, the Island could flourish and become the Hay-on-Wye of the South of England. So I got to know him, offering my services if I could be of help, and I know we could have succeeded, and his move to Bournemouth would potentially have given me an even greater foothold on the mainland too."

Philips resumed, "At some time in the early part of the autumn last year, Simeon came to see me here in the shop. He said that he and Miriam were planning to move to Bournemouth so that she could continue her architectural practice. The airport in Bournemouth would enable her to fly to her office in Paris and back in a day, and so he was intending to sell the business in Shanklin and re-establish himself on the mainland. He said that he had one or two parties who were interested in nurturing the Island as a mecca for the literary establishment. 'Are you interested in buying my business?' he asked me. It was an opportunity I could not turn down, Chief Inspector, regardless of my ties to Bembridge. He said he was happy to do a deal, leave money in the business until I could pay, and from Bournemouth he would continue doing what he did best. He felt Miriam, he and the boys would all be happier there."

Bruno listened attentively as Philips took him into his confidence.

"It was a deal I could manage with his help, Chief Inspector, so I agreed to buy the business, signing the contract, just before he was murdered, and, well – you know the rest. That is the situation today. I will take the business over once Miriam is ready, and because the sale has already gone through, it is not subject to probate. I don't expect her to be sorted out and ready for me to take over for at least another six weeks, but in view of developments with Annabel, it could be sooner."

Philips continued, "There is something I haven't told you, Chief Inspector. It's about the night of Simeon's Calafifi's murder."

Bruno listened. He knew that when interviewing people like Nathan Philips, it was often best just to let them talk.

"At 6 p.m. on that Tuesday, 28th February, I happened to be at Morrisons in Lake, just going through the check out, when Annabel called me on my mobile to ask if I could go to Shanklin and meet her as soon as possible in the Conservative Club to discuss something important. I could tell it was urgent, and I was – I admit – intrigued. I had literally popped in to the shop to get some toiletries for the holiday. The Conservative Club wasn't too far away. So I met her there. I got there about 6:20 p.m. and she came in less than 5 minutes after I got there. She got me a drink, she insisted, and then we chatted for about 30 minutes. 'I want to talk to you about Simeon's Bookshop,' she said. 'I know that you have made him an offer to buy the business.' I asked how she knew, and she said that she had read it. 'I've seen correspondence,' she said. 'He promised to sell the business to me.' To say that she was furious, was an understatement. She told me that I was to withdraw from the sale and let her buy Simeon's Bookshop. I wasn't sure whether she knew we had actually exchanged contracts – I suspected she did because it was literally the day after that had happened – but I didn't want to tell her I'd already signed a contract and effectively owned it. I cursed myself for meeting her, because at that moment I honestly thought she was going to kill me if I did not agree to withdraw. She was the embodiment of calm anger. So I drank my beer, said that my wife and the kids were waiting for me at home, and we had packing to do for our holiday, and I left before she carried on. I said I didn't have time to talk about the shop now and I'd speak to her the following day, perhaps with Simeon, and I left her to finish her drink. Basically I got out of there as quickly as I could."

"Was there anything strange about her behaviour? Or how she looked?" Bruno asked.

"She was ice-cold. When she told me to back out of the sale, she put her hand on my arm, and I noticed she was freezing. I asked her where her coat was, and she said she had forgotten her coat and had left it in the shop. That struck me as odd, the kind of thing you do when you're not thinking straight. Make of that what you will."

"Is there anything else you would like to tell us?" asked Bruno, who was making a mental note to confirm Nathan Philip's movements and thereby his alibi. It was helpful that he had been at Morrisons and then at the Conservative Club, both public places.

"As she was the manager of the business, I anticipated she would have been one of the first persons to be spoken to by the police. I admit to thinking that she might have been a party to the murder or had witnessed it, but I put that aside. Meanwhile I have kept close to Miriam regarding the completion date for my taking over the day-to-day running of the business."

At this, Bruno thanked Philips for his cooperation. He was bidding him farewell when a call came in from Andy. This was the moment when he would be sure that Annabel Wilson had murdered her employer, Simeon Calafifi.

Chapter 34

The contents of Annabel Wilson's garage further justified Bruno's decision to search the house first before continuing to interrogate not only their uncooperative murder suspect, but also Brian Lindsey himself.

There was a large double garage. Annabel's car was still parked at Simeon's bookshop, so a single space was empty. The other half of the garage contained the usual garage collection of boxes, tools and odds and ends. On a workbench lay a set of paragliding equipment in a huge rucksack. At the rear of the garage and under a black tarpaulin, stood a Royal Enfield motorbike. Andy could tell it was not an old one, but a new, Japanese manufactured Royal Enfield 250-cc replica. The possession of these items in Annabel's garage required no explanation. They confirmed her involvement with the person, believed to be Brian Lindsey, who had facilitated the sale and delivery of the books, the first by motorcycle at St. Catherine's Oratory, and the other by paraglider, from Bembridge Fort.

When Bruno had left to meet Nathan Philips, he had seen enough for the purpose of his investigation and wanted the fingerprint squad to search the house and the garage for the murder weapon, which he believed could lay somewhere in the house. They were looking for an unusual blade. Prints on the bike and paraglider would hopefully prove to be those of Lindsey, so the forensics team were sent in immediately to do their work. He also wanted Andy to complete a more detailed search of the downstairs rooms.

Andy had located Annabel's passport and a Lloyds Bank savings account statement, which showed regular monthly deposits. It confirmed the conduit for the cash received for the books sold by Brian Lindsey. Apart from the regular salary cheque and cash withdrawals, there were additional credits that Andy decided were from the sale of books by Lindsey, and to his personal satisfaction there were a number of large round sum credits during the last two weeks of March. Whilst they were nowhere near her share of the £50,000 received on 11th March from Wladimir Pivotkin, Andy was confident that further investigation would show that she had banked at least a proportion of her share.

The discovery of the motorbike and the paraglider in Annabel's garage did not reveal the identity of the murderer, nor confirm that it was her, but they did confirm that she, in some form of conjunction with Brian Lindsey, had stolen both the Talmud and the *Book of Mormon* and sold them for her own gain.

"The equipment discovered in the garage proves her connection to the person who sold the books, and who collected the cash, but not necessarily to the murder or murderer, despite our suspicions," said Andy. "We really need to find the murder weapon, or Simeon's Calafifi's 'phone, or something. And we need some fingerprint confirmations."

*

Forensics had indeed responded immediately to Bruno's request for a forensic examination of the motorbike and paraglider in Annabel's garage and had arrived there by 4:15 p.m. Bruno had already left when they arrived, to meet Nathan Philips back in Newport, and Andy had briefed the Forensics team at the property.

Using some manual techniques, combined with the prints that they had recently put on file, Tommy Dodd was able to report that they had obtained handprints from the bike, and fingerprints from the paraglider, which matched both Annabel Wilson and Brian Lindsey. During his examination of these items, Dodd had made a remarkable discovery, as a result of which he was agreeably able to claim to Bruno that the Forensics department had once again been instrumental in the success of the Island Murder Squad in solving another murder on the Island.

The garage workbench in Annabel Wilson's house had been littered with half-used packs of tissues, out-of-date packets of biscuits, a broken torch, a screwdriver and other untidy garage items. Given the neatness of the house and the rest of the garage, Dodd, very cleverly, thought that the untidy mess looked almost staged. Underneath the rubbish, hiding in plain sight, was a brown paper bag containing a ten-inch-long bloodstained kitchen knife. The bloody blade had been wrapped in a tissue, now stuck firmly to the sharp cutting edge.

Epilogue

The trial, *R v Wilson*, was held five months later. The prosecution's case and the defence submissions took eight days. On many occasions, under persistent questioning, Annabel Wilson displayed signs of psychotic behaviour. Her resolute denial of wrongdoing and attempt to blame Simeon Calafifi's murder on a mystery visitor demonstrated both a malefic personality and a mental illness. She clearly had a long-standing difficulty in sustaining intimate relationships. However, the detailed planning and execution of the theft and sale of the Talmud and the *Book of Mormon* were evidence not only of her calculated cleverness but also of her cold-hearted callousness. This allowed the prosecution counsel to block any suggestion by the defence that her mental capacity was reduced, which then might have resulted in a sympathetic jury verdict of manslaughter, or even an acquittal.

After the jury adjourned for two days for deliberations, they finally returned to court to deliver a unanimous guilty verdict for the murder of Simeon Calafifi; Annabel Wilson was sentenced to serve a term of twenty years. Throughout the trial she stuck to her story that Simeon had had a visitor on the evening of his murder who must have killed him and whose identity she did not know. The jury concluded, however, that the evidence against her was in fact overwhelming and that she was solely responsible.

Brian Lindsey was found guilty of handling stolen goods. He was fined and given a suspended sentence of two years. He was also ordered to carry out community service. His offer to teach the police to paraglide as part of his community service was very in keeping with his character but was politely declined. His gun was confiscated in accordance with the United Kingdom gun laws.

Nathan Philips took over the bookshop in Shanklin, and in honour of his friend retained the trading name of Simeon's Bookshop. The shop prospered, as did his endeavour to promote the Isle of Wight Literary Festival as the Hay-on-Wye of the south, with the co-operation of other bookshops on the Island. He and Max Carter took over the running of the festival jointly.

Miriam Calafifi moved back to London with her two stepsons where they settled well.

The sum paid of £50,000 for the stolen Talmud was returned to Wladimir Pivotkin and of £10,000 for the stolen *Book of Mormon* to Caleb White. The Talmud was delivered to Professor Kazac at the University of Tel Aviv, in accordance with the sale effected by Simeon Calafifi. The *Book of Mormon* was then officially sold by Simeon's Bookshop to Caleb White's church for £10,000.

Professor Kazac was so grateful to Wladimir Pivotkin for his part in saving the Talmud that he persuaded the board at Tel Aviv University to honour the agreement he had made to share the Talmud, notwithstanding who had paid for what. In any event, Pivotkin made generous donations to everyone so that no one involved felt that they were out of pocket in any way. He also agreed to pay for a huge event organised by Rabbi Barry at the Central Synagogue in Vilnius to welcome the Talmud's return. Everyone who had been involved in the case was invited as honoured guests, including Detective Chief Inspector Bruno Peach and Detective Sergeant Andy Bowen.

Chief Constable Barlow allowed Bruno and Andy to attend, provided that their trip cost the Island police force nothing, and that they took the three days needed for the visit out of their annual leave entitlement.

"And then, gentlemen, it's back to work first thing on Monday morning for a briefing with me. You never know when we might have another murder on the Island that needs investigating."

Also from James London...

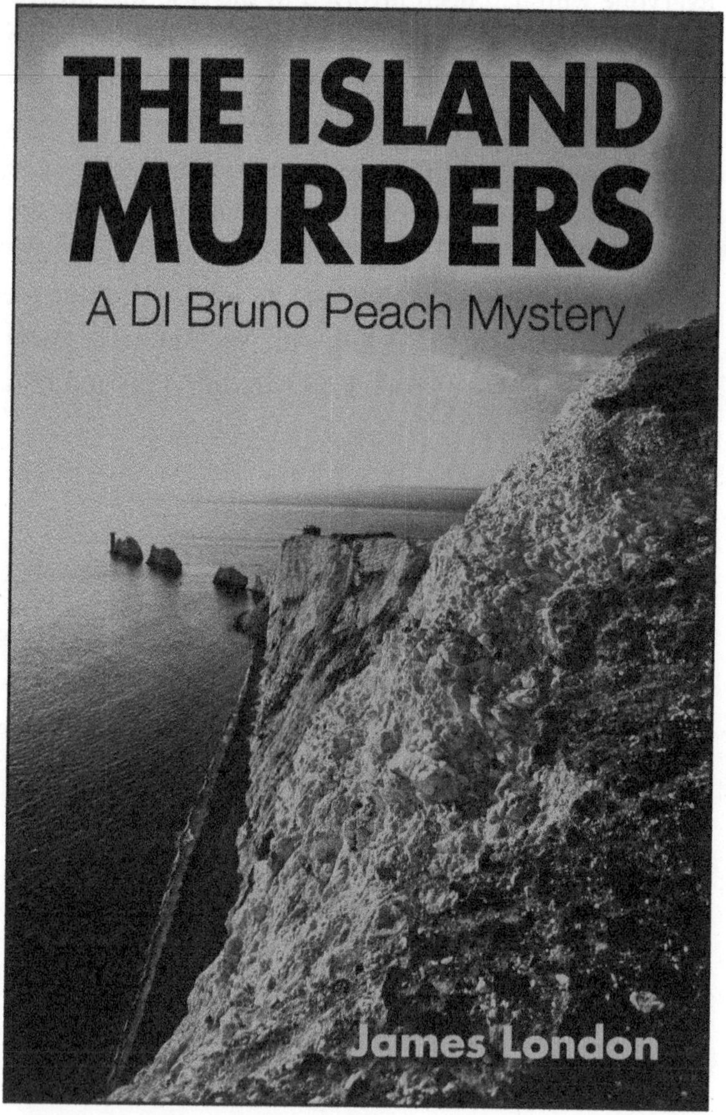